PALM SPRINGS NOIR

EDITED BY
BARBARA DEMARCO-BARRETT

BROOKLYN, NEW YORK

Published by Akashic Books
©2021 Akashic Books

Series concept by Tim McLoughlin and Johnny Temple
Palm Springs map by Sohrab Habibion

Paperback ISBN: 978-1-61775-928-4
Library of Congress Control Number: 2020948265

Akashic Books
Brooklyn, New York
Twitter: @AkashicBooks
Facebook: AkashicBooks
E-mail: info@akashicbooks.com
Website: www.akashicbooks.com

In Shakespeare, tragic heroes fall from mountaintops; in noir, they fall from curbs.
—Dennis Lehane

ALSO IN THE AKASHIC NOIR SERIES

FORTHCOMING

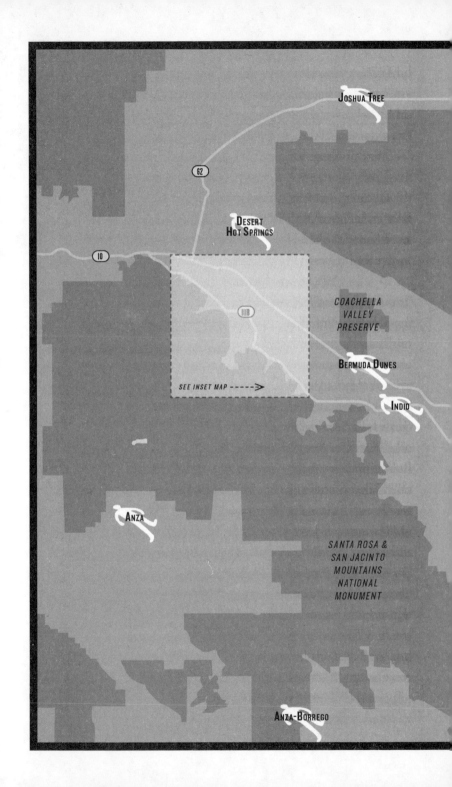

TABLE OF CONTENTS

INTRODUCTION
Between the Devil and the Deep Blue Sea

Ten years ago, when my first noir short story, "Crazy for You," was published in *Orange County Noir*, my mother-in-law asked me to define the genre. She read mystery fiction and cozies but wasn't familiar with noir.

"In noir, the main characters might want their lives to improve and may have high aspirations and goals," I said, "but they keep making bad choices, and things go from bad to worse."

Her response was immediate: "Like real life." We burst into laughter, but it was tinged with the bittersweet pain of knowing.

All of us, at one time or another, have found ourselves in sticky situations with more than a couple of ways we might go. I'd like to think most of us take the high road, the ethical and moral path. In noir, characters follow the highway to doom and destruction. They are haunted by the past, and the line between black and white, right and wrong, dissolves like sugar in water. The hero rationalizes why it's okay to do whatever dark thing they are about to do.

Crime novelist Laura Lippman summed up noir: "Dreamers become schemers." People are blinded by nostalgia as they try to outrun or escape their pasts. Afflicted affairs, lies and transgressions, and murky secrets color the world of noir. Characters end up mired in sex, greed, and murder, unable to extricate themselves.

And setting. The best noir writers make us feel the heat of the sun, the touch of a lover. Setting can be gritty but can also be sublime, no longer relegated to urban locales and seedy hotel rooms but also mansions and swimming pools. Hence, Palm Springs, which may seem like an odd setting for a collection of dark short stories—it's so sunny and bright here. The quality of light is unlike anywhere else, and with an average of three hundred sunny days a year, what could go wrong?

The area is famous for many things: 130-plus golf courses make it the golfing capital of the US; the largest concentration of midcentury modern residential architecture in the world; and with fifty thousand swimming pools at last count, Palm Springs has more pools per capita than anywhere else in the US. And nothing says Palm Springs more than the four thousand wind turbines that provide enough electricity to power the entire Coachella Valley.

While the greater Palm Springs area has its share of dive bars, its alleyways tend to be tidy and clean, and femmes fatales are more likely to be found in bathing suits than slinky dresses or tailored suits. But on a steamy summer day, the residential streets are absent of people and can possess an unsettling quiet. Where is everyone? You're reminded to lock the car and front door.

The history of the area goes back to the 1700s with the Agua Caliente Band of Cahuilla Indians. The population then—around six thousand—has swelled to 450,000, and triples during winter months when snowbirds and tourists escape from their cold homes to soak in the rays. But it wasn't until the 1930s that Palm Springs got its glitz quotient and caught on as the getaway of choice for Hollywood stars. Movie moguls instituted the two-hour rule: actors had to be within two hours of the studios in case they were needed, and Palm Springs, 107 miles east of Los Angeles, fit the bill. The desert city was also safe from the gossip columnists.

Elvis Presley's honeymoon house sits in Vista Las Palmas and offers tours. Frank Sinatra had a house here, as did other Hollywood luminaries, some of whom, along with Frank, are buried in area cemeteries. Clothing-optional resorts dot the environs and the nation's first all-LGBTQ city council governs the city of Palm Springs. This arid, ninety-four-square-mile Southern California tourist destination is a verdant patch of green smeared across the beige blanket of the Mojave Desert. The green derives, in part, from the vast underground waterways.

The aquifers are not all that goes on that you cannot see. The greater Palm Springs area has a massive homeless population, gangs, and crime. Property crime here is 72 percent higher than the nation's average. And the granddaddy of fault lines, the San Andreas, bisects the Coachella Valley. Experts say it could go at any time. That, plus the mind-numbing windstorms that hit the north end, 120-degree heat in the dead of summer, and the snakes, tarantulas, and various scorpion species would put anyone on edge.

At the far southern end of the valley, the man-made Salton Sea, currently thirty-five miles long by fifteen miles wide, with an average depth of thirty feet, threatens to dry up. If lawmakers don't do something soon to rectify the situation, the dust from the dried-up sea will wreck the lungs and sunny dispositions of the residents across the valley and many other Southern Californians. Migratory birds will lose a necessary layover. A noir situation if ever there was one.

Noir appeared in the 1920s as a reaction to the then-popular cozy mysteries. It soon distinguished itself from detective fiction with its fast-paced storytelling, gritty scenarios, and use of sex as a means of advancing the plot. In the 1940s, film noir arrived, and remained popular throughout the 1950s.

In the sixties and seventies, noir took a little rest. There was an odd sense of optimism. We believed that we'd overcome the forces of evil and anything was possible. But then something happened. It didn't go as planned. Noir returned with a vengeance, thanks to publishers like Akashic and others. And thanks to the state of things in our current political situation as well, there are wars that never seem to end. Fitting, because in noir, sometimes the problem is not so much the person as it is the government. People are always blaming someone or something else. Character disorders and narcissism run rampant in noir.

Its complexion has changed. Once the province of mostly white men, now female, LGBTQ, and nonwhite authors are making their presences known, writing powerful, brutal stories.

Are the writers and readers of noir inherently different from those who read and write cozies, thrillers, and mysteries? Are we more jaded, scoffing at the good guy winning? Noir stories don't end well. They may end *just*, but they won't end happily. And are we drawn more to gloom than the average writer? Maybe we're able to be cheery enough in our daily lives but secretly—or not so secretly—hold a dim view of the world. We have secret sadnesses and regrets nursed in the privacy of our own minds, which we funnel into our fiction.

In grade school I read Nancy Drew—not exactly noir; in fact, the opposite of noir. But in high school, as my parents' marriage went down the drain, I stayed out more than in, hung out with townies, got into drugs, and had a meth-head boyfriend who got us pulled over by the cops in his vintage turquoise '57 Chevy and was arrested. The cops told me to drive his car home. But they never arrested me or even warned me. Was I even there?

The stories in this collection come on like the wicked dust storms common to the area. More than half are by writers who live here full-time; all have homes in Southern California. They know this place in ways visitors and outsiders never will. These are not stories you'll read in the glossy coffee-table books that feature Palm Springs's good life. There is indeed a lush life to be found here, but for the characters in these stories, it's often just out of reach.

People from the past have a nasty habit of showing up, and no one is more fraught than the scientist who awaits his fate, a cyanide capsule lodged in his cheek as he prepares to bite down. A vacation rental agent trying to make a fresh start gets caught up in the lives of the vacationers, and an Airbnb landlord discovers renting has a downside. Private eyes chase down missing people and others go on hikes and never return. Local landmarks, historic neighborhoods, and the ubiquitous swimming pool make appearances beneath the glaring sun. Moorten Botanical Garden (appearing as "Morston's"), Spencer's, and the Ace Hotel are among famous spots with cameos. After you read these stories, hot tubs and swimming pools will never look the same.

Each one is a gem, and as the editor of the collection, it's gratifying to offer them to you. I hope you enjoy.

Barbara DeMarco-Barrett
March 2021

PART I

STRANGERS IN THE NIGHT

SUNRISE

BY JANET FITCH

South Palm Canyon

I like cactus. Cactus and old people, old places, things that
survive. Quiet mornings. Water soaking into sandy soil
before the heat. That's what I was doing at Morston's that
morning—watering, raking, feeding the tortoises, watering
the doves—white doves, like the ones magicians conjure out
of thin air. A nice buzz on, just about perfect.

I was pretty much done, taking a drink from the hose, that
coppery taste of summertime. Time go home, clean up, feed
Mr. Frenchy, get ready for the day. The first customers were
arriving.

What made me look up? The cigar. I hate cigars, they remind me of someone I'd like to forget. I staggered too close
to a prickly pear, but I hardly felt it as it caught my arm. I
recognized that tall trim form, long-legged in jeans, cowboy
boots, shaking a match. Even with his bald head covered with
a baseball cap and his eyes hidden behind aviator sunglasses,
I knew him.

I watched him buy tickets, him and the girl, a pretty redhead in a hat and yellow sundress.

Look at him, laughing.

The LAPD said there was no such person as Jack West.
The detective we hired came up empty. *Sorry, kids, but you're
never going to see that money again.*

His hand rested on the girl's slim shoulder, a tall man's

ease, her arm around his waist. Christ, he was old enough to be her grandfather. We thought he'd taken off to Venezuela. *Mathilde, Matilda . . . he take the money and run Venezuela.* Or Bogotá, that's where the wife was from, a former Miss Colombia, or so he said.

I found a bit of crumpled Kleenex in my pocket to dab at the blood seeping through my shirt as I watched them move through the ecosystems—all the varieties of cactus, some thirty feet high, others no bigger than your thumb. I could shove him into a patch of ocotillo, leave him crucified, like a bird I'd seen once, impaled on a thorn by the wind.

The girl screamed and batted at her flowered hat, knocking it to the ground. A hummingbird darted away, offended. Jack laughed, settling the fallen hat back on her head. So graceful, so easy. That gold watch, the only sign of his taste for fancy cars and expensive women, rented yachts, larceny.

We'd never seen that kind of flash, Gil and me. Box seats at the Bowl, house in Beverly Hills, boat at the marina, the white Rolls. By the time we knew what had hit us, he was gone. Along with everything we'd ever owned, ever made of ourselves, vanished. Like a magic act in which it was the magician, and not the doves, who appeared and then disappeared.

Had to suck it up. Our credit busted. Gil's brother doling out a grand or two like he was the Sun King.

Then came the dark days. The shit condo in Reseda, Gil on the couch playing solitaire on a TV tray, watching detective shows . . . There are things in life you didn't survive, and we didn't survive our encounter with Jack West.

You're young. Get on with your lives, the detective had said. *Chalk it up to experience.*

I sprayed water on things that didn't need it, cholla and prickly pear, watched Jack and his date make the circuit and return to the tables of souvenir cactus and succulents. I coiled the hose and slipped out to my car across the street, an Audi from the eighties that'd once belonged to my mother.

Come on, you son of a bitch.

Here they came. Walked down to a silver-bullet Porsche. He folded himself in, leaving the girl to manage for herself. Clearly he was past trying to impress. I hoped they were staying locally; I didn't have much gas. But I wasn't going to let him get away. Not even if I had to follow him to LA or San Diego. It was a sign. The universe was giving me a second chance.

I tailed him down South Palm Canyon, past the Palm Canyon Mobil Club where I lived in my grandmother's old trailer, as far as Coyote Hills Drive, where he turned and climbed. A white brick wall and a gate of frosted glass and black metal shuddering open for a quick glimpse at the house—a modernist platter with what looked like a 270-degree view over the valley. I kept going, found a place to turn around, and parked in the shade of someone's olive tree.

Jack sure had improved his taste. The man I'd known favored mirrored tiles and round Hollywood beds. That bed . . . back then, that and Sarita's lace stockings were the most elegant things I'd ever seen. What a kid I'd been.

Where the jutting roofline permitted, I could see the house's patio, an angular blue pool, the concrete limited by glorious big boulders. *That was my money.* Mine and Gil's, the money he'd stolen from us. A neighbor came onto his front patio and glared at me. Fuck you, sir. Unless he called the cops, I was staying right here.

But the gate was opening again.

I shadowed him back through town, to a sleek modern building with aqua-tinted windows. It housed a Coldwell

Banker, a medi spa, and on the second floor—Thompson + Price Design/Build. Jack climbed out of that Porsche like he was Steve McQueen. He had to be fifty by now, maybe even older. I was thirty-six, but I felt sixty. Eight years since he'd killed me. I was a ghost, and he hadn't aged a day.

Ten a.m. and my shirt was sweated through. My pierced arm throbbed. I ran the AC, listening to Rat Pack radio: *Fly me to the moon—hey!* I would wait. I was the soul of patience. I was a hawk waiting on a lamppost, a scorpion under a rock. I had nothing but time.

Meanwhile, Mauricio texted me. *Echale un vistazo, jefe.* It was our joke. Mauricio was my boss. I met him when I'd first landed here—bottomed out, tapped out, living in my grandmother's trailer. Newly widowed, having a beer and a taco and a good cry. Back when I still cried. My Spanish was pretty good—my only good subject at Birmingham High—and he seemed sympathetic. I told him my sad story.

He too had a problem, he said. He ran a landscaping crew. Recently, the California governor had announced they were going to pay people to take out their lawns and put in *plantas tolerantes a la sequía*, cactus and natives. It was the future. He was a good gardener, not an idiot with a rake. But owners didn't think Mexicans could do anything but wave a leaf blower. What he needed was *una gringa bien hablada para conseguir nuevos clientes, ¿comprende?* An ambitious guy. He wanted that business. I would be the boss, get the gig, then he'd take over. He'd give me 10 percent.

We came up with a name—Xterra Gardens. Gays y hipsters were the likeliest clients, new owners. This being Palm Springs, there was always somebody dying or moving away. I kept my white-lady wardrobe neatly together at one end of my closet—white jeans, canvas shoes, a clean straw hat. *El jefe.*

Mauricio's lead was in Cathedral City, *el profesor*, could I drop by?

Mañana. Problemas personales.

Was Jack ever going to come out of there? Was I going to have to go in? At twelve thirty, he appeared with a young man, handsome, tanned, in a blue shirt and white linen pants, carrying a slim portfolio. Jack laughed at something and squeezed his shoulder. That gesture. I almost spewed. He did that exact thing with Gil. The approving father he'd never had. Jack smelled it on us, our need.

They headed into the Historic Tennis Club, valet parked at Spencer's—that other Palm Springs of immaculate tennis courts, the members-only cabanas. The young man knew people, shook hands, introduced Jack. Suckers.

Spencer's is casual but tony, with a kind of Polynesian air, a laid-back patio. I couldn't go inside in my dirty khakis, but with my leather gardening gloves and big hat, a small rake, I could spy from the garden, where I had an excellent view.

An older woman joined them. Pale linen pantsuit, her hair a soft platinum. The opposite in every way from the redhead Jack had stashed on Coyote Hill. I watched him orchestrate. He let the young man talk, stepping in when the woman asked questions, soothing objections, making her laugh. The young one opened his portfolio, setting their wineglasses aside, their bread plates. The woman took out her reading glasses, leaned over. Diamond ring, platinum tank watch. I wanted to shout, *Call your lawyer!* but it was none of my business. I had some planning to do.

I threaded the Audi through the network of lanes comprising the Palm Canyon Mobil Club. Meticulous double-wides, even some new microhouses. *The New Palm Springs.* I liked it better when it was cheap and shitty and full of old people who hated children. Those crusty old broads. Some of them were still around, like Shirley Bliss, my grandmother Lottie's best friend, two doors down and across the street. The difference in ages hadn't been apparent to me back then—I had thought her ancient, but she must have only been in her fifties.

At home, I showered and let Mr. Frenchy out of his cage, put him on my shoulder, and grabbed my computer. My lanai wasn't nearly as nice as Spencer's, just a cover of funky green corrugated fiberglass protecting my cactus and succulents, an old aluminum glider. I turned on the fountain so Mr. Frenchy could splash. A little cockatiel, he didn't take much upkeep. Birdseed and fresh water and he was good to go.

I turned on my laptop, typed in *Thompson + Price*.

Photos appeared. Futuristic condos, walls of glass, oval or circular swimming pools set into cement or wooden decks like the water tank in *Petticoat Junction*. Good landscaping. I was wondering who did it before I realized that these weren't actual photographs. It was a projected development at the hem of the San Jacintos off South Palm Canyon, past where Jack had his house.

Sunrise. Not *Sunrise Palms* or *Sunrise Dunes*, just *Sunrise.* I hated that shit. The newest New Palm Springs, bland and generic as a suburban Gap. I preferred the hipster fakery of midcentury modern, built around fantasies of the Rat Pack and tuck-and-roll upholstery, tropical plantings with blue uplighting.

Thompson + Price. Principals Alan Thompson, Licensed Contractor, and Ben Price, Architect. So Jack was now Alan, but the same man grinned out at me, lanky and loose like Sam Shepard as Chuck Yeager in *The Right Stuff*.

I typed in: *statute of limitation, fraud.* Added *California.*

Four years. Only murder could still be prosecuted at this late date. But wasn't it murder? Hadn't he killed us?

At last, the sun drooped over the ridge of the mountain, the temperature dropped five degrees, and it was cocktail time. I crossed the hot asphalt to Shirley Bliss's battered single wide, rapped on her sliding glass door. "Yoo-hoo."

She unlatched the slider. "Just in time." She wore a little shift of white and gold Lurex. She'd once been a semifamous mobster's girlfriend. The wig of the day was a long bloodred number—Brandy. She'd been breaking out ice for a margarita, pounding the tray on the sparkly Formica. Her ancient fingers neatly punched the handle out and back, the ice falling, such a nostalgic sound. She'd bartended at El Ranchero, still had a stiff pour.

"Salt the glasses, baby."

I poured kosher salt onto a flat plate, water in another, wetted the rims, and dipped them while she shook the tequila, triple sec, and fresh lime in a cocktail shaker, overhand.

Out on the lanai with its green AstroTurf and the bird-bath I'd once made in a mosaic class, we sipped our drinks. She eyed me from behind her ombré frameless glasses. "You don't look so good."

"I didn't realize it was a looking-good occasion."

She was the only person I knew who was armed. When the nation learned that Nancy Reagan had a gun, Lottie and Shirley just shrugged. *Of course she did. Who didn't?* Child me was appalled, like when I found Poppy's revolver in his desk drawer. But that was his generation. *Don't tell your mother,* he'd said.

"Still have Nancy's little bedside gun?"

"Man problems?"

"A guy I used to know. Someone who once took something from me."

She tasted the salt on her lips. Her drawn-on eyebrows lifted. She already knew the one. "Take my advice, honey. Just walk away. Walk away and keep walking."

The smell of lighter fluid wafted over from a neighbor's lot.

I couldn't get him out of my head. The girl's laughter, his arm on her shoulder. The car, the house, lunch at Spencer's. He'd done well for himself. Out enjoying life while my husband was dead, and I was hanging out with old ladies and Mr. Frenchy. I'd waited eight years for this. "I can't. He's out there, breathing."

She gazed up at the overhang, the hummingbird feeders.

"What would Moe say? Poppy?"

She sighed, her shoulders sagging. But she rose and click-clacked back inside, emerging a minute later with the gun—squarish, chrome, no bigger than a sandwich. "So," she said in a half whisper, "I guess my gun got stolen."

I stopped in to visit Pamela at Coldwell Banker. She had a couple of tips for me, one up in Old Las Palmas, the other in the Historic Tennis Club. She especially liked the one in the Tennis Club. "A young couple from LA." Showed me the sales postcard. Where did people get money like that? Crime. Somewhere, there was crime.

I perched on the corner of her desk. "So what do you know about Sunrise?"

"A hundred town houses, high-end. Coyote Hill Drive. They're still in permitting."

"And Thompson + Price?" I indicated the ceiling.

"Yum-yum." She crossed her tanned legs in her pencil-slim

skirt, tapped her pen against her white teeth. "The architect's your age. Rich kid. Cute. But I'll take the developer. Mr. Personality. I think he's from Phoenix."

"Legit?"

She shrugged. "If it gets built, it's legit. Rule of the veldt."

Nobody was home at the Historic Tennis Club address. I left a card. Old Las Palmas was two gay guys with a schnauzer. They didn't want cactus in case the dog hurt himself, but might be open to natives. I made some sketches. Drove out to *el profesor* in Cathedral City, thinking all the while about Jack West, and Sunrise. What was a deal like that worth? He had that architect, but I doubt he'd split the profits 50/50. How much would be in the kitty as they got ready to break ground? Millions. That was when he'd strike, and vanish. I had to get him before that.

I dialed Thompson + Price. Made an appointment with Ben Price. Could he come up to the house? *Yes, it would make things so much simpler. Ilona Sonnenschein.*

The Sonnenscheins were in Cannes, and I was watering their plants. We'd put in their garden, and Ilona had taken a liking to me. Probably a poor idea.

I met Ben Price at the Sonnenschein house in the Mesa. I wore my white-lady clothes—white denim jeans, aqua shirt, maybe buttoned a little lower than usual. Turquoise bracelets, and Shirley's "Elke the Swedish Stewardess" wig, a plausible blond, roughly like Ilona's. "Ilona Sonnenschein," I gave him my hand. I'd even polished my nails. I could see his eyes widening. He hadn't expected any sex appeal.

His eyes jumped to the view, clear across the valley. Then glanced at the house dismissively. Back to the view. I saw it through his eyes—fake Spanish with sixties touches. "I know it's kind of a mishmash," I apologized in my best white-lady voice.

He indicated the valley, unrolling like a carpet, bright in the morning air. "This view is what it's all about, Mrs. . . . Sonnenschein."

"Call me Ilona. And I'll call you Ben." I rattled him for some reason. He kept staring, then forcing himself to look away.

I walked him to a secluded patio under the ramada, sat across from him at the glass-topped table. "Ben, I'm going to tell you something in strictest confidence. Is that all right?"

Now he was curious, leaning forward eagerly. "You can trust me."

"It's about your partner. Alan Thompson."

He looked so disappointed. Wounded even. "What about him?"

"What kind of business arrangement do you have with Mr. Thompson? Are you incorporated?"

"I don't see why that's any of your concern, Mrs. Sonnenschein." His handsome jaw tightening.

"Ah, but it is," I said, folding my hands before me. "Let me explain. A friend of mine, her husband actually, used to be in business with this man. His name was Jack West back then. They had a partnership. A construction company. Your partner waited until the company was flush, right ahead of groundbreaking on a big project, then drained the accounts."

He went pale. *Yes, that's right, Ben. Your partner's a crook.*

I moved into the seat next to his, put my hand on his arm. I wore a good perfume, Ilona's Dior, it rose on the heat from my body. The wind shook the bamboo chimes. Water splashed in the small fountain. "They lost everything. The husband committed suicide."

"It was you, wasn't it?"

I ran my hand over my sweaty neck and his eyes followed. Those long-lashed eyes, the color of pool water, drank from my neck, my mouth.

"Who are you?" he asked, husky. "I happen to know Ilona Sonnenschein, and you aren't her."

"Does it matter? I'm a friend. I wanted to warn you."

"Consider me warned." He pressed his lips onto mine.

It'd been a long time since I'd really wanted a man. Maybe it was his desperation I found irresistible. I unlocked the house with the key hidden in the eaves, led him by the hand through the Californio-style living room, red tile floors and pony-skin rug, down the hall to the master bedroom with its low ceiling and heavy Mexican furniture.

We fucked like fat men gorging themselves at a casino buffet, stuffing ourselves with anything and everything. I kept the wig on, he seemed to dig it. He liked playing games. Good. He'd need that. He followed my lead.

We lay together for a while afterward under the big ceiling fan. I got us some ice water from the fridge—the ice was stale.

He drank, then he ran his cool hand up my hip, my flank. "I love this curve. Like a Gehry. Do you have a name?"

I leaned back on his sweaty chest, fleshy with muscle. "You don't like *Ilona?*"

"I like her fine. I don't want to fuck her, though. What's it say on your driver's license?"

"Miranda." I licked the sweat from his shoulder. "Promise me you're going to look into Alan Thompson, Ben. Call me when you figure it out." I made him memorize the number of the cheap phone I'd bought just for the occasion.

* * *

Late that night, he sent a text while I was in the can. *Need to see you. Tonight.*

Did I want him coming here? I looked around my trailer. Ratty and unaesthetic, a seventies museum—the Swedish modern lamps, the avocado shag, the whitewashed Formica paneling, my grandparents' club chairs. He would judge it. Mr. Tennis Club, the architect. But fuck it. I wanted to see him. *Sure, come.*

It took him all of five minutes. He must have done eighty. Down from Melvyn's or wherever he drank. He smelled of Scotch and someone's cigar. I answered the door looking like a rich boy's wet dream of a trailer slut—my cherry-blossom kimono, loosely wrapped, my dark hair in a messy twist. Mr. Frenchy on my shoulder. I could see a wild despair in him, his tawny hair pulled into spikes—he wanted to grab me, but was afraid of the bird.

"Can you?" He indicated my shoulder.

"That's Mr. Frenchy. He won't hurt you." But maybe he would. I put him back in his cage. "Was I right about Alan?"

He was too unnerved to speak. Instead, he untied my robe the rest of the way.

We fucked so hard, I thought we'd crack the wall.

Afterward, we had a nightcap on the lanai's glider, shared a j, and he came clean. "He's already moved a little—to a soils company, to a grader, to a geologist, all at the same address. The same account. He's getting ready to vacuum it all out. I can't believe it. I got everybody into Sunrise. My mother. My mother-in-law. My doctor. Friends at the Tennis Club. People in my fraternity."

"Didn't you have your lawyer look at the paperwork? Didn't somebody?" We were idiots but I'd expected a rich boy like Ben to be lawyered up.

He groaned. "I trusted him."

"We did too." I stroked the side of his face, kissed his cheek, relit the j and handed it to him. "So, tell me about this mother-in-law."

He started weeping. "I'm a shit. I'm a complete and total shit, and I'm about to have a full high colonic courtesy of Alan fucking Thompson."

"You could tell them."

He shook his head.

"Ever hear of an Indonesian monkey trap?" Holding the acrid smoke.

He lay down with his head in my lap, wiped his eyes on my kimono. Those beautiful muscled arms.

I stroked him as I spoke. "You take a hollow gourd and cut a hole just big enough for a monkey's hand. Then put some rice in. The monkey comes along, sticks its hand in there, grabs a handful." I could smell him, smoky and musky, scared and turned on. "But now his hand's too big to get out of the trap. That's how you catch a monkey."

"Why doesn't he let go?"

"He won't. He can't let go of it."

"And that's me? Is that what you're saying?"

"Why don't you tell your Tennis Club buddies that Thompson's a wrong guy? That you fucked up. Maybe they can freeze their accounts, pull their cash."

"I can't. I need Sunrise to go ahead," he said, rubbing his head against my thighs. "Not just the money. I *need* it."

I understood. He needed it, to prove something. To be the big man. Beholden to no one. I leaned over him, my breasts hovering above his face. "What if something was to happen to Alan Thompson?" I whispered in his ear.

He gazed up, his pretty eyes studying me. "Like what, a car accident?" He still wasn't getting it.

"I mean cancel his library card. Punch his ticket."

He laughed before he saw the look on my face. The chuckle died. "You're serious." He shook his head. "No, I couldn't do that. Not in a million years."

"But I could," I said. "It would be my pleasure."

The next day was windy, the palms streaming. I didn't have to check on Ben, he called me midmorning. He was on board.

"I can't stand him. He's chatting away in there with the door open, talking to some contractor. I'd like to drive a stake through his heart. Talking to me like we're best buddies. What gall." I could picture Jack—cheerful, hearty, talking on the phone, leaning back in his big leather chair, cowboy boots on the desk. "What do you want me to do?"

I told him to meet me at the IHOP on Dinah Shore Drive, a place where no one was likely to know us. At that hour, it would be mothers with little kids, retirees carefully counting their change.

The IHOP was ice rink cold, I imagined a Zamboni polishing the linoleum. I took a corner booth in the back, wearing the Elke wig and a modest shirt that nevertheless clung to every curve, sending a teasing mixed message of decorum and sex.

Ben looked like money in his pink shirt and his tan. Could he have been more conspicuous? He slipped into the booth next to me, lowered his Ray-Bans. "Come here often, Mabel?"

"I meet all my daddies here." Every daddy around us was in a wheelchair.

The waitress came by with a menu, refilled my coffee. He ordered a club sandwich, mayo on the side. I got the Rooty Tooty pancakes.

His eyebrows jerked upward. He seemed actually

shocked that a person would order pancakes at a pancake house.

"What do you want me to order, the chicken cordon bleu?"

We watched the waitress retreat, the bow of her apron. He lowered his voice. "You should have seen him. Swaggering around, on the phone with the fucking city planner. I'm ready, so help me god. Let's get this over with."

Over the rim of my cup, I studied him, wearing those stupid sunglasses. Sure, he'd like me to get rid of Jack for him. Keep his Ivy League hands clean. But this was what I'd lived for these last years. The only thing bringing air into my lungs, blood to my heart. "In three nights, you're going out with him. Just the boys. You've got something to talk to him about, confessions, advice, father-son stuff. Leave your car and take his. Don't park yours at the office, use a garage. He drives, that's important. Take him somewhere they won't know you. Not Melvyn's or Spencer's. A hotel. A bar at the airport. Not a casino, they're loaded with cameras."

Our meals came. I could see the wonder on his face as I tucked into the pancakes. "No carbs at your house? Poor Ben."

He grabbed my hand. "Miranda, I can't stand the way I've been living my life. Like a stupid kid. But when this is over, it's going to be different. It's going to be you and me and the whole wide world."

"Easy, pardner."

He let go of my hand. "You're not getting away from me," he whispered. "I used to think Alan's girlfriend was hot. But you melt metal. I'd like to come over there and fuck you into next year."

You're not getting away from me. I'd have to think about that. Later.

* * *

He texted my burner every hour for the next three days. How it was torture to go to the office. How Alan invited him and Sherry up to his place for dinner, to talk to some people about a development in Laguna Canyon. *I hate this.*

Miss you.

He's making his special burgers.

I hope he chokes.

I remembered them well. Worcestershire sauce, a bit of horseradish. Those barbeques we used to have. All that father-son sharing of esoteric grill lore. Reeling us in, putting us to sleep. Well, your son's awake now, Jack. Sharpening the knives.

He called me, late, from home. Sherry must have been sleeping. I heard the water splash, the sexy rumble of his voice. "As soon as we break ground, I'm taking you to Tokyo. First class. You see *Lost in Translation?*"

I hadn't been to a movie in years.

"In that wig, you remind me of Scarlett Johansson." He loved his games.

"Anybody get killed in it?"

"Jesus, Miranda! Relax. We've got this."

Nobody slept the night before. I went out to the arroyo and shot off some of the fresh ammo I'd bought at the Gun Barn out on Indian Canyon. The blasts were startlingly loud but nobody called the cops, nobody did shit. I imagined him kneeling in the dirt. *Goodbye, Jack.*

After work they went for some Mexican food, then to a jazz bar. Good. Dark.

How's it going? I texted him.

Having a good old chat. Says he wanted to be a drummer

when he was a kid. Hemet. Jack was from Hemet. A tough little town on the other side of the mountain. A local boy. *I'm laughing with a dead man. Flying.*

I'd told him to take one of Sherry's Dexis, so he wouldn't be totally shitfaced after a night out with Jack. I hoped he'd only taken one.

At last, it was eleven. I drove up to the site in the moonlight, descended into that beautiful bowl of rock and sage and cactus that held all of Ben's dreams. I could see it as if it were already built. He'd brought me up here before—showed me where the pools would be, the firepits and tennis courts.

I didn't need any speed to feel like I was flying. Every gesture seemed symbolic now, perfect, relentless. I took an old green army blanket and covered my car so it wouldn't glow, found my hiding place behind some boulders on a rise, where the moon would be in his face. And then life would begin. The clock that had stopped would start again.

Okay, put a wrap on it, I texted him. *Showtime.*

I imagined them walking down to the car, no valet. Jack squeezing Ben on the shoulder. The drive down South Palm Canyon, past the mobile court which had been my final resting place. No more. I was going to rise, rise. Any minute they'd be turning up Coyote Hill Drive. I waited, crouching with the scorpions and the tarantulas and the snakes in the desert night. All of the hunters.

Here they came, headlights bursting over the crest. The Porsche jolted as it descended the roughly graded road. It came to a stop right where the big pool was going to be.

They got out, so clear in the moonlight. Cocky Jack with his cowboy boots. Ben yammering about something, waving his arms around. "Yes!" he shouted. "See? This is it. This is the Future Perfect."

Jack lit a cigar, leaning up against the silver Porsche, offering his Steve McQueen grin. He held one out to Ben. Long and thin, a *panatela*. *See, I remembered* . . . A last smoke, a final farewell.

"I love this place," Ben said, exhaling. "Maybe I'll move in when it's built."

"Lot of projects ahead," Jack said. "This ain't the end."

Oh, but it was, Jack. Silently, the sand slipping under my shoes, I came down from the rocks. My clothes were dark, my hair, neither of them saw me at first. Then Ben did. And Jack. The gun glinting in my hand. I would have worn the wig, but it would have stood out too soon, spoiled my surprise.

"Hi, Jack. Remember me?"

Ben tossed the cigar, moved away from his partner, skirted the nonexistent pool, giving me a clear shot, and came around to stand by me.

Jack took it in, me, Ben. He was figuring it out. No smile now. "Miranda Constantine," he said. "Not somebody I'd be likely to forget."

"Guess you didn't go to Bogotá. Bet your wife wasn't even Colombian."

Even with a gun pointed at him, he managed a laugh. "She wasn't even my wife." He hooked his thumbs into his belt loops.

The moon turned everything to bone. "Did you know Gil hanged himself?"

He sucked on his cigar. A cloud of the stinking stuff rose into the moonlight above his head. "What do you want me to say, Miranda? Sorry your old man couldn't take it."

"Put your fucking hands on your head."

He did it, his cigar clamped between his fingers.

"Kneel."

He didn't do it. "You were always tougher than him, angel," he said. "Is this what you did for eight years? Look for me? Get all wet thinking about how you were going to fix me? Think about me every night before bed?"

"That's right, Jack. I'm a good hater. I don't let go of things." The gun tugged at me. The gun wanted to have its say. But first, I'd have mine. I'd waited a long time for this.

"I know what you can't let go of," he said. But he looked awfully stupid saying it with his hands on his head.

"The million you stole? The kid I never had? Somebody's gotta pay for all that. Someone who looks a lot like you." I didn't know the last time I'd felt so good. My sails unfurling in the moonlight.

"Did you tell Benjie here about us?"

"There was no us." I could feel Ben next to me, alert as a hunting dog. "You sick son of a bitch."

"See, Ben, Gil wasn't much in the sack—"

"Shut up, Jack."

"And the lady here was so lonely. Bored. Too much juice for a weakling like Gil. But we were a match, weren't we, darlin'? We set that bed on fire."

That round bed. Wearing Sarita's black lace stockings. I'd never had a man like Jack before. A real match.

"You fucked him?" Ben whispered.

"And poor old Gil found out." He snorted. That smirk.

I raised the barrel of the gun in both hands, closed one eye, lined up the sights. "And you didn't feel anything. Not one moment of regret."

"Can't say that I did, darlin'. It's what I do."

"Let me ask you one question," I said, pulling off the safety. "Answer correctly, I might let you live. Tell me, what's it all for? You could have made that company work. You could actually build Sunrise. All this scamming and fucking people over, people who love you, who trust you. Just tell me why. Is it just money?"

Alan took one hand off his head to puff on the cigar. He grinned. "The money's the sideshow, darlin'," he said. "It's the winning. Every time I take some simpleton like Ben here, or put one over on the city fathers, those Tennis Club assholes—I win. Even if I die, I win. That's why you're always going to be a loser, Miranda, even if you shoot me and leave me to the crows. You're a great fuck, but you don't have the brains to come in out of the rain. Eight years, and all you could do with your life was think about me."

I must have been squeezing the trigger harder than I thought—the blast caught him in the chest. It shoved him backward into the Porsche. Ben shouted, "Jesus!" as the sound bounced off the rocks all around us. Dark blood gurgled out of Jack's mouth, bubbled out and rolled down his chin, staining his shirt.

The second shot dropped him to his knees. He fell onto his side, clutching his chest, his boots dog-kicking in the sand.

I stood over him, watching his blood, black in the moonlight. "Who's the loser now, darlin'?"

I'd shoot him again, but at this range I'd have blood all over me.

Ben just stood there, his hands over his mouth. Then he turned and staggered away, threw up all those expensive Scotches.

I pocketed Jack's cell phone, pried his wallet out. Credit cards, driver's license, receipts, library card—shit, Danika'd have to return his books—business cards, including one for a lawyer in Phoenix. A fat wad of cash. He'd always liked cash. I took a single bill from it—a twenty—wiped the leather on my shirttail, and put the wallet back into his hip pocket. "You done barfing?" I said to Ben.

I folded back the blanket covering my car, rolled it, stuck it in the trunk, took out a package of Clorox wipes and cleaned my hands, wiped the gun. I'd toss it and the phone into a storm drain on the way to Ben's car.

"And we just . . . leave him there?" The smell of Scotch and barf clung to him.

"He had plenty of enemies. They'll never prove who did it . . . You coming or you want to walk?"

He looked wild as he climbed in next to me. "But I was the last one seen with him."

Yeah, things get real, Ben. "Just play it cool, and remember—Sunrise is going to get built. Someone settled a score with Alan, but Sunrise is going to happen."

He was shaking but I knew I could count on him to keep quiet. If he told the cops he'd have to admit he was the one who lured the man out there. *Accessory before the fact.* But I didn't like the way he kept saying, "I can't believe you did it. How can you be so calm?"

I was more than calm. I was redeemed. I felt like I'd been driving up and down the block all these years, looking for a certain address, and someone had finally pointed to the house. My key had fit. I was home. *I won, you son of a bitch.*

I dumped the gun and the phone. Ben's teeth were chattering. "You did great," I said, talking him down. "You're free of him." He nodded, swallowing. "We'll get through the week, and then you're going to build Sunrise."

In a few minutes we were pulling up to the parking garage. Nobody around. Palm Springs, despite its legend, rolls up the sidewalks at ten.

"Miranda." He crushed me to him, burying his face in my hair. "Let me come home with you."

"Not tonight. You've got to go home and act like you've been there the whole time. Get some sleep. Be ready to talk to cops tomorrow. I'll call you in a few days."

He was suddenly on fire. "Fuck me, Miranda. I need you."

Why not? We crawled into the backseat and did it there like two teenagers.

By the third day, it was all over the news. Millionaire developer Alan Thompson found dead on the site of his latest development. Two bullet wounds. Motive unclear. A stunned-looking Ben in wrinkled linen and a borsalino. It was fine, he *should* look stunned. An innocent man, his partner gunned down.

I went to work as usual. The dog people in Old Las Palmas called. *El profesor* liked our layout. I presented the bid, broken down into labor and materials. But as I was driving back from Cathedral City, I got a call from Shirley. "Doll. It's bad. Don't come home. You got cops running all over the place. They're interviewing the neighbors. Showed me a picture of that guy Thompson. Asked if I knew you. Me, I don't know nobody— not my own mother."

Ben had panicked. All he had to do was keep his mouth shut. Fucking Ben. What did Jack say? *Trust nobody never.* But that's a hard life.

I met Shirley at the Ralph Lauren in the Cabazon outlet mall. Parked the Audi on the blank side of the mall. "They tore the hell out of your place," Shirley said under her breath, going through the clothes on the sale rack.

"How's Mr. Frenchy?"

She took out a silk blouse, turquoise, held it up to me.

"This is nice." Then under her breath: "Eleanor's got him. But you better think of someone to go visit. Who do you know out of town?"

"How far out of town?"

"Mexico?"

Fucking Ben. Just when I thought I didn't have anything else to lose, turns out I'd had a life. Her, the bird. My place. Gone. It was my hand in the rice trap, after all.

Luckily you didn't need a passport to get into Mexico, only to come back. And what was the likelihood of that?

Shirley found an ATM and took out a sheaf of bills, slipped them into my hand. "Here. I owed it to Lottie but she never collected."

I didn't argue. I put them in my wallet and texted Mauricio.

Estoy en problemas. Muy serio.

Mi casa. Veinte minutos.

I left my Audi at the mall and threw my good cell phone out the window on the way, into the wastes before Highway 111. She took her time driving to Mauricio's house, watching her mirrors, staying to sixty. She pulled up in front of his sweet suburban ranchito. I remembered when he lived in a shit RV in Desert Hot Springs. He'd done well for himself.

The vintage maroon Thunderbird drew admiring glances as we sat waiting. Her voice was huskier than ever. "Send me a postcard when you get where you're going, doll."

I hugged her, her brittle little bones.

I could still see Jack there in the desert, looking up from the dirt, laughing.

She waited with me until Mauricio's truck turned into the drive, *XTerra Gardens—Ecological, Beautiful, Sustainable.* My cell number. He was going to have to change that.

* * *

I left at sunset, in a rattling ladderback truck driven by silent Juanito, the oldest of Mauricio's crew. Sunset washed the valley in soft blues and rosy golds—the farther from the mountain we drove the more magnificent it became. The wind turbines let out their unearthly groans. Behind us, Palm Springs revealed itself only as a little cluster of lights at the foot of immense, solemn Mount San Jacinto, indigo against the oranges and purples.

Up ahead, night was coming. In the desert, night doesn't fall, it rises. The moon, great and smooth-edged, appeared, eyeing the desert, casting its magic over mean little cities—Indio, Thermal, Mecca—bathing them in a light that would never burn.

I turned on the radio, tried to find something not ranchero. The Voice of the Desert came in, crisp. Frank. *Come fly with me . . .* Always Frank.

THE GUEST

BY ERIC BEETNER

Historic Tennis Club

"We have a situation."

Randall had been renting out the pool house at his place in Palm Springs for about a year and had expected the occasional phone call like this. Grayson, his friend who watched the house while Randall worked in LA, kept the calls to a minimum so Randall knew something serious had happened. *Just not plumbing. Please don't let it be plumbing.*

"Can it wait till the weekend?" Randall said. "I'm coming out Friday night."

It was Wednesday, the worst day of the week. All the Monday haters could shut up—midweek was the worst.

"Um . . . no. I don't think so."

"What is it?"

"I'd rather not say over the phone." Grayson sounded odd. Hollowed out and monotone, which was unlike his usual flamboyant self.

"Can you take care of it?"

"I kind of need you to come out here."

"Tonight?" Randall asked.

"Please?"

He'd been only half paying attention until then, but Randall took his hand off the computer mouse and focused on the phone, the strange dull flatness to Grayson's voice.

"Jesus, you're scaring me. Did something happen?"

"Just please come out. Tonight. Right now."

"Okay." Randall looked around his desk, set designs that had a firm deadline before cameras rolled in three weeks. Still, if Grayson was this freaked out . . . "I'm leaving now."

The house was a Mediterranean style in the Historic Tennis Club neighborhood of Palm Springs. Almost fifteen years ago in a market lull, he'd acquired it for cheap in the highly desirable district. He loved the neighborhood and counted the days until he could retire there full time instead of only weekends and breaks between work, of which there had been more and more lately, putting off a permanent move further into the future.

The house was modest and a dated wreck when he bought it, but Randall had a designer's eye and no family or kids so all his extra money went into it. His neighbors were boutique hotels, homes on the historic registry and, to the west, the San Jacinto Mountains. And of course, the Tennis Club where he had yet to play in more than a decade and a half.

He'd repaired the crack in the pool and had it refilled, then remodeled and turned the pool shack into a livable six-hundred-square-foot guest space. Once the idea of Airbnb came around, it was a natural fit. He paid Grayson, his on-site caretaker, by giving him a free place to live.

In the year since the pool house became an Airbnb, this was the first time Grayson had summoned him to the desert midweek.

He crossed over Palm Canyon Drive and into the placid tree-lined streets with expensive landscaping trying to fool people and keep them from realizing they were in the desert. When he parked at the house, Grayson was there to meet him at the front door, chewing his nails. Grayson was nothing if not a vain man, always worried about his looks and whether men found him attractive, so biting his fingers was a bad sign.

"What in the world is going on?" Randall said.

"Follow me."

Grayson led him through the house to the backyard. The palm trees were uplit and the pool cast a lazy movement of blue light over the yard and back of the house from the underwater lights. A shadow moved across the patterns of rippling water. Randall looked down into the pool.

A body floated facedown.

When he turned back to Grayson, there was a smear of blood across his lip where he'd chewed his nails until they bled.

Randall tried to keep his voice even and calm, despite the sheer panic going on inside him. "What happened?"

Grayson spoke in a voice that was half whine, half pleading for his life. "He was staying here. He was fun. And nice."

Randall's pulse quickened until it made his chest ache.

"We were having fun," Grayson went on. "He liked me."

"Grayson, what happened?"

"We were drinking and then we did some poppers . . ."

"Poppers? Jesus, what is this, the nineties?"

"I fell asleep. When I woke up . . . he was like this."

Randall turned back to the pool and looked at the floating body. He was young, early twenties. His shirt floated open around him, like delicate wings catching a breeze. Beneath the fabric Randall could see he was slim and broad shouldered, like a swimmer. Someone who should never have drowned.

"It was an accident." Randall said the words out loud like maybe he was trying to make them come true. "Yes, it was an accident. He must have had a heart attack, or passed out, or maybe hit his head or something."

"Did you try to revive him?"

"It had already been hours when I woke up."

Randall crouched down, sitting back on his heels and staring at the water. "What do we do?"

A single cricket chirped from the planter bed and the sound bore into Randall's ears like a needle. For all the romanticism around a chorus of crickets at night, a solo insect could drive a person to insanity.

He pictured police. Publicity. Questions. Unwanted scandal and attention.

"We need to get rid of him," Randall said, not knowing exactly what that even meant. All he knew was that he wasn't about to deal with police and the investigation into his life this would bring. He'd be a pariah in the neighborhood. The people in this enclave took their status seriously. The Tennis Club neighborhood was where you wanted to be in Palm Springs. And they didn't have bodies floating in their pools.

And his past wasn't entirely clean. There'd been a boyfriend back east and it had ended badly. A restraining order against Randall. An order he broke on more than one occasion. There'd been violence, a thirty-day stay in jail. Court-ordered anger management. Randall wasn't proud of it, but it was in his past—both miles and years away. And he intended to keep it there.

He didn't like the police, knew what they thought about someone with a record.

He could avoid bringing up his past again, avoid threatening his relationship with his neighbors, his coworkers. If they moved fast, he could hide this.

"You fish him out," Randall said. "I'll go pack up his stuff."

"What? Why me?" Grayson asked.

"Because he died on your watch."

"It was a little bit of X and a few poppers and some alcohol."

Randall aimed a finger at him as he walked around the

pool, the blue light playing across his skin. "Exactly why I don't want the cops coming here."

Inside the pool house Randall found a single suitcase open on the floor. Some dirty socks and underwear next to it. A few T-shirts and shorts in one drawer of the chest. He packed up the toothbrush and comb and electric shaver from the bathroom. It was quick, easy work to rid the place of any evidence of the dead man's stay.

On the nightstand was a cell phone. They couldn't hide that he was there. With the way the room was rented out on Airbnb, there'd be a record. They had to show him leaving.

Everything went into the suitcase except for the cell phone. When Randall arrived back in the yard, cell phone in hand, Grayson had hooked the pool skimming net over the young man's head and was trying to drag him to the side of the pool.

Grayson winced and squeezed his eyes shut. "Oh, for fuck's sake." He put down the suitcase and stuffed the cell phone in his pocket. He took the handle of the net from Grayson and towed the body in by its neck to the steps in the shallow end. "Help me," he said.

Grayson didn't move.

"Damnit, Grayson, get over here and help me get him out. I don't like this any more than you do."

Grayson looked like he was going to be sick, but he joined Randall. The cricket kept sawing away and the sound pushed the needle deeper into Randall's spine.

They dragged the body out onto the pool deck where it seemed to deflate as the water seeped from his lungs. Now, on his back, Randall could see the young man had been hot—when he was alive.

"How many of my guests have you slept with?" he asked Grayson.

"Jesus, Randy. Not now."

"How many?"

Grayson turned away from the body. "One or two, okay? Happy?"

Randall often wondered why he and Grayson had never hooked up. He always told himself it was because Grayson was too immature. This kind of behavior proved it. He wanted to kick him out, but they'd be forever bonded by this night.

He removed the phone from his pocket. "We have to open this." He looked at Grayson. "What was his name?"

"Mickey."

Randall felt a weird pang of guilt that he hadn't thought to ask his name before, and now he regretted that he had. It gave the dead man an identity. But the body in front of him wasn't a person. It was a problem to be hidden away. It wasn't a human being, just some debris in his pool he needed to get rid of. It was the only way he could do it.

Randall woke up the phone and it asked for a password. No way he could ever guess it right in a million years. "Maybe it has that face recognition." He pointed the phone at Mickey's face. It forced Randall to look closely. The skin was blue-gray in the light from the pool. His lips parted slightly, and his tongue swollen and purple. His eyes were clouded over.

Not a person, just an object.

The phone didn't react. Randall straightened. "Shit." He tapped the home screen a few more times, uselessly. "Let's try his fingerprints. Give me a hand."

Grayson had stepped away and kept his back to the body. "What?"

"I cannot hold the phone and his hand at the same time. Just come over here."

Grayson hugged himself and shrank away. "I can't."

Randall stalked the space between them and got in Grayson's face. "You can and you will. Right fucking now. We need to fix this and do it quick, so get your ass over here and help me with his finger."

Randall spun and marched back toward the body. Halfway there he turned toward the sound of the cricket in the planter, stomping his feet as he went. "Shut up, shut up, shut up!"

The cricket went quiet. When he turned, Grayson was standing next to the body.

Randall held the phone and Grayson shut his eyes and lifted Mickey's hand while Randall guided the dead man's index finger to the small button on the bottom of the phone. Nothing happened.

"He's too bloated and pruned," Grayson said. "It's like he's been in a bathtub for too long."

"Try another finger."

Grayson pressed each finger of his right hand to the phone and nothing happened.

"Try the other hand."

Grayson shivered and leaned away. "I don't want to touch him again."

"You have to."

Randall saw a thought flash over his face.

"Wait," said Grayson. "He was left-handed. Yes. He used his left hand when he—" Grayson stopped himself and could have been blushing but it was hard for Randall to tell in the dim light. Grayson got the left index finger on the pad and the phone came to life.

Randall found the Airbnb app, opened it, and entered a five-star review for his own guest house. He left a comment: *Great stay. Perfect location. Sad to leave, but I'll be back!*

Randall powered off the phone, wiped it free of his own

fingerprints, then tossed it on top of the suitcase. He let out a deep sigh, feeling as close to safe as he had since he'd arrived. "Okay," he said, "let's go bury him."

The San Jacinto Mountains loomed. The hills where the sun disappeared each night as it sank toward the other side of the world rose in front of them now like the entrance to a dark and foreboding stadium. At each step Randall thought, *No going back now.* But really there was. There always was. The steeper the road climbed into the hills, though, the more turning back seemed impossible.

The roads didn't travel into the hills, rather they snaked around them. The dry, brown San Jacintos were too steep to be developed, not pretty enough for anyone to level the earth and make it habitable. Perfect for hiding a dead body. Not easy to get to, though.

Randall had fallen victim to a salesman when he bought his Range Rover. He hadn't needed an all-terrain vehicle. He now silently praised that pushy guy in his ill-fitting suit.

With each switchback turn they made, Mickey's body slid from one side of the back to the other, clunking against the side walls. The confines of the car felt tight around them and Randall could see each sound making Grayson wince as if he'd been touched by a lit match. Around another turn and Randall couldn't take it anymore. He steered them off-road and wound away from prying eyes into a suitably remote area.

They couldn't have gotten more than a hundred feet from the road. They weren't even a third of the way up the hills. It seemed like a terrible place to hide anything, and yet in the darkness he felt as if they could be a thousand miles from civilization.

Randall had been surprised by how malleable and rubbery

the body had been as they tried to lift it into the back hatch. Grayson had moaned and made little squeaks at every turn.

"Okay, let's go quick," Randall said.

This was really it. No going back. Last chance. As he lifted the shovel from behind the body, Randall knew this was either the best or worst decision of his life. The one that would save him from humiliation and scorn or would make him an accomplice to a very serious crime.

He was exactly that, though, whether he got caught or not. But it was always better not to get caught.

"Do we need to dig a hole?" Grayson asked. "Can't we just dump him and get going?" He bit at his already bloody fingers.

"We don't want anyone to find him."

"Yeah, but if they did, they can't link him to us. You did the thing with the phone and we cleaned up."

"How do you explain a guy in the woods who drowned?"

Grayson's anxiety turned angry. "Just come on, let's get it done."

They took turns digging. After twenty minutes and sore palms, they had the shallowest of shallow graves.

"That's good enough," Grayson said.

"No, it isn't."

"Randy, come on. I can't do this anymore."

Randall knew Grayson wanted to get home, get drunk, maybe high, and forget this ever happened. He wasn't fool enough to think Grayson had fallen for the houseguest. Not in the two days he'd been there. It was sexual, and that's all. Grayson was the hookup king of the desert. How the guy stayed disease-free was beyond him.

Randall dragged the body, still soggy and flexible to the point that it seemed like the bones had vanished, and rolled it into the hole. It would just be deep enough to cover him and probably leave a small mound. Good enough. Randall wanted this to be done too. He needed his own drink, or three.

He let Grayson weep quietly against the hood of the car while he covered the body in loose, sandy soil.

They drove down the mountain without speaking. Grayson broke the silence with a single sob that made Randall turn to him. Grayson's head leaned against the cool glass of the window but his eyes were shut tight to the lights of Palm Springs at night as they returned to the neighborhood.

It was too late for Randall to drive back to LA, plus he was exhausted beyond anything he could remember. He and Grayson said good night, then retreated to their bedrooms. For Randall, sleep was as hard to hold onto as water from the pool.

Back in LA, a week of fitful sleep went by. Randall called Grayson to find out if anyone had been around asking about Mickey. Each time he called he could tell Grayson was drunk, or otherwise impaired. He felt a little jealous. He could have done with a week of being numb himself but work beckoned.

He went to the desert the following weekend. He and Grayson barely spoke. The pool house loomed in the backyard like a monument to their crime. Randall couldn't look at the pool.

"Did the guy come and clean it?" he asked.

"Not until next week," Grayson said. The smell of weed followed him around like a cologne.

"Call him. Have him come tomorrow or Monday."

Randall saw the floating body whenever he glanced at the water. He understood how the myth of ghosts came to be. He couldn't stop seeing the dead man whenever he closed his eyes and if that wasn't a haunting, he didn't know what was.

He retreated back to LA Monday morning and considered selling the Palm Springs house.

The cleaning crew had been out, and Randall gave them an extra hundred to do a deep clean. Randall contemplated draining the pool or restricting access, but he knew it was one of the house's biggest selling points.

Another week went by and with each passing day Randall felt more confident that they'd gotten away with hiding Mickey's death. He'd never escape his own conscience, but avoiding the police was a cold comfort at least.

The following weekend they had another guest in the pool house who arrived on Friday evening. Randall felt nervous to have anyone stay there, but life went on. For some.

The new guest was a man, arriving alone. Randall, over the phone, reminded Grayson to keep it in his pants.

"How could you even say that?" Grayson responded.

"I wish I didn't have to."

Randall arrived late Friday night and found Grayson and the new guest arguing in the doorway to the pool house. Grayson was obviously high.

"I just don't know why it's such a big deal?" the guest was saying.

"I don't know what you want me to say," Grayson whined, his voice loud and slurry.

Randall dropped his bag and edged around the pool toward the two men. Fear gripped his chest and he tried to remember the symptoms of a heart attack.

"Hey, hey. What's going on?"

The guest turned to him. "Are you the owner?"

"Is there a problem with the room?"

"My name is Karl Donlevy and my son stayed here two

weeks ago. No one has seen him since and I just want to find out what happened to my boy. This man isn't answering any of my questions."

Randall felt the blood rush from his head. His vision went dark at the edges, but he fought to keep it together.

"Your son?"

"My son, yes. Mickey."

Randall did his best to compose himself, to seem natural when his guts were tangled in knots of fear. He reached for a lie, felt beads of sweat on his upper lip. He turned to Grayson. "Did a Mickey Donlevy stay here?"

Grayson began to weep. No help at all.

"Grayson, why don't you go inside. I'll help Mr. Donlevy."

Karl stepped out of the doorway. "No, no, no. I want him to stay. I think he knows something."

Grayson turned to Randall, tears in his bloodshot eyes. "What do I say?"

Randall put a hand on his shoulder and showed all the terror on his face to Grayson to try to make him understand he needed to shut up. With a deep, composing breath he turned to Karl. "I'm so sorry. He drinks. Sometimes too much." *He's going to fuck this up*, Randall thought.

Karl drilled into Randall with eyes hard as stones. "My son was here. You were the last ones to see him. Tell me what happened. Where did he go? What did he say?"

"Look," Randall said, then had to swallow before any more words would come out. A lie would never fit through the tight constriction of his throat. "He was here. I remember the reservation. Grayson said he stayed the two days and then left. I never even saw him. I don't know where he went after here, or who he might have gone to see. All I know is he checked out, left us a good rating, and that was that."

He gasped for breath as if he'd just swam ten laps in the pool. He tried for a casual smile as if this was all a misunderstanding. He studied Karl's eyes to see if the lie had worked but he could read nothing.

The man turned away from Randall and back toward Grayson. He stepped forward and put a hand on Grayson's arm and spun him. "You were with him. What are you not telling me?"

"Nothing!" Grayson said.

Randall tried to wedge himself between the new guest and Grayson. "Sir, please."

Karl wouldn't let go. "All I want is an answer."

"I told you," Randall said. "He drinks."

"This isn't just alcohol. He knows something."

Grayson ripped his arm away. "Let me go."

"You've got to tell me."

"What do you want from me?"

Randall could see the situation getting out of control. He felt the same stomach-knotting sensation from two weeks before. He tried to move between the two men again, but Grayson was out of his mind and Karl was too consumed with grief and wanting answers.

"I want you to tell me the *truth*!" Karl screamed.

Grayson straightened and looked at Randall. "I have to tell him."

A panicked *No* pushed against Randall's lips, but he held it in. He pleaded with Grayson through his eyes.

"Tell me what?" Karl said.

Grayson's bloodshot eyes turned away from Randall. He looked down, his head hanging into his chest.

"Your boy isn't coming back."

The two men squared off. Randall hovered nearby, feeling

the static charge in the air. Karl's skin reddened and a vein began throbbing in his temple.

Randall tried his best calming voice. "Okay, listen, if we can just—"

"What's he saying?"

"Nothing. I told you, he's drunk. Now if you—"

"What did you do to my boy?"

Grayson began weeping again. "It wasn't my fault."

Karl launched himself at Grayson, tackling him down to the pool deck. He straddled the weeping caretaker and smashed his head against the pool coping. Randall reared back from the sound of bone hitting concrete.

"What did you do to my son?" Karl spit out the words on a string of saliva that dripped from his mouth. His face flared sunburn red and the tendons on his neck were taut like guitar strings. He pounded Grayson's head against the edge of the pool again.

Randall saw blood drip into the clear water and dissipate into a deep purple cloud. He stepped forward, then halted when he heard new sounds of anguish and rage coming from deep in Karl's throat.

"Stop." Randall knew his words meant nothing to the grieving father.

"He was here. What did you do?"

Again, Grayson's skull cracked against the hard surface.

Randall stood rooted in place, unsure of what to do with the wild animal in front of him. He didn't want to risk having Karl turn his vicious anger on him and had no idea how to stop him.

Karl stood up, huffing out breath like a bull in the ring. He spun and retreated into the pool house. Randall went to Grayson and turned him over. His forehead had a deep dent in it and his eyes were open and glazed over. Blood leaked from his mouth and from behind his left eye.

Karl came back out to the yard. Randall looked up and saw the gun in Karl's hand.

"You tell me what happened to my son, you bastard."

For the second time, Randall found himself on Route 74 on his way into the San Jacinto Mountains. Finding the shovel had been easier this time since it was no longer buried under other unused junk in the garage. He wasn't so sure he could find where they'd buried Mickey, though. The gun pointing at him from Karl's hand in the passenger seat gave him sufficient motivation to try. One thing he was definitely not sure of was whether he would return to his beloved Tennis Club neighborhood alive.

The smell of fresh blood leaking from Grayson's skull filled the car. Randall had had the Rover detailed when he got back to LA. Now Grayson knocked around the same dark space spreading blood that would be much harder to remove.

Karl hadn't said anything since they got in the car. His mouth hung open as he breathed, and his eyes were far away. Randall didn't trust the gun in his hand with that lost look on his face. His son was dead, and two strangers had covered it up. Where was a father to go from there?

Randall cursed his foolish decision not to go to the police. A few weeks' embarrassment, a few awkward interactions with the neighbors, what would it have hurt? Now he was at risk of either being turned over to the cops looking guilty of nothing less than murder or being killed by a distraught and angry father.

Randall could hardly even blame the man.

"It's been . . . hard," said Karl.

Randall turned and Karl kept his eyes staring into the blank distance out the windshield.

He spoke, but not really to anyone. "Mickey had issues with drugs. A suicide attempt." He cleared his throat, the words seeming to get stuck there. "Two, actually. I always knew . . . I figured, anyway, that I'd find him like this. Dead somewhere. All I . . . all I wanted was for him not to be alone at the end. To tell him that I love him."

Karl fell silent again, his eyes never wavering from the dark road ahead.

"I think this is it," Randall said.

Karl looked at the bleak landscape lit by the headlights. Randall knew he was thinking how his son didn't deserve this as a final resting place. Nobody did.

He turned the Rover off the road and found the grooves his tires had left before. Around the bend and away from view of the road, he stopped. They sat in the car for a long time, the headlights illuminating a tunnel in the darkness and at the end of the tunnel—a small mound of earth.

"This is where my boy is?" Karl said.

Randall nodded.

"Get out."

At gunpoint Randall walked to the mound that hid Mickey's body. He held the shovel in one hand and stared at the ground, expecting a bullet in the back at any moment.

"He's in there?" Karl asked.

Again, Randall nodded.

"Dig."

It didn't take long. The shallowness of the grave was like an insult. He uncovered an arm first and Karl let out a pained wail and turned away.

"Get him out. You get him out of that fucking dirt. I'm taking him home."

Mickey's flesh had gone from gray to dark. The stench

was overpowering, and Randall had to stop several times to retch. Karl stood back with the gun in hand and watched.

Randall opened the back to the Rover and dragged Grayson out into the dirt to make room for Mickey. He had no choice but to bear-hug the corpse and lift it into the back.

The smell would never be out of his nose. The feeling would never leave his skin. The guilt had a physical sensation, a rank stench of death. He would never leave this moment, even if he somehow managed to live beyond the next few minutes.

"Am I supposed to put him in there?" Randall asked Karl, looking down at Grayson's body as he gestured toward the shallow grave.

"You do what you want."

Karl had wandered to the back of the Rover and stood looking at his son. Randall had placed him awkwardly in the back, a tangle of limbs and dirt-crusted skin.

Randall dragged Grayson by the ankles to the hole and pushed him in. He took up the shovel and threw a clump of dirt over the body. He glanced over his shoulder to where Karl stood in darkness, entranced by the sight of his boy coiled lifeless in the back of the car.

Taking the shovel in hand, Randall crept away from the hole. A light wind around them filled the air with a low static hum. Now and then a bird called out. They were close enough to the road that when a car did happen by, which wasn't often, they would hear it as a rush of air rising and falling in pitch.

As he grew closer, a look of resolve crossed Karl's stoic face. He was looking at the inevitable. A moment he had expected, though maybe not in this way. His son, lost to him. It would have happened one way or the other.

Randall saw his worst decision laid out before him. He'd

further tortured a man who had suffered already with a son struggling with addiction. And Randall had thought only of himself when he'd chosen to hide the boy's death from the world.

It hadn't made the problem go away. It still led Karl to his door. But after Karl, who else would there be? The one man looking for Mickey was here. The one link to the houseguest.

Randall gripped the shovel. He could still make it all go away.

He'd already done the worst, hadn't he? He'd made his choice for self-preservation.

He lifted the shovel and swung.

He crossed back over Belardo and into his neighborhood. He stood under a stinging-hot shower for a half hour. He rinsed the shovel off with a hose and stored it in the back of the garage behind several boxes of old books.

Randall poured himself a bourbon, no ice. His skin itched with the touch of three dead bodies. His head filled with the smell of fresh blood and two-week-old rotting flesh. His ears replayed the crack of bone as the shovel blade connected with Karl's skull.

A single cricket needled his song into Randall's brain.

It would be with him forever, the guilt. The memory. Stench, sound, touch of cold flesh.

He woke to the sound of the phone. The sun was up, but he didn't know if it was morning light or afternoon sun. He answered. An inquiry: was the pool house available?

"No," Randall said, his voice weathered and foreign-sounding to himself. "I'm no longer accepting guests."

A COLD GIRL

BY KELLY SHIRE

Cathedral City

At seventeen, Jessie knew a few things. Like if you knew a guy and pictured a sweaty scene of the two of you tangled in the dark, chances were good that he'd already beat you to it. He probably imagined his own version, and in X-rated detail, back when you were stalled out on how good his forearms looked in his white dress shirt with the rolled-up sleeves. Nick, for example: though he was her cousin Mia's boyfriend, she caught him looking at her since she arrived two weeks ago. And she thought about him, plenty. It was hard not to, with them all living under the same roof in Mia's tiny apartment. She tried not to stare when he came out of the shower after work, a towel wrapped around his waist to walk from the bathroom to the bedroom he shared with Mia.

So, she didn't feel guilty lying in her sofa bed at night and conjuring up scenarios with Nick, scenes of kissing and rubbing against each other, her hands braced on his golden arms. In her visions, the room was always dark except for a row of white candles in the background, and she was dressed in something filmy and flowing, something that made her look like Stevie Nicks as she wafted into the room. And it was always late, very late at night.

Compared to Palm Springs, the town that was its immediate neighbor to the west, Cathedral City was a poor relation, an awkward middle child, the last kid picked for the team. This was also how Jessie had always felt whenever she stood beside, or thought about, her older cousin, Mia. Mia and her family lived in Cathedral City, but to Jessie, her cousin had always seemed like Palm Springs: more popular, prettier, and desirable.

Jessie wasn't exactly poor, but she'd grown up in a small bungalow up in Santa Clara. Though her parents' house in the pricey Bay Area was worth more money, Jessie didn't understand that. All she knew was that Mia's parents, her aunt and uncle, owned a sprawling Spanish-style house in the south end of Cathedral City, up in the hills in a neighborhood called the Cove. Jessie had grown up having to swim in her town's public community pool; Mia had grown up with her own shimmery turquoise pool (with a hot tub!) right outside her patio door.

Jessie was staying with her cousin for six summer weeks in Mia's cramped apartment in Cat City (as she called it). The first time she'd walked in the front door, Jessie had been shocked at the size and overall run-down state of the place. Mia's dingy apartment sat a few blocks north of Dinah Shore Drive, one of those long desert streets named for celebrities nobody younger than a hundred could remember. It had only one bedroom, and thin kitchen cabinets painted white that felt sticky to the touch. The floor tiles were white too, but looked gray, and a lot of them were chipped or cracked.

For the first time in her life, Jessie felt like she might be richer, and maybe even smarter, than her beautiful cousin.

Jessie's mom, Rose, a divorcée immersed in the first stages of a new affair, had arranged the trip to get her out of the house. Jessie lobbied hard against it, but in the end, Rose had prevailed. "Between the pool and all those tourist spots, you won't even have time to miss your friends," she swore.

Jessie wondered now exactly what tourist spots her mom was talking about. Everything her mom had ticked off on her fingers was actually located in Palm Springs: the huge water park, the tram that ferried visitors up to the top of the San Jacinto Mountain, even the cool vintage Camelot theater that showed indies and midnight movies. Cathedral City had a franchise miniature golf and arcade park, and a fancy movie theater, but what town didn't have that stuff? There was literally nothing to do every scorching summer day. Mia's apartment complex did have a pool, but it was an unshaded, basic rectangle that was usually crowded in the late afternoons with rowdy Mexican kids—real Mexicans, not a watered-down half-Latino mix like herself and Mia.

Both only children, they were the closest things either had to a sibling, though separated by five years and raised in different halves of the state. With her glossy dark hair and striking light eyes against her olive skin, Mia had been popular with boys from the sixth grade onward. Jessie couldn't remember a time when she hadn't compared every aspect of her looks against her cousin's—a hopeless game, since they looked nothing alike. Jessie had white skin that resisted tans, brown eyes, and a cloudy mop of hair. She was curvier than Mia, though. Her chest formed a buoyant shelf beneath the T-shirts she'd learned to wear a size too small, and the rounded curve of her hips filled out her jeans in a way that made men on the street lift their eyebrows and turn to watch her pass.

What Rose hadn't counted on in her plans for Jessie's summer was Nick. Walking into baggage claim at the Palm Springs airport toward waiting families, Jessie spotted her cousin, standing beside a lean guy with a trim beard and shaggy dark hair. She ducked behind a businessman and swiped on a fresh coat of lip gloss. Mia hugged her, then introduced Nick as her live-in boyfriend.

Jessie thrust out her hand to Nick. "Hey, I'm Jessica. Nice to meet you."

"Nick Vitale," he said. Jessie watched the ropy muscles in his arm flex as he gripped her hand. "Mia's told me a lot about you. Nice shirt," he added.

Jessie plucked at the front of her black T-shirt, emblazoned with a picture of Jim Morrison. She'd cut out the standard neckline and turned it into a deep V-neck. "The Doors are my latest obsession," she said. "Three months ago, it was Neil Young."

"You should've been out here a few years ago, when he played Coachella."

"Don't you mean *OldChella*?" Jessie teased.

"Ouch," Nick said, pretending to flinch.

Mia hooked her arm around Jessie's shoulders in affection and looked at Nick. "See, I told you she'd be cool," she said, cocking a perfectly plucked eyebrow.

Jessie smiled at Nick, and then, wider, at her cousin. "I'm *totally* cool," she nodded. The three of them laughed together.

It began like background music, a song playing in a restaurant or grocery store that you're not even aware of, until you really listen and it's one of your favorite songs, and your attention is pulled away from the chitchat at the table, with the checkout clerk, your focus snake-charmed into this one faint melody, these words you cannot help but mouth and even sing aloud. So it was with Nick. Jessie was first aware of her stomach, the way it tightened and churned before Nick was due to return from work, the way she caught herself freshening her lipstick in the bathroom mirror, for what? At first, it seemed Nick thought of her only as Mia did, just a punk kid, until his winks and glances behind her cousin's back began to accumulate, and soon enough she couldn't stop thinking about him. And somehow, Nick seemed aware of her new realization; his winks and looks accelerated until the air bristled when they passed each other in the short hallway and cramped U-shaped kitchen.

How did he know? Jessie decided that Nick must've heard it too, the hum, the background music that tugged at her attention; heard the way his name reverberated deep in her chest like a thick bass groove; saw how she bit her lower lip not only in witless seduction, but to keep from mouthing his name and singing it aloud.

Nick was one of two bar managers at the strip club over on Perez Road; strip clubs, at least, were something you couldn't find in Palm Springs. It was one of the only topless clubs in the entire Coachella Valley, so Nick was gone a lot; his work shifts meant that sometimes he was home by early evening, and sometimes he didn't come home until after two a.m. Sleeping on the pull-out couch, Jessie tried to always be awake when he came in, but most nights he crept in after she'd dozed off and she never heard a thing.

Jessie couldn't figure out exactly what Mia did for a living—but did it matter? Her cousin was barely twenty-two, and even if it was shabby, she already rented her own place, lived alone with Nick, and drove a sweet (if slightly dented) baby Benz. She claimed she was studying to be a graphic artist and had helped design some of the event posters for the strip club.

"I've been taking computer classes over at COD," Mia

told Jessie, meaning the local campus of College of the Desert, a community college. All Jessie knew was that Mia spent a lot of time puttering on her Mac laptop, sometimes drawing animations and logos, but more often shopping online.

Despite Jessie's visions of deep midnight and flowing lingerie, on the night she bumped into Nick in the dark hallway outside the bathroom it was barely after eleven and she was wearing only a musty old Mott the Hoople T-shirt over her frayed cotton underwear. As she turned off the light, stepped out of the door, and bumped into Nick, two weeks of daydreams clouded her vision as much as the sudden black. She stumbled and Nick caught her arm.

"Oh!" said Jessie.

"Whoa there, steady," he said. "What are you doing up?"

"Um, I had to pee?" she answered, and her cheeks burned under the cover of darkness.

"Me too," said Nick, and they laughed in relief. Her eyes were adjusting, and she could make out his features and the white flash of his teeth.

"Well . . ." she began.

"Yeah."

"I'll see you in the morning, then." She stepped aside to return to the living room and her sofa bed, but Nick moved with her and blocked her path.

"Listen, Jessie, I've been thinking about you," he said.

"Yeah?"

"Mm-hmm." He edged closer, and she sensed the full weight of his body. In an instant the shadow of possibility had become flesh. A worthy reply stalled in her throat.

"I've thought about you a lot too, Nick."

"Is that right? C'mere." He took her elbow and drew her

closer, back toward the bathroom door. He looked to be thinking hard and stroked his beard with his thumb and forefinger. Jessie wanted to put those fingers in her mouth. He reached behind her, pressing against the front of her shirt to flip the light switch back on. They blinked at each other in the yellow light.

Nick sighed. "What I've been thinking, see, is that I may need to kiss you." And then the electric burr of his mustache was pricking her upper lip and there was only the soft suck of his mouth on hers and the sly tip of tongue that flicked and retreated too quickly. He pressed harder, pushing her spine into the doorframe.

She shut her eyes and tried to remember to breathe as Nick's hand crept down the back of her shirt, then under the fabric, his calloused hand warm against her skin. A thick finger wormed under the elastic of her underwear and she pulled her mouth away.

"Hey," she gasped.

"Sorry. I couldn't help myself." He ducked his head to smile into her eyes.

They were whispering. They breathed quietly, the house still except for the constant hum of the air conditioner.

"But Mia . . ."

Nick put a finger to her lips. "Don't worry. Believe me, she sleeps like a rock."

"Okay—but she's your girlfriend, after all."

"Yep, and you're her kissin' cousin. After all." He grinned. "So, who's really the bad guy now? You want me to kiss you some more or what?"

She closed her eyes and leaned in toward him.

The rest happened in a blur: they were on the floor, on the thin blue patterned rug in between the sofa bed and TV stand. Nick was everywhere, on her, in her, and then out again almost as quickly, hitching up his athletic shorts and running a hand through his hair.

"See you tomorrow, kid," he whispered, then walked to the room at the end of the hallway and the bed he shared with Mia, humming a tune that Jessie couldn't quite place.

The morning after that first time, Jessie overslept. When she opened her eyes sunshine filled the apartment, bouncing off the shiny surfaces of the cheap lacquered furniture. She listened to Mia running water in the kitchen and the grass-blower roar of the community gardeners. The night before felt like yet another daydream. She kicked off the sheets and stared up at the popcorn ceiling.

She sat up, pushed the hair from her eyes. "Where you going?" she asked when Mia walked into the room, nodding at the open map on Mia's computer screen.

"A tattoo shop Nick's mentioned, over on Ramon. His buddy works there."

"You're getting a tattoo?"

"How do you know I don't already have some?" Mia smirked. "But no, this is for Nick; it's his birthday surprise. He wants me to draw the Led Zeppelin logo so his friend can put it on his shoulder."

"Zeppelin, huh?"

"He really likes that old stuff."

"So do I," Jessie said, lifting the front of her concert shirt.

"Well, I guess you two have something in common, don't you, *chica*? But listen—Nick and I were talking this morning, and . . . ugh, this is embarrassing . . ." Mia grimaced and rolled her eyes.

"Wha—?" Jessie felt her heart thump hard in her chest.

"It's just—well, we're running a little short this month. I mean, we've been buying all of your food and stuff and—look, I noticed you have a debit card. So, you have your own bank account?"

Relief washed through Jessie. Money? It was only money? "Yeah, my mom's got access to my account, but it's mostly my dad, depositing his divorce-guilt money. I can help out, for sure. What do you guys need?"

Mia hugged her, said, "Damn, cuz, I knew you'd be cool," adding that if Jessie could lend them a hundred, maybe one-fifty, Nick would repay her soon *in triple.*

Yeah, he will, Jessie thought, trying not to smirk to herself.

She thought of their childhoods together during holidays and vacations. She pictured the framed photo in her mom's hallway, of her and Mia on a family hike up in Cathedral Canyon, right above her cousin's neighborhood. She and Mia were standing beside each other on big rocks, both smiling and wearing neon sunglasses. In the background, the valley sprawled, dusty brown against the cobalt-blue sky, like their whole lives, wide open and waiting. The photo felt like a world ago, but the trail, and the same rock formations the town was named for, were all still there, across Highway 111 and a few miles away.

She thought about how Mia had always wielded the power of her years over her with pinches and mild slugs, and how, on the few occasions when Jessie tried to fight back with a half-hearted punch of her own, Mia retaliated by landing a sly hard one on her arm or thigh, leaving a bruise that lingered after she'd returned home. Mia had always been mean.

So what would she do if she found out now, and what kind of mark would it leave? Jessie tried not to think about it.

When she felt guilt swarming her head like angry wasps, she thought of her friend Samantha, how blithely Samantha had once said that if a chick couldn't hang on to her man, that was hardly *her* problem, was it?

The days passed in a haze of pool chlorine, vertical blinds snapped tight against the sun, and an endless Spotify mix of classic rock in her ear buds. She scrolled through Instagram, checking out images of the strip club. The dancers were sexy and lithe and awfully flexible. Jessie wondered what Nick saw in her, surrounded by all those bodies every night. She wondered what he even saw in Mia, compared to those strippers.

Even so, on those nights when he came home early, Nick always managed to sneak her some signal: a wink, a private smirk. Also, there was that song he always hummed: it was an old Doors song, he told her. She didn't recognize the slow, snaky blues melody, or the one line he occasionally sang out in a mocking drawl: *A cold girl'll kill you / In a darkened room.* She searched for it online: "Cars Hiss by My Window." She loved it, loved especially how it sounded exactly like three o'clock in the morning.

When Nick was home, the hours flew by. Mia never cooked dinner; instead they'd all climb in her car, and drive for fast food, often ending up at the Taco Bell on the corner of Highway 111 and Cathedral Canyon. "Didn't this used to be a Jack in the Box?" Jessie asked once.

"Good memory," Nick said, munching his chalupa.

"This is the same road that goes up into my parents' neighborhood," Mia said. "You probably remember when we used to stop in here for chocolate shakes." So far on this trip, Jessie had only seen her aunt and uncle once, when they'd taken her and Mia out to dinner at Nicolino's, the hole-in-the-wall

Italian restaurant that was a family favorite. It was weird, to think they could all get in the car and be at their front door in a few minutes. Mia's life felt so entirely different and separate from her parents.

After eating, they usually cruised around town, avoiding returning home to the tiny apartment. Mia would turn up the radio and play her favorite rap station, passing strip malls and car dealerships and a dozen bars and dispensaries that Jessie wished she could enter. It didn't seem fair how so much fun was reserved for supposed adults.

Once, they stopped at the community plaza just off the 111, where there were lighted fountains and a movie theater named for Mary Pickford (another long-dead and forgotten celebrity). The sun was just setting behind the mountains and the colored lights of the big central fountain came on. Movie tickets here were too expensive, but they strolled around, watching the Latino kids screeching and scrambling over the fountain, their families relaxing on the nearby turf. The slight breeze tossed the tall palms lining the walkway, each strung with white fairy lights. On a night like this, Jessie could see why this part of her family had never left the desert, despite the terrible heat and retail sprawl. She dug a quarter out of her wallet and threw it into another fountain, between its two spitting mosaic frogs. In the hot night, her whole body was a wish, a yearning for something beyond words.

But lately after dinner, they often piled back into Mia's beat-up white C-class that matched her dingy white apartment and drove to the nearest Bank of America. Sometimes Jessie took out money, a small fan of twenties she handed to over to Mia. And sometimes she hung back, while Mia, armed with Jessie's ATM card and PIN, deposited a couple of checks. "Just sign the backs," she'd tell Jessie, who would obey and pay no attention when Mia turned and handed her a slippery white receipt. Over their heads date beetles shrilled in the trees, louder than the passing traffic on Date Palm Drive.

They kissed and kissed one night until her brain was smooth as a polished marble. In the middle of the thin rug they rolled and grappled until Nick's hips ground into hers with a shove.

"Take 'em off," he urged, tugging at the leg of her underwear.

"Wait—not yet."

"Damnit, Jessie." He sat up and ran a hand through his hair. "Stop acting like such a cock tease. I see enough of that at work."

"But I'm not!" she said. "I just wanted to talk a little more, first."

"Nah. Forget it." He edged away. "I should get to bed. G'night," he yawned.

"Wait!" Jessie hissed. She wriggled into her shorts, rose, and pulled down her shirt. She tried putting her arms around his waist, but he twisted away and moved toward Mia's desk.

"Let it go, Jess."

She followed him across the room and stood beside him as he switched on the desk lamp. "But it's still so early! Barely even midnight."

He kissed the top of her head and mussed her hair. "Time for good little girls to be asleep in their sofa beds."

"But . . . there's something I've wanted to talk to you about."

"What's that?"

"You know, I'm going home in a few days."

"Uh-huh." Nick scratched at his beard. "And?"

"And. So, I was hoping we'd keep in touch. Just us. Maybe you could text me or call me from work on . . . like another phone, sometime. I'd love to hear from you." She failed to keep the trembling in her knees from climbing into her voice.

"That's flattering, sweetheart. But I think you realize why I can't do that. This is all a one-shot deal here. But we've had a good time, right?"

"Well, sure, but I was thinking . . . see, next June I'll grad-uate, and then I can totally move down here for good. It's less than a year away, when you think about it." Without meaning to, Jessie's volume had risen along with the force of her words.

Nick frowned and raised a finger to his lips. "You're cute," he said in a near whisper, "but really fuckin' deluded."

Unconvinced, Jessie twined her arms around his neck. "Just a kiss good night?"

"Nick? Jessica?" Mia's voice approached from down the hall.

"Christ," Nick said, and flung Jessie's arms away.

Mia appeared in the doorway, blinking and pretty in a lav-ender chemise, her dark hair spilling around her bare shoul-ders. "What the hell's going on?" Her blue eyes snapped in bold relief against her brown complexion.

"I wanted to—well, I was showing him that Zeppelin logo you drew." Jessie grabbed at a sheet of drawing paper across the nearby desk. She and Nick both looked down at Mia's rendering of the iconic winged angel, his head and nude torso bent back and muscular arms reaching heavenward.

"This is fantastic, babe," Nick said to Mia.

"You knew it was a surprise, goddamnit," she barked at Jessie. "And," she nodded at Nick, "that still doesn't explain why your fly is down."

He looked down and pulled up the zipper. "Whoops," he said, shrugging. "We were about wrapping it up here."

"Yeah," added Jessie.

"Remind me when you're going home again?" said Mia.

"On Monday."

"That is just about soon enough for me." Mia swung around and started back down the hallway. "Are you coming or not, Nicholas?"

"Right behind you, babe."

During the night, Jessie woke. It felt very late, but when she looked at her phone, she saw she'd been asleep for only an hour. She heard a noise, and another. There was a rustle and squeak, and then Mia's voice calling out Nick's name, over and over. Jessie strained to hear anything from Nick, but after Mia's last shout there was nothing but a muffled tension that lingered throughout the apartment. She mashed the pillow over her head, but it was too late to block Mia's moans from replaying again and again in her ears, too late to stop the tangled images from forming in her mind.

In the morning, Jessie hurried to put on her swimsuit and get to the pool early. She needed to be away from her cousin.

"We'll be going up to my parents' house tomorrow," Mia told her, as she grabbed a towel and headed for the door.

Jessie stopped. "The three of us?" That sounded promising. Maybe there'd be a chance to corner Nick alone in her aunt and uncle's big red-tiled Spanish house.

"Another couple is joining us. We've got the house for the weekend; my parents are in Laguna to escape the heat. Just pack a few things, okay?" She smiled hard at Jessie and tapped at her phone, her long neon-pink nails clicking against the screen.

Trashy, Jessie thought.

Dozing beneath the lone shade tree near the apartment pool,

Jessie nearly missed the call. She saw it was her dad, Jim, and swiped to answer.

"Daddy—" she started, but was cut short by her father's angry voice. He never yelled at her, not really, but he was yelling now, all the way from the Bay Area. He was yelling about money and what in the hell, what the *fuck* was she up to, who were these people, and did she have any idea her account was over six thousand fucking dollars in the red?

"The red? What do you mean? I'm sorry! I didn't know, I swear," Jessie stammered, around and over the continued noise from her phone. He said other words: *check fraud* and *cops* and *felony*. It all sounded so bad, and she had no idea how to make it better. She thought about the trips to the bank, or sometimes the Circle K with its ATM machine beside the Monster energy drinks and Lotto tickets. All those slips of receipts she'd shoved in her pockets, or even thrown away without a glance.

"I'm coming," her dad said now. "I'll be there tonight, maybe tomorrow if I can't get a flight. Where will I find you? I'd say this is all your mother's fault, but you need to answer for this too, Jessica. And so does Mia."

And Nick too, Jessie thought. She didn't say his name, but her dad would be learning it soon enough.

The group had partied all day under the hazy white sun, diving into the turquoise pool over and over. The misters were on around the covered patio, the outdoor ceiling fans turned. Nick and Mia laughed and kissed often, their arms wrapped around each other, recounting with Leo and Cherise tales of other parties at Mia's parents', of post-Coachella all-nighters and trips to Havasu. Once, as Mia bent over the outdoor fridge rooting for a beer, Leo came up behind her, grabbed her thin hips, and started humping. He turned his face to the group and wagged his tongue. "Uh, uh, uh!" His eyes were hidden behind his mirrored sunglasses.

"Quit it, perv," Mia laughed, slapping his hands away. Jessie glanced at Nick, but he only laughed along with his friends. Later, Nick approached Cherise in her lounge chair, standing with his crotch directly in front of her face. He grabbed at himself and grunted, "Got something for you, baby." Cherise only stared up at him, one eye squinted shut against the sun, and blew out a cloud of vanilla Juul smoke. "Use it or lose it, asshole," she chuckled.

To all of this, Jessie forced an echoing laugh and whoop, accepting every beer and joint passed her way. Otherwise, Mia and everyone else seemed to forget she was there. By midafternoon Jessie felt nauseous, rocked by long hours under the sun and atop the wide pool float. The beer and smoke had helped her nerves, though.

Earlier that morning, her hands had shaken. They shook when she googled the phrase on her phone, making sure it applied. They shook when she looked up the local sheriff department's number, and when she called and spoke to the woman who answered, and then an officer. She kept her voice low, despite the thick plastered walls of her guest bedroom in her aunt's home.

Her hands had shaken, saying the words *statutory rape*. Giving Nick's full name, his age, and then her birth date. "I think he stole my money too," she said before hanging up. Her mouth had been so dry. Then she called her dad, who was stuck at the San Jose airport, unable to catch a flight until the afternoon. He was calmer than the day before, but still angry. Jessie reminded him of the location of her aunt and uncle's house; he'd visited plenty of times for family get-togethers be-

fore the divorce. Her dad said he'd called the sheriff's department too, that he'd be "bringing a posse." It all sounded so
terrible. Her mouth was so very dry.

She fell asleep in a lounge chair under the patio, beneath cool
droplets of the spraying misters. She woke with a start, though
she hadn't slept long. Did she hear a siren, way down the hill?
Would there need to be sirens for this money crime that she
barely understood? Out of habit, her mind drifted to thoughts
of Nick, to their late nights on the cheap blue rug over the
hard tile floor. Each time they slept together had been hurried and nearly silent, but in her daydreams, Jessie recast the
encounters, making their gestures slow, lingering. Would he
go to jail for what they did together? She watched Nick, out
by the pool, still drinking, talking to Leo now. His eyes, his
mouth, had not sought her out even once since that last night
in the apartment.

She turned her gaze from him and lifted her face to the
sky, darkening with clouds from the monsoons that pushed
up from Mexico in late summer. Far above, a cloud shadowed
the earth as it parked before the burning disc of sun. In that
moment, a vision descended over Jessie's eyes: her hot skin,
the bare flesh of the party crowd and the unnamed women in
her Instagram searches, the mocking eyes of Nick—all of it
cloaked in the cool, velvet dark of midnight. Over the laughter and the hip-hop she could hear the wail of a blues guitar.
She didn't have to close her eyes or plug her ears to imagine
it. Instead, this cool world opened wide before her and wel-
comed her, a moment perfect in its seamless reality.

The cloud scooted away and she squinted against the
instant return of desert glare. Was she imagining again? No.
Here they were, then. Across the pool, just on the other side

of a low iron gate, were three men. One was her father, the other two were unfamiliar, but in uniform. They had badges and guns. Things were going to happen now, and quickly.

The music stopped, the voices grew louder and angry. Was that Mia crying? It didn't matter. It was all over; she was going home, to her mom's small expensive house, her dad's modern condo, to morning fog and summer evening sweatshirts. Things would get bad for Jessie for a little while too. But she wasn't worried: she would always have music, and the perfect darkness of late, late summer nights.

PART II

LITTLE WHITE LIES

VIP CHECK-IN

BY MICHAEL CRAFT

Little Tuscany

The move, the new job, the fresh beginning, none of that was my idea. But for two men, together for years—hell, decades—the time had come to plot a path toward retirement. And to Dr. Anthony Gascogne, ophthalmologist, Palm Springs felt like the logical destination. To me, not so much.

That was seven years ago, when Anthony was dead set on relocating his practice from LA. Because I balked, he said I could join him in the business as his office manager and assistant. My lackluster career as an actor and model had sputtered to a standstill, so I tagged along to the desert. Soon after, when the law finally allowed, he asked me to marry him.

Then, two years ago, Anthony divorced me. And fired me. And my career path took another unexpected turn—a much darker turn.

Starting over, pushing sixty, I was broke, unemployed, and couch-surfing.

On the brighter side, I was now in Palm Springs.

Well-heeled snowbirds fled for the long summers, but for the rest of us, twelve months of sunshine provided a constant tan, inspiring me to stay fit. And while the sizable gay populace skewed toward the rickety side of Medicare, this demographic twist had its upside: in the eyes of the local gentry, I was still pretty hot (which had a little something to do with the divorce).

My immediate need for income and a cheap apartment led me to consider—briefly—a stint as an escort. But I wasn't getting any younger, and time would quickly take its toll, as it had on my starstruck dreams, so I settled on a bartending gig to get back on my feet. When I took the job, the manager said, "We already have a Danny." He rummaged through a drawer and pulled out a name tag. "Here you go: Dante."

The job lasted only five months, but the name stuck, trailing me as I sniffed around for more durable employment. And that's when a friend tipped me off to a vacation-rental agency that had an immediate opening for a field inspector. I landed the job, which involved checking the condition of properties before guests arrived and after they left. My duties also included occasional VIP check-ins and minor service calls during their stay.

"*Yes?*" crackled the intercom after I rang the doorbell.

"Dante from Sunny Junket."

A befuddled pause. "*What?*"

"My name's Dante. I'm from Sunny Junket Vacation Rentals."

"*Oh. Just a minute.*"

This was one of our premier properties, up in the Little Tuscany neighborhood, where the bohemian feel of steep, winding streets gave no hint of the million-dollar views enjoyed by residents behind their walled courtyards. In the gravel parking court on that rare cloudy afternoon in February, my battered Camry looked especially pathetic—huddled next to an elegant champagne-colored SUV. When did Bentley start making those?

The party of two was registered under the name Edison Quesada Reál, booked for eleven nights, the entire duration of Modernism Week. It was a prime booking in high season, costing north of a thousand a day. The office said the guy was a bigwig art dealer from LA, and they wanted him happy, so they sent me out for the VIP treatment.

I intended to greet them when they arrived at the house, but they'd driven over early, letting themselves in with the keypad code we provided. The front door now rattled as someone fussed with the lock from inside. I waited with my slim folder of paperwork, standing under the cantilevered roof of the boulder-lined entryway. A small peeping bird flitted from the top of a barrel cactus and darted into the darkening sky when the door swung open.

"Well, *hello*." His Asian eyes widened with interest as he sized me up.

I grinned, returning the once-over. He didn't fit my picture of anyone named Edison Quesada Reál. And he was too young for a titan of the art world, maybe in his thirties. He had delicate features and a prettiness about him, like a twink who'd grown up, but he'd also hit the gym and was pleasingly buff, for a short guy. I've always had a thing for short guys.

I reached to shake hands. "I'm Dante. Welcome."

"And I'm Clarence Kwon. Friends call me Clark."

"Hi there"—I smiled—"Clark."

"C'mon in," he said, stepping aside and closing the door after me. He was dressed with the casual sophistication of moneyed LA—wispy calfskin loafers, tailored slacks, and a clingy cream-colored cashmere sweater with its arms shoved up to his elbows. Nice pecs. Good guns.

By contrast, I looked dorky in dad jeans and a yellow polo shirt embroidered with the Sunny Junket logo. Gesturing to myself, I told Clark, "They *make* me wear this."

He laughed. "You look great." And I half believed him as he wagged me along, leading me toward the back of the house.

As we entered the main room, the view opened up from a wall of glass. Although I had seen it many times, the elevated vista never failed to stop me cold. Even on that gloomy day, I caught my breath as the city spread out below, peeking through the crowns of distant palms. Sloping down from one side, granite mountains muscled into the scene to wrap around the city. Above, in a vast gray sky, clouds slowly roiled, snagged on the barren shards of the horizon.

"Edison," said Clark, "the guy from the agency is here."

Seated at the center of the huge window, facing out, mere inches from the glass, a man in a wheelchair remained dead still for a moment. Then he grasped both wheels. The rings adorning his hands clanged the chrome rims as he turned the chair to face me.

I stepped toward him.

"*Stop*," he said sharply. "Let me get a look at you."

I waited. He was older than me, well into his seventies, and way too heavy to be healthy. Though stuck in a wheelchair, he was smartly dressed—to the point of flamboyance—with a silk scarf of peacock blue around his neck. I shot him a smile.

"Forgive me if I don't get up," he said. "If I could, I'd kiss you." He spoke with a worldly refinement and the trace of a Castilian lisp.

I moved to the wheelchair. "But I hardly know you."

He grinned as we shook hands. "You're quite the *cheeky* little cabbage, aren't you?"

"I've been called many things, Mr. Quesada Reál. But never a cabbage."

He let out a feeble roar of a laugh. "Please, please—it's Edison."

"And I'm Dante."

"Of *course* you are." His tone sounded almost suspicious.

Had he seen through my act, the stagey name, the swarthy tan?

Clark moved to the far end of the room, near the long dining table, where he fussed with several piles of art prints, all of them protected by plastic sleeves. While arranging them vertically in wood-slatted browsing racks, he called over to me, "Did you bring us something to sign?"

"No, actually, that was handled online. I just need to snap a picture of the credit card you'll use for payment—and a driver's license to verify the name."

Edison noted, "I don't drive. You'll need to handle this, precious."

The younger man stopped his sorting. With an impatient sigh, he pulled his wallet from a pocket, slid out his license and an AmEx, and plopped them on the table. "This what you need?"

"You bet." I went over and took pictures of the cards with my phone. I noticed that Clarence Kwon was thirty-four, which could not have been half Edison's age. I assumed they were a couple; even though their rental was one of our most expensive properties, it had only one bedroom. I explained, "For these pedigreed houses, we run the charges every other day."

Clark shrugged. "Whatever."

"Perfectly understandable," said Edison, wheeling himself in our direction. "You know I'm good for it, precious."

Clark said nothing as he resumed sorting the artwork.

Edison continued, "Truth be told, no price would be too high for *this*." He flung both arms, a gesture that embraced the whole house. Then he leaned forward, beading me with a milky stare. "Do you know who designed this, Dante?"

"Umm, I've heard, but . . ."

Edison sat back, twining the plump fingers of both hands. "Alva Kessler designed and built this house for himself shortly before he died in the late fifties. He envisioned it as a pure, modernist vacation 'cabin'—a sleek exercise in glass and steel. Truly magnificent, yes? In its sheer minimalism, it's every bit as fresh and avant-garde as it was sixty years ago. And now, for a while, it's all mine." Edison paused, turning his head toward Clark. "I mean, it's all *ours*."

"Right," said Clark, looking peeved. "Ours, when I'm not at the convention center."

I asked, "The art sale? I know it's a big deal during Modernism. I went once."

"Once"—Edison sniffed—"is enough."

Clark added, "If you've seen one lava lamp, or one Noguchi table, you've seen'm all."

Edison explained that his Los Angeles gallery, Quesada Fine Prints—which dealt in original graphic art, no reproductions—had rented exhibit space where they would offer collectors a wide selection of lithographs, engravings, and screen prints from the mid-1900s. The bulk of their inventory had already been delivered to the convention center, with two of their staffers setting up for the show. The most valuable works, however, would remain here at the house, with Clark showing them by appointment or delivering them for consideration by high-end buyers.

Listening to these details, I stepped over to one of the racks to take a look and was instantly drawn to a smaller print, less than a foot high. "This is *great*," I said, breaking into a smile as I lifted it from the bin. "It would sure be at home in Palm Springs." Bright and colorful, it was a blotchy depiction of a swimming pool.

"That's a David Hockney," said Clark. "Limited-edition lithograph, signed artist's proof, mint condition. At *this* show, it's our jewel in the crown."

Edison said, "Sell that one to the right buyer, precious, and you'll get the other Bentley." He turned to tell me, "Clark's been wanting the convertible."

Gingerly, I handed the Hockney to Clark, who said, "Edison is exaggerating." He glanced at the coded sticker on the back of the plastic sleeve, adding, "Or maybe not."

"I'm feeling peckish," said Edison. "Some trifle would help."

Under his breath, Clark told me, "He's been a bit much lately."

Edison reminded us, "I can hear you."

Clearly seething, Clark turned to the wheelchair. "I'm *not* your coolie servant."

"But you *are*." Edison chuckled. "You can leave, if you want—but you won't. And I can't *divorce* you, can I? Far too costly. Face it, precious: we're stuck."

Rain began to spit against the expansive window and drip in long tendrils, streaking the glass from top to bottom, rippling the million-dollar view.

Hoping to defuse the tension, I asked, "Is there anything I can help you with?"

Edison gave me a lecherous look. "Like . . . *what?*"

"I'd show you through the house, but you're already settled in. It's an older place, has a few quirks. The electronics are all new. Most guests have questions."

Edison said, "We'll figure it out." Then he blurted, "Pink fluff!"

Bewildered, I looked to Clark for guidance.

Still sorting prints, he spoke to me over his shoulder. "We brought a few things that need to go in the fridge—including the raspberry trifle. Could you?"

"Sure." The galley kitchen opened into the main room from the street side of the house. While the A/V system was up-to-the-minute, the kitchen had retro appliances with a midcentury vibe. The vintage refrigerator was a hulking old Philco in red porcelain enamel; the doors of the top freezer and the main compartment both featured elaborate chrome-handled latches.

Edison wheeled in behind me, watching as I hefted five or six shopping bags from the floor to the countertop. They held a few canned goods and liquor bottles, which I set aside, but they were mostly filled with clear plastic containers brimming with a sludgy concoction that Edison had aptly described as pink fluff. Two bags contained ingredients to make more of it—box after box of fresh raspberries, jars of raspberry jam and Melba sauce, several hefty packages of pound cake. A zippered thermal bag contained at least a dozen rattling cans of aerosol whipped cream.

"*Now*," Edison barked with a wild look in his eyes, "pink fluff!"

I removed the lid from one of the Tupperware tubs.

"*Smell* it," he commanded.

Whoa. The recipe had been lavishly spiked with Cointreau. The piercing boozy scent of orange melded with the tart perfume of crushed berries, making both my mouth and my eyes water.

"*Now*," he repeated, reaching with trembling hands.

I gave it to him, then slid a drawer open. "Fork? Or spoon?"

"It doesn't *matter*." He looked ready to slop into it with his fingers. I gave him a spoon.

He rolled a few feet back and gobbled the trifle. Between swallows, he groaned and gurgled.

I glanced over at Clark, who seemed unfazed by this behavior. In fact, he gave me a thumbs-up. So, I returned to the task of putting things away. I had to tug at the Philco's heavy ornamental latch (which brought to mind the hardware on a casket) and soon had the beast filled. Its condenser hummed in earnest.

Edison was now banging his spoon on the sides of the plastic container as he scraped at the last of the trifle. I asked if he needed anything else from me, but he shook his head without looking up from his scavenging.

I stepped around the wheelchair, took my folder from the dining table, and told Clark I was leaving. He followed me toward the front of the house.

When I stepped outside, he went with me and gently closed the door behind us. We stood together on the landscaped walkway, protected by the jutting cantilever of the roof. It rained heavily now—straight down, with no wind to drive it—like a translucent curtain blurring the gray afternoon. Raindrops danced wildly on the windshield of the polished Bentley. In the hushed racket of the pelting water, the world was still.

"It's . . . exhausting," said Clark, his words no louder than a whisper as he gazed into the courtyard.

"Edison?"

Nodding, Clark turned to me. "Ten years ago, I knew what I was getting into, and I was sure I could deal with the age difference. He's always been pampered and fussy—that was part of his charm. But now, Jesus. It gets worse by the month, like he's regressing into childhood. You've seen the pink fluff; that's been going on awhile. As of last week, about the only *other* thing he's willing to eat is canned spaghetti, like a kid."

I'd noticed the SpaghettiOs while unpacking in the kitchen.

Clark said, "What's next—diapers?"

"Maybe."

He was quiet for a moment, then laughed. Stepping near,

he clasped my hand with both of his. "You've been super, Dante. Really helpful. Thank you."

I grinned. "Anything else, just let me know."

He moved closer still, brushing against me and lolling his head back to fix me in his stare. His dark almond-shaped eyes appeared black in the dusky shadows that hugged us. I could hear him breathing. I could almost hear his thoughts. Was he open to a fleeting kiss? Or did he want something less innocent—something more animal and lusty?

When his lips parted, he broke the spell. "Can you fix this weather?"

I backed off a few inches. "It'll dry up. We never get much, but they say we need it."

"Yeah," he agreed coyly, "we need it."

Which left me unsure if this was small talk—or foreplay. Either way, the time was right for a quick exit. I turned to leave but paused. "Enjoy your Sunny Junket."

Clark rolled his eyes. "Let me guess. They *make* you say that."

With a wink, I sprinted off toward my car.

When the office texted the next morning, it came as no surprise that the Quesada Reál party was having trouble with the cable and Wi-Fi. They had snubbed my earlier offer to explain things, and now they were miffed, so the office told me to return to Little Tuscany at once. I was driving down valley for an inspection in Indian Wells—I'd nearly arrived—but I did a U-turn at the next light on Highway 111 and shot back toward Palm Springs.

Shortly after ten, I drove up the narrow driveway and parked in the courtyard next to the Bentley, which had been spiffed and detailed since the rain. More was on the way, but for now, tourists were getting the slice of winter paradise they'd paid for.

When I rang the doorbell, it took a while for someone to garble through the intercom. I said, "It's Dante."

Another long pause. "*Let yourself in?*"

"Sure." I tapped the code.

Inside, I walked back to the main room. "Hello?" Hearing no response, I stepped farther in and looked around. Everything seemed in order. In the kitchen, a few dishes were stacked near the sink, but the tenants clearly appreciated tidy surroundings. Although the print racks near the dining table had been rearranged, the David Hockney was still prominently displayed. On the table, boxes and bulging portfolios contained more inventory.

I turned as one of the glass doors on a side wall slid open, and in from the pool deck strolled Clarence Kwon with a towel slung over one shoulder. He was otherwise naked, far more buff than I had imagined, and still aroused from whatever merrymaking had transpired outdoors. He carried an empty Tupperware container of raspberry trifle, smeared pink. Unless I was mistaken, there was also a creamy lick of it on his inner thigh.

"Morning, Dante," he said, crossing the room toward the kitchen. "Sorry to call you back. Edison got frustrated with the TV last night. He started punching buttons, and by the time he gave up, the Wi-Fi was fritzed out." Clark set the towel on the kitchen counter and rinsed the Tupperware in the sink.

"Happens all the time," I said. "No two setups are alike. I'll restore the settings, then show him how to work the video."

"Fair warning: he'll never catch on." Clark stepped over to me while wiping his hands. "Can you tackle the Wi-Fi first?"

"Uh-huh." I paused to look him up and down, which got a rise out of both of us. A jolt of waist-level attraction nudged us closer. I managed to say, "Seems you had no trouble with the pool controls."

"Worked like a charm. But Edison was griping last night about the landscape lighting—said it was totally screwed up. I thought it looked fine."

"I'll check it out."

Clark wrapped the towel around his waist. "Gotta throw myself together. Someone's coming over from the convention center. Security—to help transport some of the good stuff. So, go ahead and do your thing." He traipsed off toward the bedroom.

I gathered the remote controls and took them to a former linen closet, now overtaken by electronics. Resetting the Wi-Fi was easy but rebooting the cable and restoring the streaming services was tedious. About ten minutes into it, I heard the doorbell ring. I also heard the spray of the shower from down the hall. Stepping out to the main room, I saw that Edison had not yet come in from the pool. The doorbell rang again, so I went to answer it.

When I opened the door, our eyes locked in disbelief. "What the *fuck*?" she said.

And I relived the scene—a shattering scene from a year earlier—when I had first encountered this woman.

After Dr. Anthony Gascogne, ophthalmologist, had fired me, thrown me out of the house, and changed the locks, he was then catty enough to give me one of his new keys—in case anyone needed access during his travels, which had grown more frequent.

A few months later, after leaving the bartending job, I was

going through several days of training with Sunny Junket. On a Wednesday morning, while touring some of our properties with Ed, my supervisor, I started receiving messages from my ex's office, concerned that he had not shown up that day. He'd already missed two appointments and could not be reached. Could I check at the house?

Later, maybe—I was in the middle of something import-ant, at the far end of the valley.

By late afternoon, after work, after a continued spate of texting, I drove to the house I had once shared with An-thony. Letting myself in, I called to him, but all was quiet. At a glance, there were no signs of trouble, and I thought he had simply taken off for a while. Spontaneity, though, was not one of his hallmarks, so I decided to do a walk-through.

When I entered his study, my knees went weak. I grabbed the doorjamb to steady myself as the room seemed to spin be-neath me. Anthony had dropped face-first from the chair be-hind his desk, landing on the white shag carpet, puddled with the blackening ooze of his blood. His skull was bashed in. A lamp with a heavy crystal base, streaked red, had been thrown violently aside, cracking a cabinet door below the bookcase.

I kneeled in the mess to check on Anthony, who was be-yond helping. Stupidly, I picked up the lamp and set it upright. Then I phoned 911.

Among the first responders was a hotshot cop, a black woman in her thirties with a street mouth and a chip on her shoulder. I assumed she was a dyke. Her name badge identi-fied her, dubiously, as *Officer Friendly*. I would later learn that her surname was indeed Friendly, that she was not a dyke, and that she was bucking for a promotion to detective.

That day at the crime scene, she must've figured she could grease the path to her promotion by arresting me on the spot.

It sort of made sense: I literally had blood on my hands, there were no signs of intrusion, I had a key, and most important, I had a plausible motive for revenge against the victim. It was front-page news in Thursday morning's *Desert Sun*, though I never saw it, waking up behind bars.

On Thursday evening, the medical examiner released his finding that Anthony had died Wednesday around noon. My salvation turned out to be Ed at Sunny Junket, who had spent most of Wednesday with me, providing a solid alibi. I was freed within the hour. Officer Friendly, however, was screwed.

And now, there she was, in a rent-a-cop costume, reduced to running security errands for the convention center. She sported a gun, a badge, and handcuffs, looking plenty pissed.

I smiled. "What happened? Lose your job?"

"None of your motherfucking business."

"Couth it up, Friendly. Our clients wouldn't approve."

"Go to hell, asshole."

"Aha," said Clark, strolling out from the bedroom, dressed for the day. "It seems you two have met. Morning, Jazz."

"*Jazz?*" I said.

She looked aside, mumbling, "Beats the shit out of Jasmine."

Nodding, I agreed. "Not quite your style."

Clark asked, "Get everything fixed, Dante?"

"Hold on," said Friendly. With a low chortle, she said, "*Dante?* This asswipe lowlife? He's Danny O'Donnell."

We were interrupted by the rattle of the sliding glass door to the pool deck as Edison struggled to open it from his wheelchair. I rushed over and helped him inside.

"Dante, *dah*-ling," he said, "too good of you."

"I've got the video up and running again. Can we take a few minutes to go over it?"

He heaved a weary sigh. "If we must. Later—when you come back to fix the lighting."

"I can take a look at that right now."

"Not in the *daylight*," he scoffed. "It has to be tonight."

Hesitating, I said, "I'll drop by around six." Not wanting to be stuck alone with Edison, I turned to ask Clark, "Will you be here?"

"Depends. I'll try." Clark was at the dining table, checking the inventory of prints against a list. As if he'd just thought of something, he looked up to tell Friendly, "I need a few minutes before we go. Make yourself at home. Check out the view."

Edison gave the black woman a haughty, disapproving look as she sauntered out to the pool deck. I followed.

A mockingbird warbled as it swooped from the fronds of a palm to the scrub of an embankment that opened to the city below. Friendly stood at the railing, looking out. I approached from behind. With her back to me, she said, "You fucked up my life."

I stepped to the railing and stood beside her, looking out. "You didn't do *me* any favors, either. The few friends I had left after the divorce—they're *gone*."

"Shit happens, O'Donnell. It happened to me, starting with the murder of your ex. Still an open case"—she turned to look at me—"but I have my suspicions."

"Knock it off. You know I didn't do it. You were wrong."

"And *you* made a mess of that crime scene. My so-called partner—a racist prick—reported that the muddled evidence was *my* doing, that the arrest was wrongful and incompetent. So, I was denied training for detective status. I lost overtime privileges. Got crappy shifts. Then my husband dumped me— said it was my drinking." She paused and looked away. Her voice dropped as she said, "Worst part, he got custody of our daughter. My little girl."

I blew a low whistle. "Sorry. That's rough."

The story had drained her swagger. I heard the tinge of fear in her words, in her uncertain future, as she explained how her standing with the police force had continued to sour. They made it clear they wanted her out. She decided to leave on her own terms and quit. Trying to start over, she opened a private investigation service. "Not much business yet"—she shook her head—"so I'm doing security at the convention center."

I shrugged. "It's a plan."

"It sucks."

Clark appeared in the doorway. "Ready, Jazz."

With a parting smirk, she went inside.

So did I. Closing the glass slider, I noticed that the front door of the house was wide open, as if Clark had already trudged through with several batches of prints. But he was standing at the dining table with Jazz, telling her, "Light load today, just this portfolio. Take it in your van; I'll follow in the Bentley."

"Got it." After signing a receipt, she took the portfolio from Clark, and they headed toward the door.

"Pink fluff!" bellowed Edison.

Exasperated, Clark asked me, "Can you take care of him?" Before I could answer, Clark walked out to the courtyard with Friendly and shut the door.

"*Now*," said Edison.

I turned to him. "You just finished a whole tub of the stuff."

"And now I'd like *you* to try some. It's quite delicious."

I wanted to leave. But I'd been told to give him the VIP treatment. Plus, I'd been wondering if the trifle was as good as it looked. So I played along.

Edison wheeled himself into the kitchen and waited behind me as I tugged the refrigerator door open and removed one of the containers. I popped the lid, grabbed a spoon from a drawer, and gave it a taste.

"Get *out*," I said, amazed. It was fabulous.

"Didn't I tell you?"

I wolfed a few more spoonfuls, then stopped myself, returning the trifle to the fridge. "Thanks, really, it was great." I stepped to the sink to rinse the spoon.

"Give me that." He grabbed it. Locking eyes with me, he licked my spoon lewdly. When finished, he sat back, whirling the spoon. "Let me ask you something. What do you think of my Clark?"

"Nice guy. Seems attentive to your needs." I grinned. "And he's hot."

"Isn't he though?" With an edge of bitterness, Edison added, "I'm not stupid, Dante. I *know* what you're thinking: I'm just a vapid old rice queen."

I assured him, "I would never say such a thing."

But that very thought had crossed my mind.

Driving back to Little Tuscany that evening, I hoped that Edison would not be alone at the house, that Clark would have returned from the convention center. He might be in the mood for a drink. He might ask me to join him. I was off the clock and felt no obligation to wear the insipid Sunny Junket uniform, so I wore tight black jeans and a leather jacket— surefire date bait.

Winter nights in the desert could be cold, and the bright, perfect day had already turned gray and windy. Clouds piled up beyond the mountains to the west, rushing the sunset. The dusk disappeared into a starless, moonless darkness.

As the Camry reached the top of the narrow drive, its headlights skimmed the parking court, which was empty. Peachy—I'd be solo with Edison. When I got out of the car, I took note of the landscape lighting and, finding no problems at the front of the house, checked along both sides, which also seemed fine. However, the most elaborate lighting could be seen only from the rear deck, and due to the embankment, the safest way to get there was through the house.

I rang the doorbell. After half a minute, I rang again. A minute later, I punched in the code and entered, calling, "Edison?" All was quiet.

The interior lights were on, as programmed. At a glance, there were no signs of trouble, and I thought Edison's afternoon nap might have drifted into the evening. But he had been expecting me, so I decided—with a chilling sense of déjà vu—to do a walk-through.

When I entered the kitchen, my knees went weak. I grabbed the doorjamb to steady myself as the room seemed to spin beneath me. Edison had fallen backward, crushed beneath the refrigerator, which had toppled onto him, covering his lower torso. The scene was a nightmarish shamble, with Edison pinned in the mangled metal frame of his wheelchair. The refrigerator was still running, its condenser humming, its door flung open. Raspberries, whipped cream, and tub after tub of pink fluff were scattered everywhere, oozing across Edison's chest. From his mouth, blood had gushed and was beginning to blacken, puddling with Melba sauce on the hard, white terrazzo floor.

This time, I knew better than to kneel in the mess and try to help.

This time, I knew better than to phone 911.

This time, I beat a path out the door and ran to my car.

Shaking, I fumbled to start the engine, then backed up to turn around, when I noticed headlights bouncing up the narrow drive. Running through my options—fuck me, there weren't any—I stopped the car and got out while Officer Friendly pulled her van in next to me, followed by Clark in the Bentley. The wind had picked up, rattling the palms in the black sky.

Friendly got out of the van with the portfolio she was guarding. With a flashlight, she swept the surroundings before proceeding. The beam slid up my backside. "Hngh," she grunted. "Nice ass, for a white guy."

Trying to keep things buoyant, I said, "I'll take that as a compliment."

"You damn well better."

Carrying a box of files from the Bentley toward the house, Clark asked, "Did you check out the lighting?"

"Uh, look," I said. "There's something you need to know. Inside. It's bad."

Clark and Friendly glanced at each other, then rushed into the house. I followed, telling them, "Kitchen."

"Holy fucking *Christ*," said Friendly, stunned by the grisly scene.

Clark dropped the files and stared numbly at his husband. "Jesus."

"No signs of intrusion," said Friendly, giving me a suspicious look.

I said, "Edison *asked* me here tonight. This *had* to be an accident. Why would I . . . ?"

"Then why didn't you report it? You were leaving."

Clark blurted, "I *knew* it." He had moved over to the print racks and held up one of the plastic sleeves, empty. "The Hockney. It's missing. It's worth more than this clown makes in a year—"

"Two years," I assured him. "Or three."

"—and just yesterday, he practically *creamed* over it."

Turning to Friendly, I spread my jacket open. "If I took it, where is it? Wanna frisk me?"

"The car," said Clark, rushing out of the house with Friendly at his heels.

I took my time. In the courtyard, Clark had flung open the doors and trunk of my car, making a frantic search, while Friendly assisted with her flashlight. I watched calmly as they trashed it, secure in the knowledge there was nothing to find.

"See?" said Clark. "I told you." And he withdrew the Hockney from underneath the Camry's passenger seat.

And Friendly was cuffing me and phoning it in and calling for backup and dreaming of salvaging her tattered career.

And I regretted that I had been so easily mesmerized by Clark's tight little body.

And I recalled that morning, when I came in from the pool deck, after talking to Friendly, while Clark was inside, fussing with prints, and I wondered why the front door was open.

And through the wind, I heard the first distant wail of sirens.

And now I said, "Yes, indeed. This old house has state-of-the-art electronics. Surveillance in every room. Up under the eaves too." I pointed vaguely toward the deep, dark recesses of the roof. "Back at the office, we can just scan through all the video. We'll see Clark planting the 'evidence' this morning. Then we'll see him again, later, killing his husband."

Clark froze, dropping the Hockney as the first cold spits of rain arrived on the wind. He hadn't planned on video—lying would be futile. With a convulsive heave, he said, "Edison was right. I couldn't leave, and he would never divorce me. We were stuck."

"Till death do you part," I said. "And I'll bet you're his heir."

Clark looked blindly into the rain. Beaten by the truth, he muttered, "There was . . . no other way."

Friendly released one of my cuffs and clamped it to one of Clark's wrists, saying, "We'll sort this out quick enough." The sirens grew louder. A gust of wind grabbed the soggy Hockney from the gravel and tumbled it through the courtyard, sending it over the embankment.

I laughed, saying to Clark, "You idiot. There's no surveillance. At Sunny Junket, we have a measure of respect for our guests."

Slowly, Clark's gaze pivoted to Friendly. With renewed fire, he stared into her eyes. "Some of our wealthier clients value their privacy and prefer cash transactions. I have forty thousand in the house. That could go a long way in the fight to get your daughter back. It's yours—tonight—if you forget what you heard."

Jazz Friendly, the ex-cop who'd accused me of fucking up her life, now studied my face while telling Clark, "But I'm not the only one who heard it."

Clark reminded her, "You've got a gun. Use it. Self-defense— if you say he tried to grab it. Case closed."

Her eyes darted from mine to Clark's and back to mine.

Clark smiled. "Just do it."

Sirens screamed nearby.

THE WATER HOLDS YOU STILL

BY BARBARA DEMARCO-BARRETT

Twin Palms

The landline rang after midnight. It had to be my mother down in Palm Springs. She was the reason I kept the line.

I picked up. "Hi, Mom."

"There was a noise," she said.

I stood my brush in a jar of water. Red paint escaped the bristles, a blood cloud. I took the phone outside, the curly black cord stretched taut as a tightrope. Ferns along the patio were wet with night mist, common here on the Central Coast.

"Houses settle at night and make noises," I said.

A few months ago, she began calling me about noises at night and the calls were coming more often.

A puff of breath and the faint strain of music—Sinatra. "Mood Indigo." She'd become obsessed with him, more so since my stepfather Jerry died.

"A coyote was outside by the pool," she said. "It was sniffing the water."

"Maybe it's bored," I said. "No little dogs around to eat."

"Greta, that's not funny."

"You're keeping Joey Bishop in, right?" He was her little red Pomeranian.

"He's in." Her voice dropped an octave. "My sapphire ring is missing. Your brother was here. Every time he stops by, something else goes missing."

"Are you sure?" Out on the highway red and blue lights whirled by.

"Last week it was my diamond earrings. I was going to give those to you."

I took it personally. My brother knew they would be mine someday. "I've always loved those earrings. Has anyone other than Ben been around?"

"Repair people. Pool cleaner. Gardener. I can't keep track."

"So, it could be anyone."

"Do you think your brother's gambling again?" she asked. "People go to those pawn shops up on Palm Canyon and over in Cathedral City to sell things they steal. Or they sell them on Clubslist."

"You mean Craigslist."

"Make fun."

"Look, Mom," I said, "if Ben's stealing from you, call the police. Turn him in."

"I can't. He's my son."

"It will only get worse." I was afraid for my mother, brother, and me. Families weren't supposed to be like this. Sons didn't steal from their mothers. But she'd complained before so there must have been some truth to his thieving. "You'd be doing him a favor."

"He'll stop coming to see me. Then who will I have?"

"You have me." I felt like that little girl again, competing with my brother for her love. Ours was a complicated relationship. Mothers and daughters and sons—oh my. She had that old-world Italian thing going: sons were gods, daughters . . . were what?

"You're so far away," she said.

"I'm not that far away, only four, maybe five hours. Come stay with me for a while."

"I don't drive anymore. My eyes."

"Then I'll come there."

We made plans for me to go down in three days and hung up. Back in the studio, I studied my many unfinished canvases propped against the walls. I'd never get another gallery show if I didn't finish already. I had done well at my first show but how could it ever happen like that again? What if I was a one-hit wonder? And was that better than becoming a follow-up failure? When Daniel and I broke up—I found out on Instagram, of all places, that he'd cheated on me with an ex-girlfriend— my confidence was rocked. Faulty female intuition. The dickhead. I lost my motivation and my creative ideas turned to mush.

By the weekend, I'd made little progress on my painting, but I had to visit my mother.

On Friday morning I threw a few things into a suitcase— changes of clothes, sarong, bathing suit—bagged a bottle of wine, got into my Mini, and headed south, Amy Winehouse crooning "Back to Black."

Past Redlands on Interstate 10, the land yawned open. The hills were curvy, a smooth velveteen. A freight train passed alongside the freeway. Blades of wind generators lackadaisically spun.

I took the exit for Highway 111 and ten minutes later the lunar landscape gave way to Palm Springs's green lawns and lush landscaping fed by a humongous underground lake.

Palm Canyon Drive runs through downtown and even though it was August, pedestrians milled about. My desert city no longer cleared out during the searing summer months. I liked it better back when tumbleweeds rolled down the streets as the theme song from *The Good, the Bad and the Ugly* played in my head.

At the stoplight near Rocky's Pawn Shop I called my brother and left a voice mail. Just beyond the Ace Hotel I hung a right and turned into Twin Palms, named for the two palm trees planted in front of each midcentury marvel. My father had bought one of the original homes and Mom had lived here through three husbands. I pulled into the curving driveway and made a mental note to ask her where her car was.

From the outside, the house looked the same: the butterfly design—sleek angular lines spread open like wings, high windows with broad panes of glass, chartreuse front door.

As I made my way up the front walk, things began to look awry. Empty vegetable and dog food cans littered either side of the cement path as if someone had pitched them out the front door instead of into the trash. And why hadn't Ben picked them up? Was he losing it too?

I rang the doorbell. Through the walls, a vague chime. I shifted from foot to foot, knocking, ringing the doorbell, and waiting. It took awhile for my mother to respond and when she did, she opened the door a crack.

"Who are you?" she said, peering out.

"I'm your daughter, remember me?" I replied, partly indignant. Still, I was freaking out inside. "C'mon, open up."

"You look different," she said, and pulled the door open.

"I cut my hair." I reached up, touched the ends that I'd dyed blue.

"Why'd you do that?"

My hair had been long until last month when I kicked out Little Dick. "I needed a change," I said.

"What the hell is with the turquoise?"

I dropped my bags in my old bedroom, which had hardly changed, put the wine in the fridge, and joined her in the kitchen. Joey Bishop spun as he barked. Yappy dogs can drive anyone right over the edge. Maybe this was what had happened to her; it was the dog's fault. I leaned down to pet his head. He growled, then snapped at me. I jumped back.

"He likes to protect me," she said.

"Not from your son, apparently," I mumbled.

"What did you say?"

"Oh, nothing."

The inside of the house wasn't exactly a shambles, but something was off. The big plate-glass windows were smudged at the bottom from Joey Bishop's snout. Big antiques were missing—the carved Chinese table my father had bought when I was twelve. A bronze mirror that hung opposite the front door, supposedly from the Tang dynasty. Then there were the missing Eames coffee table and Slim Aarons photographs.

End tables and built-in shelves were bare of artifacts she'd collected over the years from her trips to Europe and Asia and they were dusty, except for circles and squares that were varying levels of clean, the chalk outline equivalent of missing items.

A yellowing pile of *Desert Sun* newspapers as tall as a toddler stood by the sliders. I ran my fingers up the side. "You going to read all these?"

"I'll get to them," she said, and trundled to her midcentury stereo cabinet. Hanging on the wall behind it were dozens of framed photos, mostly of Ben and me, but also of the Palm Springs celeb set she once hung out with. She set the needle of the turntable down on vinyl. There was Sinatra again, singing "In the Wee Small Hours of the Morning" from his saddest album.

I poured wine into a mug with that Marilyn Monroe flying skirt image. After that long drive, I deserved a drink. It was five o'clock somewhere, right? I took my cup and wandered about the house, noting all that was missing or just plain wrong. I threw away an empty plastic milk carton on the floor by her nightstand. On the wall where a Slim Aarons photo once hung, the paint was a shade lighter.

"Where is it?" I said, pointing.

"Where is what?"

"My favorite photo of the Kaufmann house."

"That's been gone a long time."

"It was here the last time I visited. Four months."

"Seems like longer," she said. "Ask your brother."

"When does Ben come by? His voice mail was full."

"He comes over every night to swim. His new religion. What do you want for dinner?" She threw open the fridge to reveal a dismal collection of milk, condiments, wilted iceberg lettuce, and not much else.

"Let's go to the store."

"You go," she said, and handed me her checkbook. "Take one, unless you need more."

"You shouldn't be handing out checks like Halloween candy."

"You're my daughter," she said. "If I can't trust you, who can I trust?"

"Do you say the same thing to Ben?"

"He's my son," she said.

When I returned with groceries, I set them on the bench outside the front door, picked up the tin cans and threw them out, then carried the bags inside. Mom was on the sofa paging through a *Palm Springs Life*. Out by the pool the first man in some time I wanted to be close enough to smell was skimming the water, sweeping leaves, bugs, and crud into a net. He wore khaki board shorts, a neon-yellow rash guard like what surfers wear, and a wide-brimmed straw hat. He looked to be pure muscle, calves striated like rocks carved by river currents. He moved fluidly, as if to his own soundtrack, and swished the pool sifter back and forth.

"That's Ernesto," my mother said without looking up from the magazine.

I put away the frozen foods and went out to introduce myself.

He was tall with eyes the color of kiwi fruit. He said he had tended the pool three times a week for the last two months.

"That's a lot, isn't it?" I said.

"It's what the man wants," he said.

"What man? My brother?"

"Ben, he said his name was."

So, the house can go to hell, but the pool needs to be pristine. Interesting.

"And you are?" he asked.

"Greta," I said. "It's nice to meet you. I'll leave you to your work." I turned toward the house.

"*Que bonita*," he said softly, perhaps to himself.

"What?"

Rather shyly, he said, "You're much more beautiful than your picture."

I felt flustered, then dizzy, then smitten. It happened so fast, like I had just been hit with the flu. "How'd you see my photo?"

"Your mother asked me to look at her stereo. Sound wasn't coming out. Your photos were on the wall above it."

"Do you want a drink?" Was I hitting on him or had he just hit on me?

"A *cerveza* would be nice. So hot." He wiped a red bandanna across his forehead.

"I don't think there's beer, but I'll check. I have wine."

"Whatever you like, I like," he said.

I stumbled on my way inside. *What is this?* I wanted him, and that he might want me was enough to turn any whisper of the idea into a roar of demand.

I poured more wine into my mug and into one that read *PALM SPRINGS* with a palm tree, and looked out the floor-to-ceiling windows that took up the entire back of the house. Ernesto scooped water from the pool into a vial and squeezed in a chemical. Capped the bottle, gave it a shake, then dipped it in litmus paper. He was young; his face and body were absent of history. When I was eighteen, I wanted wrinkles so I'd be taken more seriously. Imagine. Now, closer to forty than thirty, I lapped up his attention like a neglected kitten.

In my old room I changed into my two-piece. Dust bunnies hugged corners. This wasn't like my mother. She used to keep a pristine home, vacuumed as if it were her part-time job.

I carried the wine out to the pool and handed Ernesto one. We awkwardly thunked mugs.

"Sí, *muy hermosa*," he said, looking me up and down as I approached in my two-piece. It wasn't like me to find a man I'd just met, my mother's pool cleaner at that, so instantly compelling. But after my lying Little Dick boyfriend—he'd even proposed!—I was game. I needed an ego boost, and fast.

Plus, this thing with Ernesto, whatever it was, would distract me from my growing concern over my mother and brother. A tryst while I was here would be sublime.

I laid a towel over the lounge chair and sat down. He took the chair beside me and we made chitchat. He told me about his mother, a green-eyed blonde from Los Angeles who lost the part to Bo Derek in that awful movie *Bolero*, but got a walk-on part and met his father, also an aspiring actor. I was only half listening as I felt a gnawing animal attraction.

I asked him how he came to be a pool cleaner in Palm Springs. It was time to leave LA, he said, and shook his head. He didn't offer more and I didn't ask. I didn't care.

I must have been nervous because I downed that wine like a ginger shot. I jumped up, padded inside, and grabbed the bottle.

When I sat back down, I said, "I'm curious. Have you seen my brother doing anything strange?"

"Strange?"

"Things are missing from the house."

He pondered this and said, "One day as I was arriving, he was putting a black table into his car. He asked me for help."

"Was it carved?"

"With dragons," he said.

The Chinese table.

"Another time he carried out a cardboard box with frames."

That Slim Aarons print.

Ernesto's cell phone pinged with an incoming text. He looked at his phone and said, "Filter emergency."

Huh? Who has filter emergencies in the late afternoon?

I got up with him. He went to shake my hand, or maybe kiss it, when I pulled him into a hug.

"How old are you?" I said, looking for a reason to stay away.

"What's age?" he responded, and gave me his card: a little graphic of a diving board with his contact info.

"Call me if you want to talk," he said, and with that, he pulled his trolley with bottles and hoses and disappeared through the side gate.

I went inside and changed. I vacuumed and cleaned the house. An hour later Ben showed up. My handsome little brother was losing his hair and had teeth in need of white strips. We side-hugged. I followed him outside. The sun had moved behind San Jacinto Peak, turning the sky a sulky violet.

He pulled a pack of cigarettes from his shirt pocket and offered me one. I shook my head. I'd stopped smoking and didn't want to start up again. My brother's hands trembled slightly as he lit one for himself.

"I'm worried about Mom," I said. "She called the other night about a noise. She's getting worse."

"She has her good days and her bad days," he said, puffing away. The smoke hung in the windless air, our own personal smog alert. I hated wind but right now I longed for it.

I waved away the smoke. "She says things are missing."

"She's imagining. Sign of early-stage dementia. What kinds of things?"

"Art. Jewelry. The dragon table—where is it?"

"What table? I didn't take a table. What am I going to do with a table?"

"It was worth a lot of money."

"Lots of people go in and out of the house," he said. "There's no telling. Old people are hungry for friends."

"That's bullshit."

"Is it?" Ben set down the cigarette and pulled off his T-shirt.

"You're growing a belly there," I said.

He gave me the stink-eye.

Three crows perched on the branch of a huge ficus tree, complaining about something or other. He stamped out his cigarette, lit another, and offered me the pack.

"Stop doing that," I said. "It took me forever to quit."

He shrugged. "Whatever."

"And the house is filthy. I found an empty milk carton beside her bed."

"She was probably thirsty."

I didn't laugh. "You were supposed to look after her. Make sure she has food and a clean house."

"I am!"

"You're not doing a good job of it."

"Why don't you move back, then?" he said. "*You* can take care of all this crap."

The underwater lights of the pool came on. Ben went into the house, returned a few minutes later in his trunks, and dove in.

I stood to stretch. My mother was on the other side of the slider, gazing out. I waved but she made no gesture to show she saw me and evaporated back into the darkened house.

"What's up with all the darkness, Mom?" I said, stepping inside, sliding the glass door shut behind me.

"The bulbs burned out," she said, and wandered back over to the slider. "Your brother thinks he's a fish. Always swimming."

When we were kids, my brother and I would swim as close to the bottom as we could, lie on our backs, and open our eyes. Above, the water became a stained-glass window to the world. Once, as we surfaced, I pushed Ben back under and held him there, wishing, in a way, that he'd drown so I'd get back the attention he took from me when he was born. I still had nightmares about it, only in my dreams he sinks to the bottom and my father dives in to save him. I always wake up before they surface.

By the light of my phone, I searched the drawers for bulbs. I replaced what I could and switched them on. Somehow, when all lit up, the house looked even dingier. I heated up a mac-and-cheese entrée in the microwave, made a salad, and as I set plates on the table, Ben hefted himself out of the pool, dried off, and came in.

"Are you hungry?" asked our mother, who was already at the table.

"Have an appointment." He kissed her on the check, gave a little wave to me, and said, "Good to see you," then scampered down the hallway and out the front door.

"Your brother always has meetings."

"At night?"

"He's a very busy man."

She got up. I heard the bathroom door close. When she was back, she said, "I can't find my ruby ring. It was in the bathroom drawer."

"What was it doing in the bathroom?"

"That's where I keep it."

I went to look, riffled through her vanity drawers, and found it, wrapped in a tissue.

"Here," I said, placing it in front of her plate.

She picked it up and studied it. "Where was it?"

"In the bathroom," I said. Hard to know what she imagined and what was real.

I drained the bottle into my mug, but I needed more than wine. I needed Ernesto.

"C'mon, Mom, you have to eat."

She took a bite. "He was such a sweet boy," she said. "I used to dress him in the cutest outfits." A bemused expression skittered across her face. "So smart."

What I remembered was a smart-ass kid who always tattled on me, who pulled scary pranks, and who once almost got me killed when we were on our bikes at a busy intersection.

I tonged salad onto our plates.

"He must be gambling," she said. "What else would he do with the money I withdraw from the bank?"

"The bank?"

"Sometimes we go to the bank so I can take out money. Last week it was two thousand. What does he do with it?"

"Dollars?"

"He says we need things. Repairs." She gestured. "House is old."

There goes my inheritance.

"I meant to ask: where's your car?" I said.

She shrugged. "Ask your brother."

"Oh my God. He doesn't tell me anything useful and neither do you."

She pushed back her chair, wandered over to the windows, and gazed out at the pool flashing blue in the darkness. "We used to have such parties. Frank would come by. He had a house a few streets over. This was before he married Barbara. Do you remember him? You were just a little girl. He'd come over and we'd sit by the pool and drink Jack Daniel's. That was his drink, you know. He was a very nice man, always nice to you. I have all his albums. He gave them to me."

I remembered Sinatra, how he would sing in our living room, all my mother's friends gathered around.

She sighed. "I'm going to bed." Before she disappeared around the corner, she said, "Where does the time go?"

I'd begun to wonder the same thing myself.

Slippers scuffed down the hallway, followed by Joey Bishop's nails slipping across the floor. Her bedroom door clicked shut. I held Ernesto's business card, kept turning it over in my hands, and finally gave in. I texted him, asked what he was doing. Watching TV, he said. Come over, I said. He lived in Cathedral City, the next town over, and could be here in a half hour.

I cleaned the kitchen and paged through a newspaper that had fallen from the stack. A feature about the growing crime of elder abuse in the desert, prevalent because there were more and more older people coming here with property and money.

I didn't want to believe that's what Ben was doing. But somebody was doing something nefarious.

Such a sweet little boy.

When did sweet turn to sour?

I flipped through the paper. Buried on page five was a story about a pool drowning from electric shock. A lot of swimming pools in Palm Springs were built before 1963 and not all were up to code. Who even knew to get the wiring of their pools checked twice a year?

I called my brother. He picked up.

"What did you do with her car?" I asked.

"Look," he said. "You're not around. You don't know what goes on here."

"Enlighten me: what goes on here?"

"She's losing it," he said.

"Today you said she has her good days and her bad days."

"You're afraid for your inheritance, aren't you? I'm the one who deserves payback. You left. You don't care about Mom."

"Fuck you," I said, and hung up. My face felt hot. I found a bottle of tequila in the liquor cabinet, probably five years old from when Jerry was still alive—maybe from their last cocktail party—and set it on the counter. There was a faint rap on the slider. A silhouette of a man framed against the turquoise of the pool. I jumped.

"You scared me," I said, hand on heart, sliding open the door.

"I have a key for the gate," Ernesto replied.

I held up the bottle. "Look what I found. I'll pour us some over ice."

We took our tumblers out to the pool along with the half-full bottle and sat side by side on lounge chairs.

"I've been thinking about you," he said.

"What did you think?"

"You in that bikini." He tapped his forehead. "It's right here."

"I thought of you too," I said. Tequila was wending its way through me, tamping down the circuits, loosening the boundaries between me and everything else.

He took hold of my hand and gave it a tug.

"Come sit with me," he said. I snuggled into him on the lounge chair as if I'd known him forever. He stroked my arm, then my shoulder, trailed his fingers over the cliff of my clavicle and kept traveling south under my tank top. He gave my chest a delicious massage.

"You have some hands on you."

"That's not all I have," he said, which is when he tugged at the waistband of my shorts and I let him. I pulled them off, pulled his off. We fucked by my mother's pool under the stars as the bats fluttered among the palm fronds.

Afterward we jumped in the pool to rinse off, wrapped ourselves in towels, and went back to the lounge chairs. I poured us more tequila and we toasted to us.

I awoke as the sun inched up over Indian Canyons. On the other side of the pool a coyote sniffed the water. I clapped my hands and he jumped over the gate and ran.

Inside, my mother was still asleep. After a shower, I tied on my sarong, brewed a pot of coffee, and checked my cell phone. A message from my brother.

"*I don't appreciate being hung up on—*"

Delete.

Another message, this one from Little Dick. "*Greta, I keep telling you, I'm sorry. It was a mistake. I meant it when I said want to marry you.*"

Delete.

Screw them. Screw both of them.

My brother continued to come over every night to swim—usually at sundown when my mother went to bed. We ignored each other. My mother was the same, ignoring me but vaguely glad I was here.

Each night as soon as Ben left, I'd text Ernesto. He'd come over and we'd have sex, and then we'd talk. Mostly I talked. Over the next few nights, I told him the long story of my past with Daniel, my painting, why I was here. Admittedly, I'd grown addicted to his silky fingers that made my body feel things it hadn't felt in years.

It was bugging me, what my mother said about going to the bank. I wondered if I'd find out anything if I went through her expandable file.

As soon as I started riffling through her file, I found papers for a reverse mortgage. What the fuck? I about exploded out of my sarong.

My mother was in the garage, going through a box of old photos.

"Why'd you take out a reverse mortgage on the house?" I asked.

Studying a faded color photo, she said, "Ben told me I should spend the money before I croak."

"But what do you need it for?"

"I don't need it but just in case."

"Unbelievable," I said, and returned to the file and the bank statements, accompanied by a huge headache that two Advils and a glass of wine helped to mute.

That night as Ernesto and I lay naked in the balmy night air, I said, "I have to do something, go to court, get power of attorney or something, so my brother doesn't take all my mother's assets."

"Court takes a long time, no?"

"By the time it goes through, my mother could be penniless. Fifty grand is already gone."

"How much is left?"

"Around a hundred grand. Probably more."

"Still, a lot of money," he said.

We watched the glimmery blue water, listened to the mockingbird that ran through its repertoire of cell phone ringtones, and sipped tequila. My eyes fixed on the underwater light.

I brought up the article. "I've read that a lot of pools here are not code compliant. Old pools, old wires." I paused before asking, "Is it painful, drowning that way? Do you think it hurts?"

"The swimmer feels a tingling, becomes kind of numb, can't get out, gets sucked under."

"My brother swims all the time," I said.

"I check pools to make sure this does not happen."

A shiver ran through me when I realized what I was thinking. I wanted my brother gone and I needed Ernesto's help to make it happen. There was a name for that, and it wasn't good.

The next evening when Ben came over, he brought Mom a

cherry pie, her favorite, and exclaimed for the universe to hear that he'd hired a cleaning lady.

He went out to swim laps and Mom went to bed. I stood over the glistening pool.

"I know what you're doing," I said.

He pretended not to hear me. Water in his ears or something.

"You don't fool me," I continued, and sat on a lounge chair with my drink, hoping to intimidate him into leaving. I watched him swim back and forth—not for much longer, though, if things went as planned. I used to like my brother more, even love him, but for years now he'd been all about Ben and I'd had my fill.

That night Ernesto and I went at it in our usual place, on the lounge chair beside the pool. Thank God for mothers who go to bed early and for magenta bougainvillea that grows tall along stucco walls surrounding properties. Sex with Ernesto was good for my nerves—better than any antianxiety medication. This thing with my brother had my nerves sheared raw.

We rinsed off in the pool, then sat on the bullnose edge, sipping tequila.

"I'd be willing to give you some of the money."

"Excuse me?" he said.

"The last straw was the reverse mortgage. He needs to pay. You can help me, can't you?"

He took a long sip. "Oh, *chica*, this can be very dangerous."

"It's a lot of money, you even said that."

"I know, but I—"

"You know how to make pools safe, right? So, you must know what makes them unsafe."

"I can't disconnect anything, but I can do something, make the wiring look frayed maybe."

"No one will ever know you had anything to do with it. I'd never tell them how to find you. Why would I?" I ran my hand over his lower regions, said, "Ernesto, I would do anything to show you my appreciation for your efforts on my behalf," and we went at it again.

Afterward I said, "I need a picture of us," and reached for my phone.

"Oh, no," he said, "I don't like to take pictures."

I leaned my face against his anyway, reached out my arm, and took a selfie. My breasts and his bare chest were in the shot. So sexy. A photo to keep me company on hot desert nights.

"I've never met anyone like you," he said as I licked a bead of sweat from his cheek.

"There's more of this for you, whenever you like."

He shook his head, kissed me hard, and said, "Tomorrow I'll come over and play with the wires. Just don't forget and jump in the water yourself."

My brother took my mother out for breakfast, just the two of them. I did errands. When I returned, I dodged yappy Joey Bishop—maybe he'd get dizzy and faint from spinning as he barked—and stood before the pool. It looked so pristine, so very innocent. I dropped in a palm frond to see what would happen. It did not sizzle. It did not fry. I wasn't going to jump in to test it. Hopefully Ernesto had been here and done his thing.

I was in the bathroom slathering on sunblock when Mom returned—shuffling down the hallway, followed by her frantic little pooch, and she said, "I'm going to rest."

"Where's Ben?" I called after her.

"Had to work." And closed her door.

Work. What work?

When the sky turned lavender, the pool lights came on. I poured a drink and heard the front door.

Ben was here, using his key, striding through the house like he owned it, heading for the pool. I purposely didn't turn on any lights in the living room so I could watch him.

The desert wind stirred up fronds and dust, sweeping them against the house and into the pool. The south end of town rarely got hit hard, but this evening the wind was wicked and sent a standing umbrella onto its side, missing Ben by inches. He jumped out of its way, then picked it up and leaned it against the stucco wall.

My mother's bedroom door creaked open.

Shit.

Out scampered Joey Bishop, who sniffed my feet, barked, and ran out the open slider toward the pool.

"Don't!" I called. He trotted back, spinning as he barked.

My mother moved beside me, watched my brother standing by the water. The room was freezing; she must have turned the air down to sixty-five.

"We saw Ernesto at breakfast," she said.

"Who?" I responded, playing dumb.

"Your *boyfriend*," she said. So, she'd seen us outside. "Ben took me to Cathedral City, some little restaurant. Your boyfriend was there, with his wife and kids."

My brother dove in, began swimming laps.

I felt suddenly hot all over. "How do you know they were his wife and kids?"

"They called him *Daddy*."

Ben slowed and seemed to struggle, as if an invisible force was pulling at him.

"Why isn't he moving?" my mother asked, her voice quavering.

"Maybe he has a cramp."

I felt awful. A mother shouldn't have to watch her son die.

"Call 911!" she cried, flailing her hands about like startled birds. I found my phone and called.

Ben gestured toward the house for help, then stopped struggling, and was sucked under. He rose to the surface and lay inert on the water.

The sirens grew close and then the paramedics were here. I let them in and said the way a frantic person would, "My brother! He's in the pool!" and three men rushed past. Joey Bishop spun like a top out of control, barking till he went hoarse.

I followed them out.

"Did your brother know how to swim, ma'am?"

"Of course!"

"Does he take drugs?"

"I don't know! He comes over every night to swim."

They mumbled among themselves, then one of them went over and unplugged the wiring and filter and whatever else was electrical; the other two used the leaf skimmer and a rope to pull his limp body from the pool. They administered CPR but Ben didn't respond.

The carved dragon table, the Slim Aarons photos. Ernesto, with a wife and kids? The world was full of rats.

As they continued administering CPR on my brother, I rushed inside. I would give them Ernesto's business card, give Ernesto to them. Mom sat in the dark of the living room and there was Sinatra again, singing about a piper man and losing someone to the summer wind. But as I held the card, I realized that by giving them Ernesto, I would also be giving them me.

I went back outside. They were loading Ben onto a stretcher. His cigarettes lay on his shirt. Oh, what the hell.

I reached out and grabbed them, tapped one from the pack, and lit up. On my phone I looked at the picture of Ernesto and me. Gave me pangs to think it was over. I flicked the card against the phone, then the thought came to me: maybe his wife would like the photo too.

THE EXPENDABLES

BY ROB ROBERGE

Wonder Valley

1981

Have you ever seen government agents feed radioactive cereal to a group of mentally ill children, just to study what would happen, and have them call it a medical experiment?

I have.

What happens when you poison mentally ill children with radiation? With dusts of plutonium? Any children, of course. We used the institutionalized. What happens? They die. Of radiation poisoning.

The ones who ingested the most, the luckiest, died fastest. The others died slowly and more painfully than you could possibly imagine unless you've ever witnessed it. There are the enormous skin blisters and burns down to red muscle and the white—with a subtle shade of light blue—bones exposed. The constant diarrhea and vomiting. Often, blood from every orifice. The organs break down and basically liquefy. The child dies a savage death.

And I thought then, and I still think: why in the world did you need that experiment to figure out what the results would be?

I'm hiding, even if you couldn't tell by looking. I sit on my screen porch here in the high desert. An unforgiving burning sun that keeps most people away is perfect for me. You spend a summer out here, and you wonder why the people stopped here on their westward expansion. A hundred and twenty miles from Los Angeles. From paradise. But it wasn't like that distance was easy back then. My guess is they rode until they dropped. And they probably got here in fall or spring, when the weather sits in the low nineties and loosens its grip on everybody when the nights are all seventy-five to eighty-five degrees.

I read and watch the clouds change the colors of the mountains to the north. From sharp grays, to, later in the day, a dark tint like on a car window, to a burst near sunset that looks like cotton candy might if it were the most beautiful purples and oranges and reds and whites you've ever seen. As colorful as an atom bomb's mushroom. The place might hold a place of love in my heart, if I didn't *have* to be here.

Out here, you never know the secrets of people's lives. My secrets are more guarded than most—as they are murderous secrets I've been keeping since 1953. My actions were born in secrecy, and it's what I've lived in ever since then. In the 1950s I participated in the CIA's mind control experiments, known as MK-ULTRA. I worked in what were called "subprojects," but they were all under the ULTRA umbrella. I told myself, at first—before I'd seen or known of the scope of it—that I was doing this as a patriot, knowing the Russians were doing the same experiments. And we in the agency could not allow them to be first. To be able to control people's minds. Our soldiers. Our POWs. Our spies. Hell, possibly our president. And we did these experiments, I now regret deeply, so we could, with our rapid advancements, be able to control *their* minds. Any other enemies of the state, domestic and global.

A good man would have told the government and screamed

it to the *Times*. A good man would have risked his life. But while it does nothing to ease my guilt, I have never thought that was an option. To want to quit made you a national security risk. If they didn't kill you right away, they would torture you and destroy your mind until you were of no use. And then they'd kill you. Or, worse, leave what was left of you alive.

But still, the man I should have been would've known he couldn't keep torturing and killing people and remain a human being.

If I'd become a true security risk by talking, maybe I could have saved thousands of lives by trading my own. Though sometimes I think one man's word against the CIA's worst is hopeless.

I became a monster with a useless conscience. What you think of yourself is nothing when you stand it next to what you actually do.

But I could easily be disappeared. People in the project were tortured and killed—though sometimes just killed—and nobody would figure out it was a murder. The CIA was *built* on the desire for no one to know what they were doing behind the scenes. It's in the very DNA of the CIA's birth. It *is* the CIA.

Even in the agency, though, we were a particularly evil—I think I can use that word sincerely—tributary off the already poison river.

In the previous eighteen months, I've leaked as much information about MK-ULTRA as I can. It's probably what helped the agency find my trail again. When I was silent and on the run, they had better things to do. But now, it's a matter of time. You can be very hard to find in this world. But never *impossible* to find.

My best chance is why I originally came to live out here—a

hundred and twenty miles from Los Angeles, as I say, and northeast of Palm Springs, fifty miles into the empty high desert.

Wonder Valley is a world where you don't have neighbors. Or want them. This valley is for people who don't like or want people in their lives. No one gives a shit about you. The only places I go are the gas station seven miles into town, the grocery store near it, and a little crap bar called the Mouse Trap down Highway 62, away from town and even farther east than I am. It's not really a bar—not in any legal sense. It's in a converted garage. The owner Leo built a small bar, put in five mismatched stools. There's only one beer on tap—whatever keg he got from the liquor store. And even with only five stools, the place is mostly empty during the day. I drink there when I'm sick of drinking alone. Sometimes the generator power shuts down and the swamp cooler stops. And there you are, left to drink in total darkness—opening the door would only bring more heat. Drinking quickly because out here even a cold keg can turn the temperature of a cup of tea in no time.

Leo and I talk. We talk but we don't communicate. Who does? Neither of us knows anything about each other's lives. I'll never know his story, and he'll never know that I spend my time sending the secrets of the agency to the world in hopes they will be read and heard.

When I started writing all this information down—when I started releasing this information—I signed my death warrant.

More than 90 percent of the ULTRA files were destroyed in 1973 by the director of the CIA, on the order of my old boss, Sidney Gottlieb. Nothing we did was legal, according our government, the CIA, or the Nuremberg Code. If any other country were outed for doing this, our president would call them war criminals. Instead, Eisenhower knew about it and let it go on. After my time, Kennedy endorsed it. Nixon.

It seems impossible to me that it's stopped at all since. There is permanence to the subterranean horror that lies hidden from this nation.

They only ended the Tuskegee Airmen Syphilis Study in 1972, after more than forty years. Did it end because someone with a shred of ethics came to power? No. It ended because it was uncovered.

The people will only ever know—if they find out at all— long after the damage has been done. Long after what's being done and will be done in the future.

If people knew the truth about the scope of this shadow world, they would realize what a fragile endeavor society actually is.

My death? The agency may torture me—but electroshock and isolation aren't practical for a portable assassination. LSD or another drug would be too unpredictable, even if quickly administered by IV. There's no twenty-story hotel to toss me off. I'm guessing a beating with a bat. I only hope it's not a sniper. I need to see the assassin's fear when they walk in the door and realize I'm not the only dead man in the room.

1953

I was hired because I was an expert in biochemical developments, and I was excited to have funding for what I thought I was there for—national security. Over time, I would collaborate with major advancements, but all of them were meant for defense, as far as I knew.

Very soon after being recruited and receiving my security clearance—which I was granted despite being a Jew who'd attended, after I'd immigrated to save my life, communist meetings with a girlfriend in the 1930s. She was more possessed with a revolutionary spirit than I was. I thought the American government could be trusted to a degree. Certainly more than the Germany which I'd fled. But I learned painfully and relentlessly that there was not an honest or benevolent government in the world. Savage men run everything. Everywhere.

As Abigail Adams wrote to her husband: *All men would be tyrants if they could.*

Yet, at the time, I was still a patriot. No one is more in love with this country than the immigrant. I wanted to spend my life in service to the ideals, the promise, of my new home. The agency taught me early that the ways to reach closer to that perfect American ideal were as far as you could get from those ideals. A *lie in service to the greater truth*, a colleague said. No matter how much that truth went against everything people thought the country stood for. They didn't even have a country. They just never knew.

1981

You do have to understand it was a different time, which excuses the fear, but not the experimenting with human subjects. The agency—the whole government—was terrified at how advanced the Russians might be at controlling a person's mind. We had no idea and, as people tend to do when they don't know anything, we feared the worst. And, as is always the reaction, we acted with blind rage over what we didn't know. So, this was mainly about beating the enemy to discovering the secrets of mind control. And it made for what should have been strange bedfellows.

First came Operation Paperclip. The agency brought over Nazi space engineers, rocket scientists, chemists—anyone who could give them an edge in the Cold War.

And there were doctors. Nazi doctors—mostly Nazis, anyway—who performed experiments on human beings. The

Nazi doctors and chemists and others experimenting on prisoners from the camps. POWs. Several of the Nazis who had tortured people to death, reduced others to permanent vegetative states, exposed them to poisons and illnesses, were given one of the great moral mulligans of all time. Some of these men were about to be sentenced to death at the Nuremberg trials.

Project Artichoke would protect those guilty of war crimes and, in trade for their knowledge from inhumane studies, the US government brought them to America to share their information with the CIA. The other, perhaps main, reason they did this was to keep the doctors and scientists and biochemists away from the Soviet Union.

My first mentor was a Nazi. Hans Krieger. My family had fled Poland in the thirties and would almost assuredly be dead had we stayed. I studied how to experiment on human beings from this man. I never could reconcile that our national security meant we had to protect war criminals and put them in positions of power.

If Nazis taught me my first lessons in how to destroy the human mind, what does that make me?

People think there's nothing to see in the desert. No life to speak of. But it's all here. You just have to know where to look. Lizards hide under any shelter they can find so the birds of prey don't get them. Sidewinder rattlesnakes that move in a way that will always creep me out. I'm not afraid of death. But I'm still afraid of that damn snake.

Mesquite trees. When it rains, the whole desert smells of ozone. There's nothing quite like it.

The bones left to the elements out here? Some of them easy to identify as human, for someone who knows too much about remains. They turn whiter than other bones. They fracture up and down their sides. Somehow, they are the loneliest bones I've known. Stories behind all of them.

1953

After any training, the way Sidney Gottlieb trapped you into silence was to bring you in. The moments you were in a room where these experiences took place was when you became one of them forever.

Gottlieb had me present to study their mind control and interrogation techniques so that I might have a better idea of what they were looking for from my field of expertise. I designed nothing for the test. I didn't administer any of the tests—I was later put on strategies for assassination of foreign leaders, including Castro.

At the experiments, I was sickened by what I saw. Nothing in my imagination prepared me for any of it.

I witnessed how a man responds to interrogation while he's sealed in a low-pressure chamber. The pain builds. The body is stressed beyond belief. What did I learn about how a man responds to a high-pressure chamber while he's being interrogated? I learned that his eyes pop out of his sockets while he's still alive and screaming and begging to die, which he does.

At first, all the experiments were in Europe. Then Gottlieb managed to start them in the US and Canada—at hospitals and institutions. All of the unwitting test subjects were known, casually and on the paperwork, as *expendables.*

Some of the other techniques I saw were tests in how a man reacts to hypothermia while interrogated. He freezes to death. How he reacts to 130-degree heat until he, too, can no longer speak and slips into a coma and dies.

Other expendables? Prisoners. Heroin addicts. Children.

Mentally ill children and adults. Anyone in a mental institution, no matter how minor the reason they were admitted. It didn't matter if you were white, so long as you were expendable. But you mattered even less if you were black.

1981

There was a saying in the agency. *It's good to have someone you can trust to have your back; it's better to trust no one.*

Along with an elaborate system of getting information to various destinations, I trusted my mentor, Dr. Hans Krieger. The Nazi. I wouldn't call it true trust, however. I figured, if I had secrets, his were worse. If the agency taught me nothing else, it was to always have the most leverage in any situation. I didn't trust Hans. But I trusted Hans to keep his mouth shut for fear that I'd expose him.

If anything happens to me, I've left paper trails all over.

1953

I've seen the lifeless eyes of a woman who entered a hospital for postpartum depression and then had ten times the normal electroshock dose twice a day for forty-three days in a row. The hope was to empty a person's mind and then implant thoughts that would make them helpless to protest, or even reflect on, the agency's commands. They weren't supposed to be people anymore. They were only vessels for orders. They could be used to do anything, no matter the person they used to be. The goal behind this was to create unwitting assassins. The result, in this case, was a woman with no history. No knowledge of a millisecond of her life. With the cognitive skills of a child. Destroyed.

I've seen expendables driven insane, given massive doses of LSD for fifty days or greater in a row.

I've seen pregnant women intentionally infected with malaria to see if their babies are born with it. Almost always black women and children.

I have seen people put to sleep for 172 days and played the same recorded sentence every second of it. A command that would replace one's mind.

I have been, as with the entire inner circle, experimented on.

1981

Hans contacts me via a PO Box in Palm Springs. Over an hour away, but a PO Box in Twentynine Palms would only be useful if you lived a hundred miles away, let alone fewer than five miles from my cabin. Everything is a code. We haven't spoken or written a word to each other in almost thirty years. If we don't truly have trust, we share an enlightened self-interest in staying alive.

But with the information I've already released, the agency has known for a while that I'm responsible. Hans has told me this much. I have no idea what else he's told them. Among all the deaths, secrets, double lives, the actual scope of the information could only be from the inner circle. And I am the weak link.

Though I have no idea if they've already reached Hans and let him live the rest of his anonymous life in trade for the end of mine.

1953

In my first two months on the job, I was invited to a meeting with Gottlieb and much of the inner circle.

After dinner, the seven of us retired to a large living room with books lining the walls. Every chair some dark wood with deep leather seats, looking as deep and ominous as a Bacon painting.

Gottlieb and a man I didn't know poured drinks from a carafe. This was used for just five of the drinks—emptied, and then he poured mine.

I had no idea I was given LSD. A dose that was twenty times what would later become a common recreational dose. I lost clear vision. Everything became exaggerated and looked like a funhouse mirror on every side of me. I remember the laughing. Then the menace of two men approaching me, taking me to another room with only a simple chair in the center. It was the brightest-lit room I had ever been in.

I was ordered to strip.

They tied me to the chair. I opened my eyes and saw an enormous mirror on the wall to my right. I'd seen enough subprojects to know, even in my compromised state, that it was a one-way mirror and I was being observed. There had to be an audio recorder, as well. I tried to prepare to die and prayed the torture wouldn't last long. I couldn't fathom what I had done. A man I recognized—Thomas Somebody, or Somebody Thomas—from the chemical studies came in, bent down, and gave me a shot at the base of my penis. It burned immediately and my penis swelled beyond anything I'd ever experienced. Enormous pressure, like my blood was trying to escape through my increasingly pained skin. It felt like it could split open at any time.

Then, a different shot, this one rough, as they tied off my bound left arm with rubber, and injected into my vein, after trying many times. I realized I should be feeling pain with the needle's crude hunt, but I felt nothing. Just fingers and the pressure of the needle.

But once it was in me, even with the acid fracturing my brain, I knew immediately what it was. They'd been testing ketamine as a truth serum. And I'd felt a light sample once. This was not a light sample.

A young man—maybe eighteen—was escorted by two men into the room and they closed the door behind him. He stripped and came over to me, got on his knees, and began sucking my penis. I'd seen this, or something like it, happen to others in the program. The point was to compromise the agent by documenting him in certain positions—and homosexual activities were a popular way to leverage your total loyalty. I stared at the light and felt the boy's mouth up and down the length of my penis. It felt amazing, and my head rolled back, and I moaned for what seemed like a very long time. He didn't stop. I heard the door open. I heard cameras flash. Their light exploding behind my eyelids at irregular intervals. But I didn't care. Nothing but lights and the feeling I'd be blind soon when I closed my eyes, and this blurred, distorted, beautiful boy in my lap when I opened them. I felt on the verge of orgasm for what seemed like an hour, but I never had one.

A man's voice ordered the boy to stop.

I was already compromised. Whatever footage and recording they had were plenty. I felt the boy's hands on my thighs as he started to stand, and I asked him to wait. I felt his erect penis hard up against my ribs as he got up and pressed into me.

"Please kiss me," I said.

He sat on my lap and we kissed, my mouth open to the glorious invasion of his tongue. The ketamine had me floating endlessly—one of its effects was that it made you feel weightless and like you were drifting down slowly into a void without any bottom. My head grew cloudy with images. I tried to touch the boy, but my hands were still tied. I'd never felt someone lick my neck and I couldn't believe the feeling. He kissed me again, and it was like we were alone, together, drifting and falling ecstatically through endless floating space and

I never wanted to leave. Someone pulled him away from me.

I stayed locked naked and bound in that room. My mind stayed bent. The ketamine leveled off and faded about two hours later, but the grip of the acid was suffocating. I wanted it over. More than anything.

They turned the room temperature below freezing. I lost all control and shivered and shook while they interrogated me for an hour. My penis remained embarrassingly erect from whatever the chemist had shot me with. I tried to think of a chemical that would have this effect, but among the acid and the cold and the rapid aggressive questions, I couldn't focus on any thoughts of my own. I saw my breath. The concrete floor that agonized my feet seemed somehow even colder than the air.

A man brought in a strobe light. Another came with a small table that he put down in front of me. The first man positioned the light in front of my eyes. They fastened a neck brace on me—one that totally restricted my head and left my eyes helpless to whatever assault they had planned. The over-head light went out seconds before the strobe started.

From a speaker in the wall, the faceless interrogator barked questions at me.

"What is your name?"

I had no idea at first. I laughed.

The strobe light made me sick. I tried to swing my head away, but I was completely bound. I vomited all over myself and felt it grow shockingly cold on my chest and legs. I could barely talk, but I finally answered my name.

"Have you ever betrayed the agency in any way?"

Answering was so difficult. I had no control of my body. I was falling into hypothermia—that much I knew. Every breath hurt. And the strobe light relentlessly attacked what little control I had of my mind. I spasmed repeatedly and lost control of my bowels and they left me in my own mess, never cleaning me the rest of the day. It turned cold. Soon, I would sit in my own frozen waste.

The interrogator said, "Answer me. And open your eyes."

When I pushed my thighs against my bindings, I found that my vomit had formed a fragile skin of ice. When I moved—as little as I could—the sound of ice quietly cracking came from the vomit falling on the chair. I faded in and out of consciousness.

"Open your eyes!"

I did as I was told. With what little control I had left, I fought to not say anything that could make me a security risk.

He yelled the question again.

The strobe light had turned me blind. The questions kept coming. *Are you trustworthy? Would you ever betray your country? Would you ever betray your country for the country you'd left? You're not walking out of this room until you're broken. Tell us that. Tell us you're not walking out of this room until you're broken.*

I knew enough. They might be killing me, but I wasn't giving them the satisfaction of a reason to do so. Plus, I was barely able to form a sentence. Whatever their plan was, they'd rendered me useless. I tried to think. To tell myself all drugs have their half-life and will fade. That I was a chemist. I knew this. But still, life kaleidoscoped and strobed and attacked. Light was a glorious enemy. Beautiful one second, jackhammering the brain the next.

I struggled to speak. "Then I am not walking out of this room."

The cold was close to killing me. I screamed in pain. I screamed, thinking it was my last chance to be saved. I screamed. It was all that was left of me. Two men came in the room and untied me and brought me to a warmer room and covered me in blankets. I was going to live. And that could be very good—or very bad—news. The men stood over me. I still couldn't make out faces. Objects I knew were stationary—bookcases, unoccupied chairs, a vase of flowers—swelled and moved like trees in a windstorm.

Maybe thirty minutes later, they brought me back to the room and tied me to the chair, the strobe light away from it. The room was comfortable with the heat cranking. Maybe eighty degrees. But I knew the room would shortly be heated to a hundred and five degrees and the interrogation would resume. The strobe came back on. The room grew hotter and hotter. A hundred and ten. A hundred and fifteen. By a hundred and twenty, I'd seen men start to die of heatstroke. One twenty-five or thirty, and you were sure to die.

I don't know how long it lasted. I passed out.

I woke naked in a sealed box no wider than a couple of coffins. Tall enough to get on my hands and knees, but that was all. I'd been shot with ketamine again and it was starting to peak. The acid still raged inside of me. I was overcome with my own stink. I threw up.

Lights lined the walls and a voice kept repeating the phrase "You can stop this at any time." How many times can you hear a sentence repeated for over an hour? Maybe thousands? *You can stop this at any time. You can stop this any time. You can . . .* It could have been ten hours or ten days. I thought about those we left to sleep for six months of this. I would live in this box and listen to that sentence until I died. I screamed and wept constantly and begged them for it to end. Never an answer, just the same recorded message over and over. I'd vomited so often it was impossible not to crawl or lie in it.

Telling them anything they wanted started to feel like a welcome manner to end this hell.

Every hour, they opened the box. I heard it and saw blurry figures. Muffled men's voices. I would feel another shot, and the familiar floating sensation of ketamine would come raging back. They would close and lock the box again.

I felt myself suspended, drifting down again. But without the boy. I was locked in the box, *my* box, and set off to drift in the infinite loneliness of the universe.

At some point I was removed. I couldn't stand. Weak and disoriented. I screamed again, weeping and gulping breaths as a man carried me to a bed and placed covers over me. I didn't sleep all night. I think it was night. I remember hearing my constant screams. At one point, I collapsed on the way to the bathroom, dragged myself onto the tile, and then couldn't stand or see shapes, and I passed out in my spreading pool of urine, only understanding my situation when I was dragged back to bed and tied down, still wet and stinking in all my waste.

I'd remember that boy forever. Maybe there have been only a handful of days that I haven't thought about him. I still feel him on my skin. He lasted forever.

I don't feel the torture anymore.

They didn't break me. They didn't kill me. But they be-came my silent enemy, and I knew I would try to destroy them if I could.

1981

It took a year after the interrogations for me to find an open-ing to leave the agency. That life. To begin my series of new identities and new lives. But every new person I became al-ways looked over his shoulder. Though I don't think I ever knew fear again after they'd finished with me in that room.

They tried to destroy all of the MK-ULTRA papers in 1973. Helms, the head of the CIA, did it at Gottlieb's request, and Helms knew this was something that could never become public. However, twenty thousand pages were misfiled and never destroyed, and they were released under the Freedom of Information Act in 1975. Congress held hearings. People were shocked. But nothing happened. More hearings in 1977. The same—brief horror followed by everyone forgetting about it and moving on.

A couple years later, I started sharing the stories with some investigative reporters who I trusted could keep a secret. I knew experiments that were not covered in those twenty thousand pages. But my attempts at anonymity, I realized early, were futile. And the stories have yet to appear.

I've sent copies of everything to Hans. I've sent copies to a PO Box in Portland, Maine, and one in Lincoln, Nebraska, and mailed the keys to the *Times* journalist, who's mailed it to a friend. A friend now at risk. I hope there is no way the agency can know about that. But I also know they are everywhere. Nowhere and everywhere.

1951

I was a graduate school chemist at Northwestern University. I remember snow, which I know I will never see again. I wasn't *this* man. With only one different choice somewhere along the way, maybe I would have never been *this* man. I don't remember the man I was before the agency. He disappeared when the man from the agency appeared.

1981

A new message from Hans told me to call him and he left the number and time. We hadn't spoken in decades. When I called, all he said was, "I can't protect you anymore. They're on their way."

When I went to hurry home, I burned my hand on the car handle. And on the steering wheel again. It can be damn near impossible to even drive out here.

Still, this cruel landscape has become my home.

Since I heard from Hans, I haven't so much as left my cabin in three days. Nor have I slept. Methamphetamines are one of the easiest drugs to make. My brain slips here and there from sleep deprivation, but I have enough control to see this through.

They'll come soon, and I'll make sure I'm awake.

And when they open my door—front or back—they will be dosed with one of the early experiments with the VX nerve agent. I've carried it and made deadly gasses for years. The hard thing was picking one that would kill them within a minute or less, but have its power dissipate to safe levels so that when we're all found, no one else will be in danger.

Never leave an institution that seeks to kill you without the means to kill them.

I have a gas mask for the VX. I put it on, and the vision glass fogs. I wear two pairs of latex gloves. Even though this is mainly an airborne weapon, you can kill yourself if you break the skin.

I've turned off the swamp cooler. It blows too much air for me to hear them coming. I spread the nerve agent over the middle of the floor and by the doors.

I have a cyanide capsule in my mouth that will end it soon after I watch them take their last breaths. My life is over. Somehow, this brings waves of relief.

Inhaling twenty-five to thirty micrograms of this VX strain is enough to kill a person in minutes. Once they open my door, they'll be dosed with over two hundred micrograms. It immediately begins to paralyze the muscles. And then freezes the diaphragm, which causes the suffocation and death.

A car pulls up outside. I sit in my corner chair.

I'm covered in sweat. No swamp cooler, and in the confining rubber of the mask. The increasingly sweltering wet mask limits my vision a bit. But I can still make out their faces and thick, cruel bodies. They are the same as the agency killers I knew in the fifties. One replaced by a clone, and so on. A seemingly enormous supply of men with no skills other than to overpower and kill. Any agency with enemies will forever need these limited men.

The sunlight through the window illuminates dust specks in the air. The nerve agent hits them as soon as they fully enter. They shout at me to hold up my hands. Which I do, but the gas is already starting to kill them. They can no longer speak. The coughing has started. I watch to see if they will be able to step forward and try to beat me to death. The shorter one holds a gun on me—the taller man a baseball bat. The gun falls out of the short man's hand, and he drops to the floor. The man with the bat takes two steps toward me and collapses. They look at each other. At me. They gasp for air that will never again come, terror in their eyes.

Briefly, I wonder whether or not it matters if I witness them die, or if knowing is enough. I close my eyes. I breathe. My face slippery from the sweat. I keep my eyes closed. I have seen enough death, caused enough death, to ever want to see another one. I bite down on the capsule and wait for it all to end.

PART III

Everything Happens to Me

THE STAND-IN

BY J.D. HORN

Deepwell

"I learned about the Kennedy assassination while I was stripping for the prison guard." Donna waited for the line to land, then sensing a tough room, stepped it up. "Tits out and squatting in front of this Mack truck with a vagina, and she just bursts into tears."

The kid sitting across from her—couldn't be more than thirty, corn-silk hair, weak chin, done up like a newly minted missionary in a white short-sleeve button-up—shifted in his seat but said nothing. Donna didn't make a habit of letting just anyone into her house, but after the kid called two days earlier and asked to meet her, she got help at the senior center looking him up on the Internet. She found his résumé—a fancy school, followed by a meandering mishmash of jobs, pictures of him and his girlfriend drinking beer in Puerto Vallarta, pictures of him and his girlfriend drinking beer in Portland, videos of their tiny muttsy, whateveradoodle dog. The kid seemed rudderless, but harmless. He was interested, and Donna was bored, so she figured why the hell not? She'd talk to him. Besides, Sally was waiting nearby if Donna needed her help.

It was July. She turned off the AC to discourage a too-long visit. Outside it was a buck twenty, and even with the shades drawn and the ceiling fan turning, it was pushing ninety in her kitchen. The smell of fresh paint—one of her boys had talked her into letting him paint her cabinets white and the wall behind them chartreuse, because one or the other would "pop"—lingered a full week after the work, growing sharper in the mounting heat. It was starting to get to her, but the kid didn't seem bothered.

A fat fly that had followed him in buzzed overhead, circling like it was waiting for permission to land.

"A grown damned woman," she mumbled, her own enthusiasm waning. "Bawling." Donna had been dining and drinking on the story of her incarceration and the events leading up to it for fifty-odd years. The kid's dubious stare wasn't the reaction she'd come to expect.

"I wasn't aware," he said, enunciating with the smarmy cool diction of an NPR correspondent, "they had prisoners squat as part of the intake process in 1963." He folded his hands on the table next to the white robot-looking microphone recording their talk to his laptop. Across from him sat the box of chardonnay she'd demanded as compensation for speaking with him. If she knew he was going to be a pain in the ass, she would've demanded bourbon.

Donna raised her eyes to the faces of the Rat Pack staring down from a black-and-white photo on the wall behind him and offered up a silent prayer for strength to the city's patron saints. "I don't know. Don't remember." She scratched her temple at the edge of her lace-front wig's nylon cap. "Maybe they did, maybe they didn't."

"Details are important to establishing the veracity of your account."

"Veracity?" she said, rolling her eyes at the kid's shameless sincerity. "You can't tell a story as long as I have without embellishing a point here and there."

"The unembellished, and with any luck verifiable, truth

will go a long way in helping me help you set the record straight."

Donna swatted at the fly. "This is Palm Springs. About the only thing left around here anymore that's straight is the record." She allowed herself a cackle at that one. "Not that I mind the boys. My boys. They adore me. They see me as dangerous, glamorous. Beautiful, like I used to be. Not this wheezing colostomy bag I've become."

The kid tapped his fingers on the table's Formica top. *Genuine midcentury modern*, a succession of her boys had cooed about her chrome dining set when first they laid eyes on the "antique" Donna had bought new. The kid stopped midstrum, as if he realized the sound was being picked up on the recording. Or maybe he misread her contemplation of herself as another midcentury modern relic as irritation. He polished a spot with his shirt cuff.

Donna felt an inexplicable flash of sympathy for him. She sighed. "Maybe it is the truth. Who the hell knows after all these years? Who the hell cares? After this long, it's the story that matters, not the truth."

"The truth is why I've come."

"Then I'll sow a few grains in from time to time." She placed her cup beneath the wine box spigot and held it there till it was half full. "So, this program you're doing . . . ?"

"It's a podcast. You are familiar—" he began, the obvious—given her age—question forming.

"Yeah, yeah." She waved her hand like she was training a pup to sit. "The old lady knows what a podcast is. Have even listened to a couple."

She must have flipped some switch because all at once the kid was on. "Ours examines organized crime, but from a different angle." He leaned in, his formerly passive features animated. "It's an anthology focusing not on made men, the gangsters themselves, but on the women who, often through circumstances not of their own choosing, find themselves caught up in the gangsters' world." Each word came out with a polished enthusiasm, addressed, it seemed, to an imaginary audience of thousands rather than one old woman at her kitchen table.

Donna waited till his evangelical fervor cooled. "Not my cup of tea, but you think people will listen? A lot of people?"

"We haven't released any episodes yet. We want people to binge, the first season at least. But with stories like yours, I'm sure we'll pick up a massive following in no time."

"With stories like mine." Donna laughed and saluted him with her drink. She sipped her cup, dribbling wine on her chin. She wiped it away with the back of her hand. He watched her, patient, impassive. Maybe he hoped the wine would loosen her tongue, but the joke was on him. If her tongue got any looser, she could slip it out with her dentures.

He slid the mic a touch closer to her. "Perhaps we could start a bit earlier? What brought you to Palm Springs?"

Donna feigned surprise. "Why, you must know. I was an actress," she said, rolling the word in deep plush drama. She read his noncommittal expression as skepticism. "I had some roles. Look it up. They were small but they were speaking. You should've done better research before showing up at my door." She rose, her knees protesting. "I've got something I can show you." Donna shuffled, her steps heavy, tired, to the bookshelf in her living room, and took down the thick coral-colored scrapbook—a gift for her seventy-fifth last year from her boys. A warmth filled her chest as she thought of sharing it with the kid. It was crazy. He wasn't anything special. Not a prize by anyone's standards. But he was here, and she wanted him to see her as she'd once been. She made her way back, pausing at the threshold. The kid sat there, futzing with his phone, kicked back in his seat and looking bored.

"Sorry for the wait," she said, chagrined not to be returning to a rapt audience. "You're going to like this." She set the book before him, detesting the sight of her mottled hand as she flipped open the cover. She watched him, studying his face, waiting for his reaction to the decades-old headshot.

His eyes scanned the photo but didn't warm at the sight. "This is you?"

Donna examined the photo. It was glossy. Black-and-white. Even so, it was clear that her eyes were crystal blue, her hair a buttery blond—natural.

The kid turned the page, flicking it over with the nail of his index finger like he was afraid to touch the book.

A couple of candid snapshots. Donna in a zebra-stripe one-piece that gave her the look of a vintage Barbie. A faded color shot of Donna lounging in an aqua-blue peignoir set. That one was a warm-up to a few private "artistic" nudes that helped her make rent when the roles didn't come rolling in.

"I bet you would like to get together with her." The kid's eyes darted to her, then away. "She's still in here, you know." Donna's tongue grew thick and heavy, feeling like someone had pumped it full of cement. She felt the pulse in her temple. "I don't mean . . ."

The fly buzzed past.

"You were beautiful," the kid said, then looked back at her and flashed a grin. "And you wouldn't have looked at me twice."

Donna didn't feel gratitude often, but she did now. She'd stumbled into deep water, and he was offering her a chance to surface. She shifted around the table to her chair. "No, I wouldn't have." She nodded at the scrapbook. "Go ahead."

He turned the page using the same odd nail flick.

A call sheet. Her two lines from the same movie, a western, cut from the script. A clipping showing the movie poster—on which she had not been featured. "So, you were performing—"

"I was putting in my dues. Just like everybody else back then." She removed the lid from the ice bucket, and with her forefinger and thumb plucked out two fresh cubes. She dropped them into the wine. "You couldn't pop out a sex video and become a star. You had to work for it."

"You believe you had the talent to succeed?"

"I sure as hell did. And the backbone. That right there." She nodded at the scrapbook. "Shows you I had the looks too. All I needed was to get noticed. That's what brought me here . . . in answer to your question."

The kid's head jerked back; one brow raised, telegraphing his incredulity. "You're saying you came to Palm Springs to advance your career? Can you explain what led you to believe spending time in the desert would improve your chances of stardom?"

Donna chuckled. "Sure, it sounds crazy now, maybe, but back then this town was something special. Glamorous. Everywhere you went there were producers, directors. Stars. Even here. In Deepwell." She looked around like she was taking in the whole of the neighborhood. "Liberace. William Holden. Tippi Hedren." She flung up her hands and mimicked Tippi's batting away the birds from her bouffant. The kid froze and stared at her like he thought she was having a seizure. She dropped her hands. "Tippi Hedren? No?"

The kid shook his head. "Sorry."

"Elizabeth Taylor? You have to know *her*."

"Everyone knows Elizabeth Taylor. She lived in this neighborhood?"

"Yeah. For a while. Over on Manzanita, back when she was trying on Eddie Fisher."

The kid's eyes narrowed.

"Fisher. Eddie. Princess Leia's dad."

"Oh." His eyes widened with recognition. "Yes." He leaned back, seeming pleased with himself. "So, you came to Palm Springs to make . . . connections?"

"Connections. Is that what whoring yourself is called these days?" Donna laughed. "Yeah, I started coming every weekend or so. I figured it would be easier to catch a director's eye prancing around a swimming pool than it was on one of those god-awful cattle calls they used to do. Do they still do those?"

"I wouldn't know."

"No, of course you don't." She returned the lid to the ice bucket. "You don't know Jack." She paused for the punch line. "Webb that is. Jack Webb. He lived around here too."

The kid shrugged. "I'm not familiar with him."

"Shame. You two would've gotten on. He was all *just the facts ma'am*, too."

The kid pretended—poorly—to be amused and rewarded her with a polite for-the-recording laugh. "Did coming here work for you?" Again, the NPR diction, punctuated by a precisely timed pause. "Did you get noticed?"

Donna was beginning to get a feel for this podcast business. She leaned into a well-polished contempt. "Oh, I got noticed all right." Then allowed a beat to pass. "But not by any movie people."

"By Joseph Fiato."

"And others, but Joey was special."

"Were you aware from the start that Fiato was involved in organized crime?"

Donna grunted. "I was."

"This didn't concern you?"

"Listen. Back then—here—it didn't concern anyone. The Hollywood crowd, the mafiosos, even some of the police. It all blended together. A cocktail with a killer kick." She pointed at the mic, then whispered behind her hand, "That's pretty good. You can make like you made that up yourself if you want."

He closed the scrapbook and studied her with his gray, unblinking eyes, his gaze lingering on her hairline. Donna straightened her wig. The kid seemed as embarrassed as she once might have been. "May I?" he said, gesturing to the shaded window.

"Sure. Just drop a token in the slot."

"I'm sorry?" His head tilted like a dog's at a high-pitched whistle.

Donna waved his question off. "Never mind. Go ahead."

He rose and went to the window, tugging the chain with a smooth hand-over-hand motion. Sunlight flooded in, and in an instant Donna could feel the temperature rising. The kid stood there, in silhouette, taking in the view. "That's a shame."

"You stop seeing the wires," Donna said, knowing he was speaking of the power lines garroting the mountain view. "After a while you do. But they're always there. In the background. Humming. It isn't so noticeable when people are around, but this time of year, the whole street is empty. It gets pretty damn quiet around here."

"Quiet enough to hear the hum of the power lines?"

"Quiet enough to hear a mouse fart. You can hear them now if you listen hard enough. The wires. Not the mice."

"Why don't they bury the lines?" He began lowering the shade. "Save the view?"

"Maybe it'd cost too much. Or maybe someone's afraid what might get turned up once they got to digging." She leaned in toward the mic. "That's a joke. I repeat, a joke."

The kid returned to his seat.

"It's Deepwell," Donna said. "They've always been here."

"Always have been doesn't mean always have to be."

"Aren't you the philosopher?" She pasted on a parody of a smile and batted her eyelashes at him. "Listen," she said, letting her voice drop an octave, "if they aren't gonna hide the wires for Elizabeth Taylor, they sure as shit aren't gonna hide them for me."

"You have a point." He glanced down at his computer. "Let me make a quick adjustment to the balance." He fussed a bit, his focus on the monitor. "I'm curious," he said. "The intake guard. What did you say?"

"I said she was bawling—"

"I'm sorry. I meant, what did you say to her? When she began crying in front of you?"

"What could I say? *Sorry for your loss?* I said, *That's terrible.* Or something along those lines."

"Were you worried that she might mistreat you later to make up for this display of weakness?"

"Damned straight I was worried," she said, the memory of her vulnerability turning prickly. "I was terrified. I was in prison."

"For the murder of Joseph Fiato." He looked up from the screen, his eyes locking in on hers. "A crime you didn't commit even though you confessed to doing so at the time."

She snorted. This kid thought he was so flipping smart. Pretending to mess with his computer. Jumping her around in her story. Poking around for a sore spot and trying to catch her off guard. "Don't be stupid. Why would I say I killed Joey if I didn't?"

"Why don't you tell me."

She sloshed the wine in her cup, then rested the cup on the table. "What makes you think I wasn't the one who killed Joey?"

"There were rumors—"

"There've been rumors since Eden. You want the truth? The unembellished and verifiable truth? Here it is—the son of a bitch needed killing. I did it."

"Why?"

"Rumor has it . . ." she drawled out the words, "he was cheating on me, and stealing from me too, though he called it 'investing.' Claimed he'd lost it. That same night I saw him out with this bimbo. My investment was hanging around her neck." She shrugged. "I snapped. Crackled. Maybe even popped a little too. I shot Joey in the gut. Twice." She lifted her hand and feigned a tremor. "My hand was shaking. I was aiming for his balls." She stilled the trembling and reclaimed her wine. She lifted the cup to her lips and wet her mouth. "No regrets. No regrets at all. No, wait, that isn't true. I do have one. The DA offered me a plea deal if I waived a jury trial. I would've enjoyed a chance to go on the stand before my peers. I could have given Susan Hayward a run for the money. All I got was an old gray judge flapping around in his black robe."

"Wasn't she executed at the end of the film?"

"Ah, so Susan Hayward you know."

"I've seen the movie."

Donna nodded. "Based on a true story, it was. Could've been me." She rapped her knuckles on the table, a practiced move she often used at this point in her account. "The DA told my lawyer he'd pursue the gas chamber if I didn't accept his largesse. I knew he meant business, so I plead down."

"You were convicted of willful manslaughter."

"Yes. That was the plea."

"And you were sentenced to three years." His words hung between them for a moment. "A light sentence—"

"Not if you're the one serving it."

"Your actual incarceration lasted only four months. I understand this was before mandatory sentencing, but—"

"They take time off for good behavior." She swirled her cup, watching the diminished ice cubes spin. "Mine was . . . exemplary."

"This degree of leniency implies you had influential friends pulling strings for you."

Donna shrugged her response.

He slapped his palm on the tabletop and leaned in, turning all bad cop. It was almost cute. "Someone was protecting you. Who was it?"

The kid was trying to trigger a response. All he got was her indulgent stare. "Nobody was protecting me. Joey was a bastard. Maybe someone was grateful to me for taking him out."

"Was that somebody Johnny Giancanna?"

"Never heard of him."

"I'm sure you have." The kid riffled in his beat-up messenger bag and pulled out a manila folder. "You used to date each other. I've come across photos of the two of you together. Here, in Palm Springs." He took a pair of photocopied pictures from the folder and slid them to her. The images were a bit grainy, but it was certainly her own foolish young face staring back at her. To the mic, "Donna is now looking at the photos."

"Yes, indeed, Donna is." She raised her eyebrows. Shook her head. "I don't know. There were so many men back then.

Did I date some guy name Giancanna? Maybe. Probably even. But I don't remember him if I did." She placed her hand over the photos. "You should let me keep these for the scrapbook."

"He's dead. Giancanna." The kid opened up the folder once more and took out a clipping from a newspaper. He passed it to her. Again, to the mic, "I've given Donna a copy of Johnny Giancanna's obituary."

The article was from some local Long Island rag, dated two months earlier. She scanned the piece and handed it back to him. "My condolences to Mrs. Giancanna."

The corner of the kid's mouth twitched. He returned the clipping to its folder and the folder to the messenger bag. He looked up. "I think you were alternately pressured and bribed to admit to a murder you didn't commit."

"Manslaughter. Court said it was manslaughter."

"You were covering for a mob-related killing. At Giancanna's behest."

"Now you're being ridiculous." She slapped her palm on the table and leaned in, mimicking his tough-guy charade. "There was never any kind of mob activity here."

"It's been well-documented that many mafiosos spent time in Palm Springs in the 1960s. You yourself moments ago said—"

"Yeah, sure, but they were here vacationing. That's why there were never any dirty deeds. You got to understand. Palm Springs was the goddamned Switzerland of organized crime. The guys came, brought their nearest and dearest with them, the wives, the kids, the mistresses, sometimes all of 'em hanging out together at the El Mirador's pool. That's why I stayed on here. After my parole ended. I figured I'd be safer here."

"You feared reprisal?"

Donna nodded.

"I'm sorry, could you answer aloud."

"Yes. I was afraid of *reprisal*."

"From Fiato's associates? Or from someone else?"

She studied the liver spot on her hand. "I still spend a lot of time at the El Mirador. I go there for trysts with a handsome younger man. I am sad to say that man's my doctor, and he's only interested in checking my blood pressure, not raising it." A transient wrinkle formed between her visitor's brows. She guessed she'd lost him. "The old hotel is a medical center now."

"All right." He gave a slight nod that, combined with the softening of his gaze, seemed more to signal a decision to change tack than an expression of satisfaction.

"All right," she echoed him.

"Fiato," he said, dragging the name out, "was made in Detroit."

"You make him sound like a sports car."

"He was rumored to get around like one. My source says he liked going fast and taking chances."

"There you go again with your gossip."

"Annalisa Scarpa."

"Another stranger," Donna said, modulating her tone between amusement and contempt. "Is she your 'source'?"

"Miss Scarpa was the niece of the head of one of the New York families."

"So?"

"I've found reason to doubt your account of the evening, and to believe that you weren't the one following Joseph Fiato the night of his murder. It was Annalisa Scarpa. She watched Fiato slip away from another woman's hotel room. She followed him to the house he rented. Miss Scarpa shot him twice in the stomach, then turned to her uncle to clean up the mess."

"Strange that I didn't see her there." The fly found its way to the rim of Donna's glass. She swiped at it and almost upset the wine. She'd about had enough of both of her pesky visitors. "Check the police records if you can find the stone tablets they're engraved on. I was there. I called the police. That's why the DA went easy on me. 'Cause I turned myself in."

Tiny lines formed at the corners of his eyes. He was enjoying this. "She left him," he continued, ignoring her, "with a tricky situation. He needed to cover up the crime, but he couldn't make it look like a hit by another family. As you have said, Palm Springs was neutral territory. An allegation against the member of another family could have triggered a war between the families. Worse, it could've broken the peace and ruined Palm Springs for everyone."

He leaned back and crossed his arms. Donna knew a thing or two about bluffing. He was trying to project ease and confidence.

"Someone got the idea to present the act as what it was. A crime of passion, only with a certain struggling actress in the lead role. I'll bet you never laid eyes on Joseph Fiato before the night you called the police from his home." The kid's desire to push her into a confession was rubbing his NPR plating clean away, leaving him like every other too-hungry, know-it-all punk. "But you were quite familiar with Annalisa's cousin."

"I don't know what you're going on about. Where did you come up with this stuff anyway?"

The kid shook his head and sat up straight. He bit his lip. He folded his hands. "Doesn't it bother you? Johnny Giancanna stole your life," he said, almost as if he was determined to be outraged on her behalf, even if she couldn't be herself. "You wanted to be famous. To be a star." He reached for the scrapbook and flipped it open to her headshot. "But nobody remembers you. Those roles you talk about—I bet half your scenes ended up on the cutting room floor, and the other half have crumbled to dust." Donna fought the urge to throw her wine in his smug, lineless face. "I did try to research you. You don't even rate a mention in the IMDb, and my old roommate who shoots green screen shorts in his garage is listed."

"You sure do know how to charm a girl." Donna closed the scrapbook's cover. She felt ridiculous now. Regretted she'd even thought to show it to him.

"I'm one of maybe a handful of people outside Palm Springs who even know your name, much less care about your story."

"Why were you so hot to talk to me if no one cares?"

He nodded at the mic. "You tell me what really happened that night, and I'll make people care. Really care. Not just a group of gay guys dragging out an elderly woman—a washed-up never-was—to tea dances. Presenting her as an amusing oddity. Laughing at you behind your back."

His words stung. "They don't. That's not true."

"Perhaps not, but you fear it is."

Donna's aging refrigerator hummed in agreement. She glanced back at it, wondering which of them would outlast the other.

"Annalisa Scarpa died twenty years ago. Cancer. Johnny Giancanna is gone. Why not clear your name? Get your story out there. Who knows? It might even get picked up for TV or a movie. You know that happens, don't you? People will know who you are then."

Donna snorted. "TV or a movie. Right. I was Joseph Fiato's girlfriend. One of them anyway. I killed him. You've come up with quite the scenario, but none of it's true."

"All right," the kid said, rising. "If you insist on sticking to this fabrication, I can't help you. People would have listened to your story. They would have cared about it. They would have cared about *you*. You might have even become famous." He stood and made to close his laptop. "Thank you for your time."

The truth. It was supposed to set you free, right? She'd always envisioned lying on her deathbed, spilling her guts to a priest. Her eyes fell to the closed scrapbook. Not a god-damned thing in there worth anything to anybody. Maybe this way she could spare the padre's ears and even gain something other than absolution for her trouble.

"Wait." Donna reached out to him. He tilted his head and looked down at her, but remained silent. "Maybe you're right. Who's left to care anyway?"

"I'm listening." He slid back into his chair. "In your own words. What happened?"

"Johnny promised me he'd take care of me. In and out of prison." She snatched up her wine and took a deep sip. "See to it I was set up for life."

"If you stepped in," the kid prompted her when her silence went on too long for his liking, "and took the blame for the murder his cousin committed." A moment passed. He raised an eyebrow and reached out to turn off the mic.

Donna caught his hand. "Yes."

"He guaranteed you would receive a light sentence?"

"Yes."

"How do you believe he arranged this?"

Sinatra stared bug-eyed at her from the Rat Pack photo. *Never rat on a rat.*

"That I will leave to your own conjecture. You know as much about it as I do."

"But you trusted that Giancanna would deliver on his promises?"

The fly buzzed by her ear. Donna swung at it. "Yes. I trusted him. Somewhat. I also trusted things wouldn't work out so well for me if I refused, if you get what I'm saying."

"He threatened you."

She shook her head. "Johnny never threatened. He made examples of the people who disappointed him. Made it clear to all that there were severe and lasting consequences for letting him down." The heat was getting to her. She cast a glance at the thermostat. "He asked me to take the truth of what happened to my grave. I promised I would, but it's been more than a minute."

"Did Giancanna keep his promises?"

Johnny had kept his word, though not in the way Donna had thought he meant. She never laid eyes on him again, not after the night he pressed the pistol into her hand. "Yes. I came out of prison with a hundred and fifty thousand tax free in the bank. May not sound like much now, but it'd be like someone handing you a cool million today. I bought this house with it. Invested the rest. I did okay."

The kid reached over and gripped her hand. "To be clear, you are saying Annalisa Scarpa murdered Joseph Fiato, and Johnny Giancanna offered you an easy sentence and what amounted to a fortune if you'd confess to the murder."

Donna snatched her hand from his grasp. "Yes. Yes. Yes." She glared at him. Angry with him. Ludicrous. Why should she be angry? "Yes," she said again, concentrating on speaking in a calm voice, "for taking the rap for his precious cousin." Donna broke out in a cold, oily sweat that had nothing to do with the temperature. She felt a sharp shock of nausea, like the time when a fall dislocated her shoulder and the ER doctor snapped it back into place.

The air around her grew thick, suffocating. She'd been lying so damn long. Until that moment she'd never realized the lie was like the boy in the old story, with his finger plugging a dike to hold back the ocean. The utterance of one truth ushered in a plague of others.

She was no goddamn actress. Never had been.

She would have never made it. Everyone had known it. Johnny had known it.

Deep down, she knew it too. That was the real reason she'd made the deal. And that was the reason she'd kept the secret. Not from fear—not this long, at least—or because of a promise made, but because without the lie, who was she? The lie made her somebody. Without it, she wasn't dangerous, she wasn't even interesting. She was just another goddamn never-was.

"How does it feel?" he said. "After all this time, finally speaking the truth?"

"How does it feel?" A jolt of remorse rocked her. She'd always expected to feel relief, but what she felt was nothing like truth's promised freedom. What she felt felt a lot like loss. Like grief.

The kid watched her, seemingly unaware, or maybe just unconcerned. He got what he came for. She recognized the look in his eyes, it was the same she'd seen in Johnny's when he realized she'd given in, that she'd agree to all he wanted. But Johnny, prick that he was, had given her something in exchange. More than a guarantee of a comfortable life, he'd offered her an identity. A mystique. All she'd ever had, all she'd ever been, was the story Johnny gave her, and in mere minutes, the kid had taken it away.

He took and only offered the flimsiest of maybes in return.

"It feels like I lost a part of myself."

"I'm sorry?"

"Nothing." She couldn't bring herself to look him in the eye. She focused on the sparse gold stubble on his chin. Probably not even man enough to grow a full beard. "You at least owe me one thing. Who is this 'source' of yours?"

A beat of silence. "I apologize for misleading you," he said. "I was going off my intuition more than anything else. News clippings. Old photos. Of you and Giancanna. Of Scarpa and Fiato. But none of you and Fiato. Something didn't add up. When I started to dig . . . well, there really were rumors—"

"I don't think I want you to use this." She pushed up from the table, ready to up the air-conditioning. The room reeled around her. She grasped the edge of the table and closed her eyes, waiting for the sensation to pass.

"Are you all right?"

"I'm fine." She held up her hand. "I'm fine." She opened her eyes, and realized it was true. She once again stood on solid ground. "I want you to stop recording."

The kid watched her but didn't move.

"I said stop recording!" she shouted at him.

He jolted, then tapped the computer screen. He stared up at her, his lips parted, the tiny line returning to his forehead. "Are you sure I shouldn't call someone?"

"I'm fine. I just don't want you to use me in your . . ." She waved at the mic.

"All right," he said. "It's clear you've had a change of heart, and I don't want to upset you any further." He turned off the mic and unplugged it from his laptop. "I need to get back to the city soon anyway." He closed his computer. "Maybe I can call you in a couple days? See how you're feeling then? Maybe you'll change your mind after you've had time to relax. To reconsider."

Donna nodded.

"Okay." The kid gave her a smile that landed midway between reassurance and condescension. He slid his laptop into his bag. "I want to say, though, that even if you decide not to let us use your story, I hope you'll be happy knowing there's at least one person who doesn't see you as a killer. I know the truth. You're just a nice—"

"Old lady."

The kid's face flushed. "I was going to say—"

"It's fine. We're dealing in truths here, aren't we?"

"Yes, we are." The kid rose and shrugged the strap of his bag over his shoulder. "I'll be in touch."

"Hold on," Donna said, and the kid stopped, a look of hopeful expectation spreading across his face. "I know you don't understand, but there's one more thing I should show you. Maybe then you will."

The kid hesitated but sat back down.

Donna crossed the kitchen and made her way to the cabinets, tugging open the drawer where she'd left Sally. She lifted the pistol from the drawer and turned it on the kid. For a moment he looked intrigued, but then his eyes popped open wide. All color drained from his face.

"What—" he began, jumping up and knocking his chair over.

Donna shot twice, catching him first in the stomach, then the shoulder. He fell back on the floor with a thud, then started kicking his heels against the linoleum, trying to push back, away from her.

Donna went to him. Looked him straight in the eye. "Truth is shit. The story's all that matters. The story Johnny gave me was all I ever had. He didn't steal my life. You, you little son of a bitch, you're the one trying to do that." She aimed at his head and pulled the trigger, then laid the gun on the table.

The fly landed on the kid's parted lips.

Donna stood there for what seemed a very long time listening to the whir of the overhead fan, watching the fly crawl over the kid's face. Then she began to move, her own body on automatic, her slippers making squishy, sticky sounds as she traipsed through the kid's blood to reach the phone. She punched in three numbers.

"I need to report a murder. Yes, I'm safe. I'm the killer."

THE ANKLE OF ANZA

BY EDUARDO SANTIAGO

Anza

I t took awhile for the concerned neighbors to settle down. After the scraping of metal chairs on the worn linoleum, and the greetings of neighbors who rarely saw each other, an expectant silence swept the room. This was Anza, a small community as far as population, but huge in terms of land. Most of it was worthless mountaintop—high desert they called it. Sand and scrub, and too much damn gravity.

But those of us who live here wouldn't trade it for anything. It's peaceful and quiet, save the occasional meth lab explosion. And God-fearing country for sure. I turned to face them, each of their dirt-worn faces. There's a look to us here, beady eyes from squinting against sand and wind, white, weathered skin, thinning hair, even the women, whose long gray strands clogged sinks all over Anza Valley.

The last time they gathered, Jimbo Lure's cousin had come to propose solar farms. There was an expectation of wealth, as if everyone had an oil well in the backyard just ripe for the picking. But the more the proposal got into crystalline vs. thin film vs. photovoltaic, and words like *extrapolation*, the audience began to glaze over. Even if they all pooled their money and their land together, as Gordon Lure suggested, he was talking a million-dollar investment before profits. No one here was worth a thousand, let alone a million. No one here was willing to risk the rewards. Coming up on five years ago, that was. There are solar farms here now, but none of the people present were making the money. No one knew those who were profiting, silent partners and all that. But these people whose eyes were on me now, I knew them chapter and verse.

"I want to give you people a heads-up," I said to them. I'm not used to public speaking, in fact I don't speak much at all, but these were all people I know. "We have a cat burglar up in here. There's no denying it any longer."

There were many *what*s and *what he says* and *speak ups*. This is what's called an aging community, too many of us on the sliding slope to eighty. We became hard of hearing from wearing old ears and having no one to listen to anymore save for the TV, which can be turned up or down depending on mood or need.

I repeated myself with a bit more vocal power.

"What's with the cat shit, Dave? Ain't she just a plain ole fucking burglar?" asked Don Donner, who had never uttered a sentence without a *fuck* or a *shit* in it.

"She has the nasty habit of sneaking into your home when no one's there, locking up when she leaves," I said. "Opens up your vehicles, takes a few things, locks it all up when she leaves. She's meticulous, leaves the place like you left it. You just think you've misplaced things, but she took 'em. Will slip into an unlocked door, take your things while you're asleep. She has taken important things from several people that I know, including but not limited to car titles, the key to your PO Box, birth certificates and death certificates, property documents, phones, tablets, laptops, knives, flashlights, food, stuff like deodorants, prescription glasses, wallets, whatever she can carry. Never breaks nothing, not a window, not a lock She's stealth."

"That don't make her no cat," Donner said, then cleared

his throat. I could practically smell his phlegm swirling down the sagging esophagus.

"Don't believe me if you don't want to, but she's a wily one. She will use your electronics, try to access Google accounts, try to get a reverse mortgage just to mess with you."

Whenever I'm in the same room with Don Donner I find myself trapped in an argument. I try so hard to avoid him, at least to avoid talking with him, but it's like he sets a trap and I traipse right into it.

Thankfully, a hand went up that wasn't Donner's. It was Jasper Grosch, ninety if he's a day. Came down with Parkinson's twenty-plus years ago, he's shaky as hell but he's still here. I nodded at him to speak.

"This young lady from these parts?"

"Has no permanent address. Made some friends out behind Circle K, betrayed them, robbed them, upset them. They threw her out. She will break into your garage, sheds, storage buildings. Takes small things, doesn't drive so it has to be stuff she can carry concealed. I'm sure she's hoarding a lot of the things. I would love to locate her lair, see about recovering some of the loot."

Don Donner opened his mouth to speak, but I spoke first and I spoke forcefully.

"She's a goddamn cat burglar, Don."

Don Donner's eye roll was so severe that it would have been kinder if he'd told me to fuck off. "Fucking birth certificates," he spat out.

"Is there camera footage?" came a small voice in the back. Marci Day, born again and dumb as a box of lint. "Maybe post office, bank."

"She's not the type to visit either one of those establishments, Marci," I answered.

"Probably lives in a box somewhere," Marci said, her head cast down as if to elicit the pity of the Lord.

"A litter box!" shouted Jimbo Lure.

"Seriously, Jimbo?"

Jimbo's our one and only barber. Every man goes every couple of months and endures jokes Jimbo makes up all on his own, or so he claims. Example: *Hear about the girl who wanted to have sex all the time? She had get-down syndrome.* I knew Jimbo from school, class clown, disruptive, lonely. Never changed.

"This is a wild animal we're talking about here," I said. "We need to be on the lookout as if there was a brown bear out there, or a wolf."

"With all due respect to wild animals." Jimbo again.

"Has a police report been filed?" asked Marci.

"I filed one," I said. "But you know how it goes."

Everyone murmured agreement. As an unincorporated area of Riverside County, there are no police here, never have been. From time to time a sheriff's cruiser will travel through. If there's a serious crime, something to do with bodily attack, a shooting, what have you, they'll come up and investigate. But calling the cops here is an exercise in faith and patience because it will take them at least forty-five minutes to an hour to get here, depending on where they are. We don't have cops and we don't want cops. We've learned to take care of our own up here, which is why we all have big dogs and why all these people showed up today.

"Whoever it is gonna go into the wrong house with dogs, protective ones, and get her bony ass tore up but fucking good," said Donner, who had traded bounty hunting for herding mountain goats fifteen years ago.

"She's too smart," I countered. "She'll just avoid houses with dogs."

"What if it's one of them quiet dogs?" Donner said.

"There's no such thing as a quiet dog, Don. All dogs bark, particularly at strangers."

"Not all of 'em. My dog's not a barker. Whenever he tries it I blast him with my cane."

"I don't know a single person, other than you, who will hit a dog for barking," I said, feeling like an idiot for letting Don Donner trap me into one of his arguments again. What type of man admits to hitting his dog for barking in public, just to win an argument? He knew I had him, so he launched in another direction.

"You know, if any of you dumb cocksuckers gave a shit you would post a description of this low-life piece of shit," Donner said, his eye on me. "If she is doing what people claim she is, then she will get what's coming to her. I guarantee this person isn't stealing my keys."

"And here I thought it was my neighbors, the ones with the cabin tent and the too many kids," said Denver Abernathy, an unlit cigarette in his hand. "We have two sets of keys missing . . . time for new locks, I guess."

Having said what he had to say, Abernathy sauntered outside for a smoke.

"How you all so sure she's a she?" asked Marci Day.

"I seen her," I said. "Loiters at Circle K, hair same color as a banana."

"If you seen her why didn't you catch her?" said Donner.

I took a deep breath. "Because, Don, you gotta catch her in the act. I can't just lasso her and force her to confess. That will get *me* arrested."

"Jesus can help her if only she'd ask," said Marci.

"Come off it, Marci," Donner said. "What the fuck has Jesus ever done for you?"

"Plenty," countered Marci with a puff of her chest that would have made a pro wrestler weep.

Talk of Jesus always brought these meetings to a halt and Marci Day knew it. Donner would have none of it.

"The broad's an ankle," he said, "which is 'bout two feet lower than a cunt."

Donner narrowed his eyes at Marci now, waiting for something sanctimonious, but got none. Unlike me, she knew better than to argue with Don Donner.

"May I suggest we do the right thing," Marci said, her eyes fixed on Donner, "and leave the poor creature be. The level of desperation driving her to a life of crime, I hope we never know."

"I say we find her and stomp her out," Donner said. "But everyone just wants to chew the cud, hear theyselves talk like words matter."

"They do matter," I said. "It's why we're all together. We need some good ideas, we need ideas that are legal and aren't going to land any of us in jail."

"Lock your doors!" shouted Jimbo Lure, then let out a big dumb laugh. No one joined in.

I looked at Jimbo. Poor man can't help that he's an idiot. "Thank you, Jimbo," I said. "In a perfect world that would be a great suggestion. But all it takes is that one day you're in a hurry. That one day you get careless."

Jimbo looked at me with a strange expression, not used to anyone actually talking reason to him when he flies off with one of his idiocies.

Teddy Elderberry, resplendent in tie-dye shirt, tie-dye pants, and tie-dye do-rag, made his way to where Firth was standing. Elderberry had done time before cannabis was legal. Now, he wants those years back, but he's not going to get them. Elderberry whispered in Firth's ear and Firth nodded his head up and down in agreement.

"Our friend Teddy Elderberry picked up a lot of useful info in the clink," Firth said. "I suggest you all pay close attention."

"Thank you for that introduction, bud," Elderberry said with a wide grin. He was proud of the time he had served and survived. "What you guys need to do is send in a decoy, friend her, hang with her, find out where and with who she is affiliated. Then you set her up with some keys and an addy. Have authorities waiting to take her down. Don't just sit around waiting to see who gets hit next. Operation Ninja Takedown's what you need. Fight fire with fire, you dig?"

"That's the fucking stupidest idea I've ever fucking heard," said Donner, picking up his cane and ambling out the back door, his cane making a *tap tap tap* sound because he thought rubber tips were for dicks. "You wanna catch her," he called from the door, "you fucking go get her. Where you say she go, that Circle K?" He pointed across the highway, the convenience store being set right across from the meeting hall.

"Yeah, right over there, Donner," I said. "Go get her, man. Take her down."

Donner lifted his cane and swung it through the air like a golf club meant to clobber. I had meant to be funny, but no one laughed, not even Jimbo Lure.

The cat burglar was not at Circle K that afternoon. Just as the meeting was wrapping, Kimberly Miller (her actual name) was riding shotgun in a truck, sailing down the mountain on her way to Indio, the lowest of the low desert, with every intention of getting to the night market before the sun came up. The truck wasn't new, and she'd had to cram her shit in the space not occupied by bags of chlorine and leaf skimmers, but it took the mountain roads with ease.

Behind the wheel was Justin Alvarez, the only friend she had left from down below. Even as she got in the truck she knew he wouldn't be her friend for long. She just needed him to stay her friend long enough to get to Indio. They'd met in Palm Springs five years ago, when she still had a house and a husband, a kid and a teenage pool boy.

Justin was no one's idea of what a Palm Springs pool boy might look like. At least he wasn't *her* idea of what a Palm Springs pool boy might be. Bernard had passed on the tanned and muscled blonds who applied and hired the one that mostly resembled an adolescent garden gnome. He was a fully bearded man now and taking the mountain roads with ease. They were well out of Anza in no time and traveling through the pine tree forest that links Anza to the desert floor. She wondered how much fighting and screaming Justin had witnessed in that house with the manicured cactus garden, the crystalline pool.

"You're going back to Betty's!" Bernard had shouted the last time she'd been in that house.

"I'm not going to Betty nothing," she'd slurred. She didn't want to go to rehab. Rehab is where the party ends. She was too young for that. Sure, she'd regretted that Baby Carol had seen her like that, and on Mother's Day, no less.

"You're disgusting." Bernard brought it down to a defeated whisper.

"What she's going to remember is . . ." She stopped to see if she could find the point to what she was saying. ". . . is you shouting."

They had both looked at the baby who sat calmly playing with Legos. Go figure, a sixty-year-old man, just lost his wife of thirty years, no children, meets a desperate desert rat at the

7-Eleven on Vista Chino. He gets her pregnant, which shocks her because, well, he's decrepit. So now there's Baby Carol.

He wanted to name her after his dead wife and Kimberly just shrugged. If she couldn't name her miscarriage, or abortion, what did she care what people called her? He dressed her up for Mother's Day, all in pink, even the little shoes. No matter. Baby Carol was only three. She'd never remember any of this. There were plenty of Mother's Days to come. Next year would be better. Stick to wine, ditch the blow.

That had been May. By August she had been to Betty Ford's twice. Insurance covered most of the cost, but she hated it there. While sneaking a smoke out by Lake Hope, the immaculate man-made lake that is the centerpiece of the "campus," she had looked up to the mountains bordering the valley and imagined it was more peaceful up there. Rehabs like to believe they are peaceful places, but that's just because they paint everything beige. It's actually exhausting—in the morning they get you up before you're ready to get up, make you eat with other people, and participate in what they call their "wellness activities." The mountain, as high as she could go, was the answer. Fewer people and it would be a lot cooler out. She scaled the fence and in less than four minutes was in the back of an Uber (Toyota Camry, navy blue).

"Get me as far from this place as quickly as you can."

The Uber driver asked if she was sure she wanted to go all the way up the mountain.

"Yes, wherever it's cooler. I can't breathe down here."

He'd turned to look at her and at a glance had tagged her as trash.

"How about Anza?"

He drove her up the mountain in the dark, the car winding and twisting through the hairpin curves, her stomach not reacting to it well. She could only see as far as the headlights let her. About an hour later, he stopped at a Circle K.

"Here it is, beautiful downtown Anza."

Before he left, she blew him in the backseat. When he'd come, she asked him for a twenty and he told her to fuck off and left her in the dust. She was going to write him a lousy review but caught a glimpse of herself in the convenience store window and changed her mind. *I have to start eating*, she thought, *I'm all skin and bones. And my hair! But a Circle K's better than a circle jerk.*

Welcome to your new life.

Except for the fluorescent lights of the Circle K, Anza had been dead dark that first night. Some bum told her there were abandoned buildings all over Anza. At first light she started looking for a place to crash. She settled into an old toolshed at the ass end of Dusty Road—that's what it was called and that's also what it was. That's what Anza was like: no frills.

No thrills either.

Until she started robbing them. What else could she do? As soon as the Uber charge showed up on the statement, Bernard canceled her credit cards. She called him. He wanted to know where she was. She refused to tell him, so he canceled her phone.

"The only way to get your privileges back is to return to Betty's and do what's best for this family," Bernard said before he hung up.

She hated that he called it a family, not a favorite word of hers. And she hated most of all that he called the place Betty's, as if the former first lady would be waiting behind the counter, like at a diner.

Hi, hon, what'll you have?

An ounce of crank and a cup of Joe, Betty.

Now, Justin Alvarez was halfway down the mountain, halfway to the desert towns she knew better than she knew herself: Palm Springs, Cathedral City, Rancho Mirage, Palm Desert, Indian Wells, La Quinta, and finally Indio. She had money but no credit card. No credit card, no Uber. The sunset turned the mountains orange. She wished it was dark so she could pretend she didn't know where she was or where she was going or who that guy was beside her. Justin was holding onto the steering wheel hard.

"You okay?" she asked him.

He took forever to respond. "Yeah, twilight driving makes me sad."

"It will be dark soon," she said.

In the last light she'd seen the change in the terrain, from pine trees to mesquite to striped rocks to stretches of sand littered with what her mother called malicious plants—creosote, ocotillo, barrel cactus. Justin had to drive the last stretch of switchback curves in the dark, and as they twisted their descent, she could feel the heat rising up to greet her. *You thought you could get away?*

By the time Justin dropped her off outside Indio's night market, she had four hundred and sixty dollars in her pocket. She'd asked for five hundred, but Justin needed some of it for gas.

He had convinced her to let him keep the loot and sell it on his own a lot farther away. "For your own good, Kim. Sell this shit near here, they'll pop you before you start."

He got off cheap. Hell, he could get five hundred just for the birth certificate down in Mexicali. He worked a blow job and tittie grope into the deal and she went along. The pool boy had been waiting all this time. Kimberly no longer looked as she had when he was cleaning her pool, but she was still Kimberly to him.

"You're all the same," she said before lowering herself on his rod. Soon as the transaction was over, she said she needed a beer.

"I don't think so." He didn't sound like Justin anymore, he sounded like a total asshole.

"Get the hell out of here," Kimberly growled, then hopped down from the truck and slammed the door.

It was August and Indio's swap meet could only function at night when the temperature dropped from 117 degrees to a tolerable ninety-five. The night market was all too well lit, too nicely organized. The blacktop parking lot too clean. Was this Indio? You'd think it was Rancho Mirage or some other pretentious desert community. It irritated her to walk past dozens of vendors waiting for someone, anyone, to buy a trinket, some silver jewelry, purses, shoes, mattresses, blenders from 1995, Aztec suns made of pounded tin, and about a mile of Mexican food and drinks. Kimberly wanted beer but they had none, so she bought horchata in a cup with ice and it was the most delicious thing she'd ever had. She could have drunk down the whole dispenser.

As if drawn by invisible strings, she made her way to the back, beyond the light cast by the stalls, to where the blacktop ended and the sand and the weeds began. She smelled them before she saw them. They smelled just like the men who loitered around the Circle K in Anza. What was that smell? If she could bottle it, she could sell it as a pesticide. They were standing in a circle, talking in low voices. They were all colors; no one was exempt from the strings, the hooks. Take her for example, a white and, until recently, middle-class woman, until recently a pretty girl, naturally blonder than blond. Banana blond, some people called it.

"You're wasting your life away serving tacos to tourists,"

her mother had said. "You're certainly pretty enough to be a stripper."

She'd said so more than once, but stripping wasn't for Kimberly. Too complicated. Too many routines. Too much competition from women who wanted to show off, who swung from those aluminum poles like glittering tether balls. These men, at the edge of the night market, were all shirtless and no one was tipping them for it. They looked up when she approached: the prey.

It's amazing how quickly a pack of men can size up a woman walking alone, in the heat, in the desert, in the night. But just as quickly they looked away. Had she become that hideous? Just a bit ago Justin hadn't thought so. But Justin lived on memories; the moment he'd started with *remember this* and *remember that*, she knew where they were headed, and it wasn't Indio.

"Remember that time when I came over and you were pregnant and wearing an orange bikini?"

Hell yeah, she remembered. That week there'd been no way to get comfortable other than floating in the pool all but naked. And Justin had come stomping in with his leaf skimmer and his jugs of chlorine and just about scared the baby out of her. And her wishing he had. But it would be two more long, hot weeks before Baby Carol popped out. Baby Carol just a few miles from here. To hell with Baby Carol.

"Go away, *esqueleto*," one of the brown men said.

She looked up at the mountain behind them. Atop that mountain were Anza's high desert, homes without alarms, and men who weren't so rude. Those men took your money, made the transaction quick, and the stuff was all good, always.

"I got money," she threw back at him.

* * *

"Shit's still missing," Don Donner said.

I had to look to make sure he was talking to me. Unfortunately, he was. "It's history, Don, let it go," I said, and I meant it.

"She was holed up in Dusty Road."

"Yeah, I heard that." I'd heard it but I didn't believe it. So they found some things that might have belonged to a homeless person. What does that prove?

"You let her slip through your fingers. You ever think about that?"

"What would you have done with her, Don, if you'd caught her?"

We were at the post office. Anza doesn't have mail delivery. We all go to the post office to get our mail and parcels and to run into the neighbors we mostly don't want to see. The post office is next to the town hall, which is across from Circle K. Farther down the road is our Dairy Queen and farther down the road is the rest of California.

"I'd bring her to justice," he said, and he said it so casually that for a moment I took him for a reasonable man.

"She's hardly worth the trouble, considering all she took."

"That ain't the point, Dave. Nobody appreciates a person walking through their house, going through their things."

I shrugged and sifted through my envelopes—Senior Fitness, Senior Dating, Reverse Mortgage Lender, Assisted Living, Retirement Community, Burial Insurance, and without fail, the American Association of Retired People. *I'm not even sixty yet!* I wanted to scream every time. But I knew the envelopes couldn't hear me. They had started arriving just as I turned fifty. As if turning fifty wasn't depressing enough.

I looked up—Donner was still there, his little blue eyes glowing, his eyebrows sprouting white tentacles that reached out to ensnare me. "Then there is no point," I said. "If someone is taking stuff you don't really want or stuff you can easily replace, then where's the crime?"

"There were valuable documents."

I nodded in agreement. Sure, there had been a couple of birth certificates. That was about the most valuable thing.

Donner spoke like he was reading my mind: "Them birth certificates are more than just paper."

"You ever hear of the Internet? Those things can be replaced, all you got to do is contact the hospital where you were born."

"What about the fucking Mexicans?"

"What about them?"

"They can make themselves legal with them. You want some Mexican walking around with your name on 'em?"

He wanted to argue but I didn't, so I made for the door. He tap-tapped behind me. "They can make themselves legal with them," he said louder, as if I hadn't heard him.

I was at my car and he was right there behind me. He was looking at me like he expected an answer, so I gave it to him. "All right, Don, I hear you. So two Mexicans are now legal because they got ahold of some birth certificates. Two."

"Yeah, two today," he just about shouted, tapping his cane hard on the gravel, "but the way those people fuck, there'll be twenty by Sunday."

I drove off but I was sure he was still talking to me. People come up to Anza for all sorts of reasons. Mostly good ones. When I called that meeting a couple of weeks ago, I felt I was doing my civic duty. All I wanted to do was alert the neighbors that there was something going on that might affect them. I did not count on reactivating Don Donner. I did not anticipate that lynch mobs would be formed, like it was up here in the 1860s when this was all Cahuilla land. All because a woman got desperate enough to go klepto. I'd heard talk at the barbershop that Donner and some old guys had decided to waste their time dragging the mountain for her, had found some stuff in a shed on Dusty Road. Stuff that could have belonged to her.

"Empty beer cans," said Jimbo, while snipping away at what was left of my hair.

"Could be anybody's," I shrugged.

"Oh yeah, get this—rag, used."

"You mean like for the period?"

Jimbo nodded, a big grin across his stupid face. "Could be anybody's," he repeated. "Donner's sure it was hers."

"Oh yeah, did it taste like her?" I said, appealing to Jimbo's subtle sense of humor. It worked. He about took an ear off, he was laughing so hard.

I couldn't help thinking about her, at least whenever I drove past the Circle K, which was all the time. She hadn't slipped through my fingers. I saw her, that's all. Plenty of people had. She was always there, sipping a beer or a cherry Froster, smoking, minding her own, watching the traffic go by. I wondered if she had plans, dreams, a past. I guess everybody has a past. It was her present that sucked. Not much of a life. Who can blame a woman like that for sneaking into houses? Seeing how we lived gave her something to do. I blame myself for what happened because I'm the one that made a big deal out of it. I'm the one who tagged her as a cat burglar. I'm the one who brought Don Donner into it.

Kimberly Miller was lying on human skin, warm, moist, a chest moving up and down beneath her own. How long had she been here? No matter, it was nice. She kept her eyes closed. Better not look at him too close, there was no telling what she was cuddled up to. She used the same technique she had used when at Bernard's—she had developed the ability to see without seeing. She could, for example, put on makeup without really looking at her face. She could walk by mirrors, shop windows, anything with a reflection, without seeing herself. It was better that way. She did remember things, though. She remembered handing money over in the dark, she remembered the small packet in her hand. She remembered an arm around her shoulder.

Suddenly she had a boyfriend! Who's a ratface now? Ha ha. She liked having an arm around her, she liked being led this way and that, to a car, to a park, to blankets. There were stars and cicadas and she felt so good it was as if her whole body had become a young, lovely vagina. *This is what God must be like, this arm around me. What is the matter with people?* She had giggled at the thought last night, and the night before, and the night before that, when no one needed to sleep or to eat. If everyone got some of this there would be no wars, no murders, no sadness. Everyone would be a vagina and live free. She felt the sun on her face. The desert sun she knew too well, the thing that reveals everything that should be kept hidden. She could feel it burning her through the leaves, each ray a laser beam. She had to move, go find some real shade.

She opened her eyes a little bit, just enough to see through her eyelashes. Not too old, and in his sleep he appeared beautiful. Thank God he was beautiful. There he was again, God.

She managed to extract her arm from under him. He grumbled but continued sleeping. Standing up was difficult, but she clawed at a tree and it was as if the tree wanted her to get up, it stood strong for her. She felt her body—parts ached but she didn't have to pee. Okay to get up, okay to walk. She couldn't recall the last time she'd peed, she couldn't remember how many days had gone by—could be two, could be twenty. She walked in the scorching sun. There was nothing anywhere. She thought of her homes, with her mom, with Bernard, her room at Betty's.

None of them had been her home. A person without a home was always disoriented.

She looked up to the mountain that had always centered her, but the mountain was gone. Where the hell'd the mountain go? The sand was gritty and packed with boulders and the kind of trees nobody loves.

Her thoughts furiously arranged themselves into coherence, switches flipped, lights went on. Vision came into sharp focus and she regretfully knew where she was: back in Anza. *Fuck me.*

How did this happen? There was a vague memory of the back of a car and curves and a sense of nausea, stopping to barf. Just as well, she could always get money here without tending beejays. Her knees cracking and her guts wrenching, she pulled herself upright and headed for the comfort of the Circle K's parking lot. She'd figure it out there. It was a good place to make a plan. Her brain hissed and sputtered with every step. Someone was walking behind her so she strengthened her resolve. The scent of goats and a tapping sound followed her, *tap tap tap.* Closer. Closer. And then she felt it, the pain, the back of her head, her body pitched forward, dropping fast, hard, and for good.

"Ah, but you're a sad fuck of a creature," Don Donner said with an uncharacteristic touch of sorrow as the cat burglar of Anza writhed in pain on the desert floor. The hair was still banana yellow but the rest of her looked like someone had taken a hooker, buried her alive until she died, then dug her up and brought her back to some sort of life. He'd hardly touched her with the cane and down she went.

Kimberly's thoughts sliced through like ice shards: *Go back to Betty's, be a good mom to Carol, change Carol's name to Destiny so you don't hate her every time you look at her, divorce Bernard and take no money, talk to Eric about a job at Chica's in Coachella, stay straight. Get a home of your own.*

Forget Anza by never talking about it.

EVERYTHING DRAINS AND DISAPPEARS

BY ROB BOWMAN

Bermuda Dunes

"Do you have a better plan?"

I didn't.

"Then this is the plan," Monique said.

We were broke, sitting at the counter in our apartment, a tilting slab that the ad had said was a breakfast nook but was really shellacked and cracked plywood that managed the gloomy trick of always being damp, always, 115 degrees outside, AC broken, water shut off for not paying the bill. But everything in that place still clammy and sticky, damp without cooling or quenching, like a board made of swamp.

Meanwhile, you drive up and down through the desert and every gated community here sucks down electricity, whirls their AC turbines as the windmills churn just next to the mountains, the wind slamming down the slopes and crushing along the fans, chopping down the birds. Not that I care. I wonder about coyotes running along there, eating the obliterated birds.

Fly through this valley and get knocked down and eaten.

Ever seen the entrances to those neighborhoods? Waterfalls of the clearest water you've ever seen, crashing and slamming down or tripping down little stone steps or shooting straight up, and burbling down. Endless gallons of it in the desert in front of the homes of men who haven't gotten it up without prescriptions in decades.

Those entrances.

Those gates.

Guard booths and cameras, spiked walls, sign-in sheets, parking passes.

I didn't have a better plan.

We went to the library where you can get on the Internet for free and we were a hundred bucks and a half-hour drive away from a used massage table. I call Monique "Mo" and she says she doesn't like it, but she never tells me not to say it. I thought it was cute but maybe not. We talked the old lady down to seventy-five because it was all we had, and she could tell we meant it. She looked Mo up and down, rubbed her craggy face with her gnarled knuckles, nodded but it made her whole body move up and down because of how her back was bent and humped. She looked at Mo and asked if we needed lotion and oil bottles. They looked disgusting. We took them.

"Get what you need, honey," the old lady said.

We didn't know what she meant but we knew what we needed. And we intended to get it.

Between us, Mo is the smart one. And the driven one. And the tougher one. So, what do I bring to the table, or to the cracked bar top? I exist. I show up. It's more than most guys, Mo would say. It didn't feel like much of a compliment.

We met not quite three years ago, when she came through the burger place where I worked as little as possible while selling weed to the other people who worked there. I was sitting at a Formica table on my break when I saw her come in with a friend. I liked her right away and I offered her a joint.

"How much?"

"It's a present."

"Why?"

"'Cause I want to."

Later she would tell me that was why she took it and why she gave me her number. Because I said I wanted to. She thought it sounded cool. What the hell did we know? You know what happened then or can figure it out.

It was good. It was really good. The furniture was old and lumpy, but we never noticed, curled up, smoking up, watching the TV and people living bigger than us, but it never seemed better than what we had. I'd cook her dinner; she'd do the dishes. We were happy. She would push me onto my back and lean over me, her long, dark hair falling over the edges of her face, like a curtain closing us in, our own little escape. Her hair would tickle my face and my chest, then fall more heavily onto me as she leaned closer, until she'd kiss me or blow a cloud of smoke into my mouth or both. It was really good.

And then six months goes by, a year. And we are doing okay. It's not like when we first hooked up but it's okay. Then I get fired but so what, the pot floats us by and her job answering phones for the extermination shop runs out when the owner goes to jail for poisoning some guy whose wife he was fucking or something, I don't know, just that a hell of a lot of bug spray ended up in some guy's body and he died something horrible, leaking from his goddamn eyes. So that job ends but we are okay.

Then the legal pot shops open and all the weed dealers are investment bankers and guys with MBAs and a clean criminal record to stand behind a counter, and I don't know anybody with that where I come from.

And I'm not dealing in anything heavy. That's how you find your way to the wrong side of the Loco Burros or the Bang Bang Boys, and last time I checked I don't have an army.

And that's how we started to get thin.

And that's when Mo came up with her plan.

"Don't you need like a license or some shit?"

"Who's going to ask?" she said. "We're not opening a shop somewhere, some fucking store. It's just a drive and that's it. *Knock knock, motherfucker.* Give a back rub and get out."

"Is it safe?"

"How do you mean?"

"You are just going into some guy's house," I said, "and it's just you and him? A stranger? I don't like that. Seems way too fucking dangerous."

"What are they going to do? Chain me up? You will be right outside. If I don't come out, you call the cops. Or just charge right in, tough guy."

She kissed me on the cheek and I felt a little better but not much.

We get the table and then it's another trip to the library to post an ad online after we both sell plasma at the clinic for a little extra cash. Between us we got fifty bucks, a few stale cookies, and two miniature cups of apple juice. At the library we read a bunch of ads before we posted ours.

Sensual In-Home Massage. Satisfaction Guaranteed. We found a picture of someone who kind of looked like Mo, close enough to avoid someone flat out saying it wasn't her even though it wasn't actually her. Posted it with the phone number of a little burner phone we bought with the absolute last of our cash on our way to the library, after having bought a bottle of generic baby oil and a couple washcloths from the dollar store.

The fucking dollar store has everything you need to begin your own disgusting little start-up. Aisle after aisle of toxic plastic and stale food and discount Bibles. You ever seen someone buy one of those Bibles from the dollar store? Me neither.

Then we just waited for the phone to ring.

I drove.

Those first houses, those first guys, are all a beige, lumpy blur in my mind. I'd stop, help her get the table out of the back as she slung her bag over her shoulder, then get back in the car, lean the car seat back while she went and rang the doorbell or knocked or whatever. I would peek up, curious about these men. They were always men. They answered their doors in sweat suits, robes, khakis, football jerseys, without shirts. One guy in a full suit and tie. One guy with what looked, I swear to God, like a cape. Then I'd lie back in the car with the motor and the AC running, listen to music or sleep. Daydream. Worry.

I didn't ask until after the third one. Because I already knew and I didn't want to know.

"What happened in there?"

"What do you think?" Mo was double-checking the money. One hundred per hour and a forty-dollar tip. "Rubbed him down. Listened to him talk about a lot of nonsense. I'm pretty sure he was lying about all of it. Trying to sound cool or something."

"Then what?"

Mo turned to look at me. "What are you asking?"

"Are you doing anything else? Who pays that much for a fucking massage?"

"Did you read the ad? It said *sensual* massage. What do you think happens?"

"You tell me."

"Don't boss me. You don't own me. Who's paying for your fucking lunch?"

"I drove. I did something."

"Fuck you, you did something. You didn't have to jerk off some guy, folding his gut up with one hand while you jerk him off with the other. Listen to his bullshit while wiping off your arm. Fuck you. What did you think was happening in there? Or did you just need to hear me say it? Is that what you want?"

I didn't know what I wanted. I just drove on. We had another lined up for after lunch. And I still drove her there.

At night I would massage her hands and her forearms and her shoulders. She was sore all the time. I thought about her washing those hands, what she was washing off, I thought about the hunched-over old woman and her hands like tree roots. She told Mo to get what she wanted. I wondered what Mo wanted and if she was getting it.

I understood how it was and how it was reversed at night, me rubbing down Mo after a day of pulling and pressing flesh. Her sex drive pretty much disappeared. And so did mine. Then some days she would be all charged up, needing to fuck, to grind down against me until she came. She'd turn my face away, tell me to stop breathing, to not exist until she was done. Or she would hold my face with both hands and stare into my eyes and we'd feel fully in love. Then she would finish and curl up against me. Or she'd finish and leave for the couch. Or she wouldn't finish and she would stomp out of the room and stand naked in front of the open refrigerator, the cool air chilling the sweat on her.

One time, as she stood naked in front of the fridge, I told her that having the door open would cool her off but the rest of the room would get hotter, that that's how it works—it seems better but just gets worse all of the time.

"Shut up," she said. "Go to bed."

* * *

Then one day she said she had a new plan.

"You need to start pulling your weight," she told me. "And we need to pull in more money."

We were in a nicer place. New cell phones. No more going to the library to post ads. Bought a fancy new camera to get shots of her that would bring in more money, went out to eat, bought our pot from the places that had put me out of business. She'd chew down a gummy before going into the houses of the repeat guys she thought were disgusting. I hated those days. She'd lose track of time on the job, anything could happen. I had stopped asking questions, but I hadn't stopped wondering.

"I hate these guys. Every one of them. I hate their stink. I hate when they touch me. It needs to be worth it. And that means we need to go bigger."

"What does that mean?" I said. "Raise your rates? We could but we'd lose a lot of people. Probably just come out even in the end."

"No. We need to make sure they tip more. Lots more. We need to get you better with that camera. And we need to get you some dark clothes."

It wasn't a sophisticated plan. I'd drop her off, unload the table, lie down, and wait, like always. Then, halfway through the massage, when she went to get the hot towels to wipe them down, she would open up the curtains, just enough for me, now hiding in the backyard, to get a shot with the long lens, a shot of them getting jerked off while rubbing her ass, make sure to get their faces, make sure to get their cocks, make sure to get wide shots and make sure to get close-ups, make sure it is obvious what is happening, make sure who it is happening to.

Then I'd text her the pictures.

She'd finish the job, collect, and ask for more. Then show them the pictures. Say she noticed the tan line from the wedding ring that was now sitting next to the bathroom sink. Say their wives might want to see these pictures. Say their bosses might want to see these pictures. Say that their HOA would probably be interested in these pictures. The HOA thing scares the shit out of rich people. It's crazy. Then she collects more. She'll take a personal check, sure. Write it out to *cash*. If it bounces or if it's canceled, she still has those pictures.

And it worked.

Who were they going to tell? What would they say? They'd pay out.

And for some reason, there was still repeat business. They seemed to think it established something, made her safer in some way, made it certain she wasn't a cop. They'd tip big and call again. Some guys seemed to love it, the danger of it, the torture of it. They wanted to see the pictures, asked her to be even meaner to them. That was mostly in Indian Wells, where the richest of the rich live. Something demented going on over there. She was asked to work a party there once. Turned out to be an orgy. They set up a room for her with her table in the middle and audience seating all around. She told me all about it. A crystal bowl for tips, larger bills for taking suggestions. I never saw the insides of these places, just slices through the curtains, backgrounds to all of that skin and hair.

She got calls from all over the valley, to the fancier parts of Indio, to Palm Desert, to Palm Springs, Indian Wells, Desert Hot Springs, off in the hills. We never went to Cathedral City. We lived there and didn't want her to work where we went grocery shopping but pretty much never got calls from there anyway. We went to La Quinta, by the golf resorts, PGA West, called to the hotels but rarely went with no way to photograph the men, and too many cameras that didn't belong to us that could photograph her, photograph me. Gated communities with their waterfalls and lighted xeriscapes, their tumbling plants and shooting fountains. She never gave her real name. The name she gave them would be sent to the guard house or she would be given a gate code and we would roll right in, without question. Sure, they had cameras, but so what? No one was complaining. They knew complaints would mean photos getting sent around.

I kept them all on a computer we had, every photo dropped in a folder with an address for a name. We never really knew names, not real names. No one knows anyone else if that's the agreement, even now, even these days. Every day starts to feel that way, that you never really know anyone, even someone you live with.

It's a cash business in a world of plastic people.

But we never went to Bermuda Dunes.

There's something wrong with that place. It's not a real town, it's not a real anything. It's an unincorporated island in the middle of the valley without any roads that go through. They pretend they are a town but it's more like a fiefdom with its own security force instead of police. Some rich guy wanted to build the golf course of his dreams and named it after his favorite island getaway and the sand all around. Which, fine, whatever, there's plenty of delusional assholes.

But he kept it completely private, completely isolated while surrounded by the other towns. Different electric company, different water company. They don't even share sewage with the valley, every pipe leading straight down to septic tanks, seeping down through rock until they hit sand and

194 // PALM SPRINGS NOIR

then more sand, all of that water gurgling out while the shit builds. Centuries of drought and they throw their water away while everyone else struggles to clean it, filter it, pipe it back out, and Bermuda Dunes pisses it all away. But the golf course is green and the lawns are thick and the fountains at the gates gush twenty-four hours a day. The lords and ladies sit in their pools and suck on ice cubes while they flush all of their shit straight down and sit on it, float above it. When there is too much of it, some poor bastard with the worst job in the world sucks it all out, hauls it away.

The septic thing is terrible, sure, but is it really that different from the other communities? Yes. There are levels to the HOA there and the higher up you are, the more freedom you have. There are neighborhoods inside the neighborhood, low-income apartments and low-slung mansions, gates inside of gates. For some houses you need three separate codes and cards to get through. And all of it with private security that doesn't give a shit about police because there aren't any. The county sheriffs have jurisdiction in theory, but I've never seen one in there. Bermuda Dunes may as well be a private island, a banana republic, off the fucking map. And there's only one way in and out for nonresidents. The traffic backs up for blocks with work trucks, nannies, deliveries, visitors, on and on. I didn't ever want to go in there.

We had a year and a half of this built up. Then she gives me the address for the last stop of the day. I don't know it, new client, and I don't even know the street, so she tells me it's in Bermuda Dunes.

"Fuck. Fuck that place. You should cancel."

"The hell I should," Mo said. "I looked up the street. It's one of the big classic places. Sinatra shit. Deep-pocket money."

"That's even worse. Old money is drained down and low tips. They have no sense of what a dollar even is anymore. How old did they sound on the phone?"

"Not old."

"How old?"

"I don't know," she said. "Fifty, maybe. Hard to tell. Gravelly voice. You know. Hard to tell. When did you get so precious? When did you go back to giving a shit?"

It had gotten strange between us. Once it becomes routine to watch your girlfriend jerk off a guy while he sucks on her tit, something has gone really wrong. And I was certain she saw clients without me. I'd come home from a night out and she'd look far away from me while she was right next to me on the couch. Her silhouette looking blurry while we watched television. I didn't say anything. I knew which variable could be dropped in our equation: I was the disposable one.

So I drove.

The entrance to Bermuda Dunes isn't much different from all the others except how abrupt it feels, a sharp right turn into the gates. Some obscure provision about the point where Bermuda Dunes met La Quinta and Indio meant no one wanted to pay for a stoplight, so the four-way stop turns into a disaster about thirty times a day as everything backs up, waiting for the gate to let through guests and repair trucks and the endless chains of pool cleaners and landscapers.

Here's a fun game: drive through the valley and count the beat-up white pickup trucks with a plug-in pool pump hanging off the bed, bungee strapped to a hand cart. And the wheels of the hand cart will be wrapped in duct tape. They clean the pools and sweat through the days, scrubbing down the walls with fifteen-foot extension poles because they aren't allowed in the waters.

196 // PALM SPRINGS NOIR

We were in line, the four-way stop lurching us in, when Mo leaned her seat all the way back, turned her back to me.

"What's wrong?"

"I have a headache. All this stop and start."

"Want to go home? You can cancel." I was going to push on this point if she let me. Anything to not go in there.

"No. We are already here. I just need to rest my head."

"You sure?"

"I'm sure."

"Okay."

We continued to slowly roll into Bermuda Dunes, in pieces, as though the gates were taking bites from a long chain, chewing, swallowing, biting again.

"Different name today."

"What?" She had a new standard fake name for gates. They never check it at these things, just look for the name on the list and wave you through, maybe print up a ticket for the dashboard. Veronica Hayworth. She said it was an inside joke, but I never got it.

"Yeah, they check IDs here," Mo said. "So it's under your name."

"Fuck. We should get out of here. This whole thing feels like shit."

"Come on, baby. Let's get paid." She looked at me and said it, something she had stopped saying to me a long time ago: "Please."

She said please but it didn't feel right. *Please* always feels like a pulling, like they are in front of you, leading you. But this time felt like a shove from behind, a hand between the shoulder blades. I stumbled forward.

And the cars kept worming up, chunk by chunk.

When we finally came to the booth, the guy looked

straight at the list, barely glanced up at me at all. I thought he was just slacking off but then realized he was watching me the whole time, on a computer monitor linked to a camera above the door, pointed straight at me.

"Name." Not a question.

I told him.

He handed me a printed-out card with a bar code, my name, and the address we were heading to. "Put that on the dashboard."

I thanked him, pulled forward, listened to my phone tell me what turns to take. Mo sat up, suddenly feeling much better.

"He didn't ask for my ID."

"What?"

"You said they check IDs here. He didn't ask for mine."

"Maybe he forgot," Mo said.

"Maybe."

"It's busy. Probably trying to get people through faster."

"Maybe."

"What's wrong?" Mo looked at me.

I could feel her eyes on me, my cheeks grew hot. "You know what's wrong. I don't like it. I don't like this. I don't like this place."

"Pull over."

I did.

"Baby." Mo hadn't called me by anything other than my name in a long time. Then at the gate. Then this. I felt it in my chest but also between my shoulder blades. "It's the last one of the day, baby. We are already here, already checked in."

"So?"

"I hear you, baby. I do. Listen, just this one and then we go home. We can put on a movie. Make you feel good. Then I will take off all of tomorrow. Turn off the phone. Hell, if tonight pays out like it should, I'll take the week off. We can drive out to someplace nice. Maybe the beach. Come on."

A week on the beach. Calling me baby. Cocktails and bikinis. It sounded pretty good. I felt like I could become myself again.

"Okay. Let's go."

I finished the drive to the house. It was a nightmare for me. I glanced at the address on the card. It wasn't the same one that Mo had told me. Blocks away. And a different street. Everything felt wrong. And that's before I saw the house.

Most places out here are how you think of a house: front yard, house, fenced-in backyard. Most of Mo's clients had pools out back, covered patios, which are good for me, they cut down on window glare, make it easier for me to get the shots. I can lie back on a pool lounger until the blinds open, get set up, take the pictures, and shoot them over to Mo.

The Bermuda Dunes house was a nightmare. A walled-off place where most of the house is the wall itself, a home built like a fort, a residential Alamo. Each house sits in a hollow square, a sharp-edged circle with the pool in the middle and no backyard. Probably some midsixties idea about how to party, shutting out the world from seeing what a swinging shindig is all about, steel gates and decorative spikes on the walls. They feel like prisons, these places. And Bermuda Dunes is full of them.

"Fuck. I can't even get a shot here."

"What do you mean?"

"There's no backyard. It's a courtyard place. This is a bust."

"Bust? There's no cops here," Mo said. "It's the Dunes."

"I mean busted. Like broken. It's shot."

Mo thought for a second and then spoke again. "I will leave the gate not quite closed when they let me in. You can get a shot from in the courtyard, right?"

"Maybe," I said. "Depending how the rooms are laid out."

"I'll put him right where you want. In a good spot. Just be on the far side of the pool so he doesn't see you."

That's exactly where I set up and waited for the blinds to open.

I didn't need to hear anything while waiting and usually had on headphones, listened to music, waited. The music kept me awake—I worried I would fall asleep otherwise. I sat in a chair and waited. The pool was nice but old, cement with dinner plate–sized chunks of slate around the edges, a different color above and below the surface, decades of residue and grit above the surface, while the water, constantly stirred by the filters and pumps, kept the sides more or less clean. Maybe some algae here and there.

There's algae growing in the desert. That's how much money there is here, rich people with their oases.

The furniture was all old and sun-bleached, the fabric strained and stretching on the loungers, so eaten by the heat that the cloth was crumbling, turning to dust. Sit on those things and take half the chair with you in your clothes, and that's if it doesn't collapse under you. I sat at an old café set—metal table, metal chairs, painted aluminum.

The vertical blinds moved but didn't open, swayed a little, like something had brushed by them. It seemed early to be picture time, but I hadn't looked at what time we set up. Maybe this guy wasn't pretending to even want a massage. My eyes caught something scattered and dark in a jangled line. They looked like paw prints. Maybe the guy had a dog. I hadn't seen any other sign of one, no dog tried to escape out of the front door, didn't hear barking when Mo rang the doorbell. Could have been a coyote running through. But how did they get in and out of there? Over those walls? I wondered how they knew not to drink the pool water, how to resist something so blue and sparkling, how they knew it would make them sick, dry them out the more they drank.

Who ever thought to name them blinds? Why not *hides*? Why not *screens*?

The blinds moved again but not gently, not in a careful breath; there was a hard crashing and it seemed like something was pressing up against them, they shook and then parted, and I saw what it was.

It was Mo.

Her face was pushed up against the glass, her dark hair spilled all around her and strings of it between the blades of the blinds.

I stood still for a second, shocked, paralyzed.

Replayed that sliver of time in my mind. *Oh no. Oh no.* I jumped up from the chair, knocked over the table and the camera flew into the air, dropped down into the pool. I heard it splash as I ran past, went to the sliding door but it wouldn't open, tried the next one over, locked. I kicked at a brick planter against the wall with my heel and a loose brick came free. I grabbed the brick and threw it against the glass, which wobbled and shook but didn't break. The blinds jangled again.

Picked the brick back up and threw it with everything I had into the glass, aiming for where the first throw had scuffed and scraped it. The brick sailed through the glass and continued into the house where I heard it clang into something and thunk onto the floor. The glass held its shape for a second and then fell down like water in a fountain, splashing down onto the floor.

I ran into the room, a kind of family den, pictures of a couple all over the walls, hiking in the mountains, in front of a small plane at the tiny private airport. No massage table. I looked down and saw Mo, lying facedown on the floor halfway into the room. Her dark hair swirled out around her. I couldn't figure out for a second what was wrong with her outfit and then realized she wasn't wearing the same clothes as when I'd dropped her off. Her shape seemed wrong. She was arched up and bent, a tiny broken bridge. But I was moving fast and couldn't stop. I grabbed her by the shoulders and turned her over.

There was a knife sticking out of her chest, the lone pillar arching the bridge. Every alarm in my head was screaming but nothing was making sense. I shouted her name and heard her voice, a kind of involuntary yelp, but it wasn't coming from her. It was down the hall. I looked at her face.

It wasn't Mo.

Some other woman, in different clothes and with a different shape, just dark hair and a knife in her chest. I peered around the room and realized it was the same woman from the pictures on the walls, smiling in front of some Vegas fountain, pretending to hold up the Eiffel Tower, standing so as to trick the viewer into seeing something that wasn't there, wasn't true. I looked at the knife again. It was mine—how many times had I cooked with that knife? I had just the night before. Mo said she'd clean up.

The Bermuda Dunes security has sirens exactly like cop cars and they are always roaming around, looking for problems and excuses to flex as though they are real cops, like white blood cells, like vultures: clean up and tear apart. How were they already here? I hadn't called, it had just happened. And then I knew. They were called before Mo's face hit the glass and before I smashed it in.

I looked around and there was no place for me to go. Only one way out, straight through the front door, where security was already heading. I swept the room one more time, hoping a new door would magically appear, and there was Mo, standing and looking at me. She seemed a little sad but not very. Resolved.

"Sorry," she said.

Then she was gone. I heard someone's voice, a man's. He was telling her to get in the car while she still could, get in the back, lie down. Then I heard him running out the front door. The sirens louder and louder.

I ran out of the broken window, leaped up and grabbed the edges of the wall, slicing my hands, pulled myself over and felt the terra-cotta spikes cut and scrape and pierce me as I went over, landed hard on the xeriscape rocks.

Those security guards got to me before I could stand back up, with HOA-issued Tasers and privately owned pistols. They dragged me across the stones and into the street and I was thinking as they did so that I needed the real cops to get there, that they would follow some kind of rules. And then I was on the pavement and it was hot as hell and there was so much shouting and my body shaking from the fish-hook barbs of the Taser in my skin. Then I saw a boot and it took forever to come down and it went past my eyes and past my face and into my throat. And I knew I wasn't leaving.

Because nothing gets piped back or returned in Bermuda Dunes. It all just sinks down underneath. That's when I felt everything in me do what happens to everything here: drain down and disappear forever.

A CAREER SPENT DISAPPOINTING PEOPLE

BY TOD GOLDBERG

Indio

T hree hours out of the hospital, his left foot too swollen for a shoe, Shane's car breaks down. It's July, a trillion degrees outside, Interstate 10 a gray ribbon of shit unspooling east out of Palm Springs toward Arizona. Not exactly where he wanted to go, but who the fuck wants to go to Arizona? It's what was on the other side of Arizona that mattered to Shane, the chance that there might be another life in that direction. He never liked being on the coast. The one time he ever even tried to swim in the Pacific—back when he came out on vacation with his dad, so, over twenty years ago, half his lifetime now—he was gripped with the ungodly realization that unlike a pool, there were no sides. You were always in the deep end out there.

It was a feeling that stuck with him, even when he was in one of those towns in the San Fernando Valley that sounded like an escape route from an old western: North Hills . . . West Hills . . . Hidden Hills . . .

The Honda was the one damn thing Shane thought he could depend on. But as soon as he pulled out of the parking lot at Centinela Hospital in Inglewood, the *check engine* light flashed on. A hundred thousand miles he put on that fucking car and not a single problem, and the one time he really needed it, it was telling him it couldn't comply. He didn't have the time—or the money—to swing by the mechanic, considering he'd left the hospital before the nurse had filled out the paperwork for the cops, which was a problem. Not as big a problem as staying would have been. It wasn't the kind of thing that would have the cops trawling the city for him, especially since the wound did look self-inflected, since it was. Someone else holding his fucking hand while he shot himself with his own damn gun.

Shane couldn't remember if he still had AAA, but he called anyway.

"Looks like you canceled your account six months ago," the customer service agent said.

Rachel must have done it after she moved out. Like how she canceled their shared credit cards. Or how she took their dog Manny to get his teeth cleaned on the same morning she kicked him out of the house, knowing full well Shane wouldn't have the cash to pick the dog back up.

God, he loved that dog. Probably more than he loved Rachel. No *probably*. *Actually*. If he got out of this fucked-up situation, he was going to buy another dog that looked like Manny and name him Manny too.

"How much is it to re-up?" Shane asked.

"It's sixty-eight dollars, which gets you seven miles of towing service."

"What if I need to go farther?" Shane asked, thinking, *What the hell, maybe I'll have AAA tow me to Arizona, give me someone to talk to.* Or maybe he'd just steal the tow truck. He could do that. He was capable of anything now.

"You'd need the premier membership for that," the customer service agent said, and then began to tell Shane the particulars of how amazing the premier membership was. He had $274 in cash in his pocket—Gold Mike, the fucker who shot him in the foot, that's what he gave Shane as a parting gift after he'd asked him to stop by their storage unit over by the Forum; Shane thinking it was to plan the night's job, Gold Mike with other ideas.

"It's not working out," Gold Mike told him. The storage unit was half-empty already, Gold Mike's van filled with their deejay and karaoke equipment, all their locksmith materials, plus their three industrial-sized lockboxes filled with pills. They'd been coming up light lately, but for a while it was a good living. Black-tie weddings in the Palisades, bar mitzvahs in Calabasas, retirement parties in Bel-Air. How it worked, one of them would be inside at the wedding, singing or dee-jaying, the other guy parking cars and collecting addresses. Three-hour wedding meant they could get as many keys made as they wanted. Spend the next couple days casing a house, go in and steal all the pills, which wasn't a crime any cop gave a shit about, particularly when there was no evidence of breaking and entering. Plus, it was a victimless crime, Shane not feeling too bad about taking a cancer patient's Klonopin, knowing full well CVS would hook them back up in thirty minutes, maybe less. They didn't steal jewelry or TVs or cars or any of that shit. Just pills.

Then this whole opiate crisis started getting on the news right when weed got legalized, so people in California started loading up on edibles and vape pens instead of Percocet and benzos.

"It's just an ebb," Shane said.

"I'm moving my operating base," Gold Mike said. "Got a friend in Reno. Says everyone's hooked on something. He can get me into the hotels. That's next-level."

"Cool," Shane said. "I'm down to relocate." His only

steady, legal gigs were running karaoke at Forrest's Bar in Culver City and a honky-tonk in Thousand Oaks called Denim & Diamonds.

"You're not hearing me," Gold Mike said. "You can't hit the high notes anymore. If you can't sing, this whole operation is moot." *Moot.* Where the fuck had he learned that word? "Jessie's Girl"? "Don't make it weird, all right? Ten years is a good run."

"Who needs a high note? You think Mick can hit a high note?"

"Bro," Gold Mike said, "I don't even like music."

"So that's it? No severance?"

"You think you're getting COBRA up in this bitch? Come on, man."

"Manny's chemo put me back ten grand," Shane said. Manny had a tumor on his ear that turned out to be a treatable cancer, in the sense that the dog could get treatment and still die, but he hadn't yet, as far as Shane knew. "I've been upside down ever since."

"That was like eighteen months ago." Gold Mike took out his wallet, thumbed out a few fifties, put them on an empty shelf next to a broken turntable.

"Couple hundred bucks?" Shane said. "How about you give me 50 percent of everything or I walk into a police station. How about that?" And then Shane pulled out his gun, which had actually been a gift from Gold Mike. A little .22. He'd given it to Shane after a robbery went sideways, a Vietnam War vet came home and found Shane in his bathroom, beat the fucking shit out of him with a golf club, Gold Mike coming in at the last minute and knocking the fucker out with a Taser.

You pull out your gun, mentally, you gotta be ready to kill a guy right then, no talking shit, no cool catch phrase, no *freeze*, no *hands up*, nothing, just *pop pop pop*. That's what cops are always saying, it's what Gold Mike had taught Shane too. Which is how he also had all of Gold Mike's credit cards and his driver's license, in addition to $274.

"Seven miles is fine," Shane said to the customer service agent, and gave him his location on the 10. "I need a place with a karaoke bar, if possible." He had a hustle he liked to do where he'd bet people that he could make them cry and then he'd bust out "Brick" by Ben Folds Five and every girl who ever had an abortion would be in a puddle. It didn't make him proud, but he had bills to pay.

"Let's see what we have here." The agent made a whistling sound. "Well, the Royal Californian is 6.7 miles from where you are. They have a sports bar with karaoke. If that works, shall I charge it to your existing credit card and get the truck to you?"

"How about I give the driver cash," Shane said. He needed as little paper trail as possible.

"I'll need to check with my manager," the agent said, and put Shane on hold.

He was parked beneath a billboard that advertised *The Wonder of Waterfront Living in the Desert!* and showed a happy couple of indeterminate race walking into what appeared to be an Italian lakeside villa surrounded by palm trees. He looked to the west and could make out the obvious signs of civilization: the billboard for a Starbucks, an RV park called the Long Run, a billboard touting an upcoming concert by Rick Springfield at the Fantasy Springs Casino. That fucking guy. Twice in the same day. Had to be a harbinger.

"Cash is just fine. We'll have a tow truck to you in about twenty minutes," the agent said.

It was nearly four o'clock. He was supposed to be singing "Come On Eileen" in a couple hours, always his first song over at Forrest's, everyone always losing their shit when he did that "*Toora loora toora loo rye aye*" bit, like it was 1982 and they were thirteen and it was the eighth grade dance.

That fucking song.

More trouble than it was worth, that was for sure.

He couldn't think about that now.

He needed to get Gold Mike's body out of the trunk.

Or, well . . . choice cuts of Gold Mike's body.

2009 and Shane's working the Black Angus in Northridge. They've got something they call the "Fun Bar," a relic from disco years, lit up floor, big dark booths, great sound system, but no one dancing. Just frat boys over from the college drinking vodka and cranberry like they all have UTIs. At first, he's just doing karaoke like anybody does karaoke, stand up there, let some drunk come up and sing "American Pie," help him out when he realizes the song is eight minutes long and he doesn't have the wind. Flirt with the bartender, maybe get a hand job in the dry storage. Woman or man. Hand job was a hand job, Shane believed in equal opportunity back then, because of all the coke and a profound lack of giving a fuck. Love is love, friction is friction.

Maybe a little guilt now, thinking about it, thinking about how he did Rachel wrong, staring at the ceiling fan twirling in his room at the Royal Californian, eleven p.m., still a hundred degrees outside, giant flying roaches committing suicide against his window every couple minutes, Shane dying for a fucking Percocet, a million of them still in Gold Mike's van, Shane could hit himself for being so stupid, not thinking this all through, his foot throbbing, sweat sticking his shirt to his chest.

His own fault. Rachel, that is. A lot of lying. *Fuck it* had been his point of view back when he worked at the Angus. Go home with a hundred bucks for the night and an empty load? *Fuck it.* Problem was, he'd kept that point of view long into his relationship with Rachel and she was not a *Fuck it* kind of person, so he pretended it was just how performers were, though by the time Rachel came along, he wasn't a performer anymore, he just performed.

"Baby," he'd tell her, "you gotta just say *Fuck it* when you're in this business, otherwise, every night would crush your spirit."

And Rachel, she'd say, "Then you should get another way to earn a living."

And so he had.

Kind of.

Thing was, Shane could really sing. All this other shit was ephemeral. His talent, man, that was in his genetic code. His dad played in the Catskills back in the day, singing in cover bands, even came out to California one time and brought Shane with him, doing a night at Melvyn's in Palm Springs, which was the last time Shane had been anywhere near here. Typically, his dad would come back home the first week of September with a roll of cash, and for a month everything would be good between him and Shane's mom. Dinners out. New clothes. Shane's mom falling in love all over again, talking about how maybe this year they'd get married, maybe she'd go to college, then maybe law school, Shane's mother always talking about how she was going to be a lawyer, but by the time she died, she'd spent twenty-five years as the lunch lady at Rensselaer Point Elementary down in Troy. She'd had Shane when she was fifteen. Dead by fifty-one. Got diagnosed with early onset Alzheimer's and put a fucking noose around her neck two hours later. Shane's dad saying, *Maybe she didn't really have the old-timers, because wouldn't she have forgotten?* His dad was still alive, that was the irony, doing what Shane thought of as the Dead Man's Tour: Buddy Holly and Elvis tribute shows at Native American casinos in Connecticut, Shane keeping track of him on the Internet, that fucker doing pretty well.

But the Angus.

In comes Gold Mike. Sits at a table right by Shane's kit, nurses a Diet Coke. Really gets into it when Shane sings. Tapping his foot. Bobbing his head. When Shane busts out "Come On Eileen" and hits his full register, Gold Mike stands up and whoops.

When he goes on break fifteen minutes later, Gold Mike follows him outside, where Shane is having a smoke and watching the traffic on Corbin Avenue.

"You got a nice presence," Gold Mike says.

"Thanks man," Shane says.

"Wasting it out here, if you want my opinion," Gold Mike says.

"Just waiting to be discovered."

"That's not ever gonna happen," Gold Mike says, like he knows. He's maybe twenty-seven, but he's one of those guys who talks like he's been around the world fifty times. Gold Mike fingers a diamond-encrusted V that hangs around his neck.

"Whatever," Shane says. He takes one more drag from his cigarette, then puts it out on the bottom of his shoe, like it's a thing he does all the time, which it isn't.

"Whatever?" Gold Mike says. "I insult you and you say, *Whatever.* Passivity, man, that's an illness."

"You want me to hit you or something?"

Gold Mike laughs hard. He's one of those Armenian dudes who shaves his head just to look tough, Shane making out the outline of a full head of stubble. Shane isn't much of a fighter. He's the kind of person who will stab a guy, though.

"I been watching you," Gold Mike says.

"How long have you been watching me?"

"A couple weeks," Gold Mike says, like it's perfectly normal. "You ever do any time?"

"*You* ever do any time?"

"A couple days here and there," Gold Mike says.

"That must impress some people."

Gold Mike laughs again but doesn't respond.

"What's the V stand for?" Shane points at Gold Mike's neck.

"My last name is Voski."

"Okay."

"It means *gold* in Armenian. What's your last name mean?"

"Solomon? It means peace. From the Hebrew word *shalom*. That's what my mother said, anyway."

Gold Mike leans forward, motions Shane to lean in too. "You want to make some real money, Shalom?"

Shane finally fell asleep after one a.m., woke up again at 5:47 a.m., sunrise filling his room on the second floor of the Royal Californian with orange light, his foot like an anvil at the bottom of his leg. He unwrapped the gauze and examined the wound. His foot had swollen to twice its normal size, at least, even though the wound wasn't that big. An inch around. The nurse told him yesterday that the bullet shattered two of his cuneiform bones, that he'd need surgery to stabilize his foot, a couple pins would be inserted, and then he'd be in a hard cast for six to eight weeks. But he was going to need to speak to the police before any of that happened.

That wasn't going to work.

Not with 66 percent of Gold Mike rotting in his storage unit, the other 33 percent in the Honda's trunk, Shane thinking 1 percent was probably drying on the floor, blood and viscera and whatnot. He'd chopped Gold Mike's head off using the fire hose hatchet inside the storage unit, then cut the head up into smaller pieces to make it easier to shuttle around, then took off Gold Mike's hands and feet too, because he thought that would make it harder to identify him, but with DNA, fuck, it probably didn't matter, but Shane hadn't been thinking too terribly straight.

He'd taken the battery out of Gold Mike's van and poured acid over the rest of the body, but that was really just cosmetic. For sure Shane's DNA was in the unit and the van and on Gold Mike's body, but then his DNA was all over everything regardless. They were business partners. That was easy enough to explain. Plus, he had no *legitimate* reason to kill Gold Mike. Anyone who saw them together knew they were a team. Really, the only proof that it was Shane who'd plugged him an excessive number of times was probably the hole in Shane's fucking foot and the gun itself, which Shane had tucked under his mattress.

Well, and Gold Mike's head and all that, which was now in his hotel room's safe, zipped up inside a Whole Foods freezer bag filled with ice.

Shane stepped out onto his second-story balcony—which was just wide enough to hurl yourself over—and lit up his second-to-last cigarette. He'd given up smoking when Manny got cancer, truth be known he sort of blamed himself for that whole thing, but it was the only drug he had on his person and he needed about ten minutes of mental clarity to figure out how he was going to get himself out of this situation.

He needed to get rid of Gold Mike's body parts.

He needed to get rid of the gun.

He needed to get himself an alibi . . . or he needed to change his entire identity, which didn't seem like a plausible turn of events, though he was open to whatever reality presented itself to him.

He needed to go across the street to the Circle K and get some disposable phones.

He also was in a fuck-ton of pain and under normal circumstances might go find a dispensary and get some edibles, but he wasn't showing anyone his ID. He'd get some ice and soak his foot in the tub; that would bring down the swelling. He'd get some bleach from housecleaning, put a couple drops in the water, maybe that would disinfect the wound? Then he needed to get a new car.

The Royal Californian sat on a stretch of Highway 111 in Indio that could have been Carson City or Bakersfield or Van Nuys or anywhere else where someone had the wise idea to plant a palm tree and then surround it with cement. This wasn't the part of greater Palm Springs where people came to actually visit—it was nowhere near the leafy garden hotel he'd stayed in with his dad, the Ingleside Inn—unless they were going to court or bailing someone out, since the hotel was a block west of the county courthouse and jail. He hadn't realized it at first, not until he was checking in and the clerk gave him a brochure of local amenities. Page one had all the dining options. Page two was local entertainment and information about how to get to the polo fields a mile south. And then page three was all bail bonds, attorneys, and AA meetings.

Made sense, then, when the clerk didn't seem bothered by his bloody foot and that he didn't have ID when he gave him Gold Mike's Visa to check in.

He'd given the AAA driver an extra fifteen dollars to park his car just down the block, in a neighborhood of taupe houses called the Sandpiper Estates, the word *estate* apparently one of those words whose meaning had been lost to insincerity, since all Shane saw were a lot of children standing by themselves on front lawns made of rock, staring into their phones. Shane left the keys in the ignition and the doors unlocked. If he was lucky, the car would be stripped clean in a few days, best-case scenario. Worst case, it would get towed to some county yard and there it would stay, forever.

Now, Shane counted seven cars in the Royal Californian's parking lot. A van with a *Save Mono Lake* sticker faded on the bumper. A white pickup truck missing the tailgate. Two Hondas that looked just like his dead Accord. A red Buick Regal, probably a rental, no one bought fucking Buicks. An SUV. Another SUV. He tried to imagine who owned each car, and what their favorite song might be, Shane always interested if people picked a sad song or a happy one. Gave you a sense of how people viewed their own lives. Real or imagined.

Rachel's favorite song was "American Girl" by Tom Petty. His mom's favorite song was "Suspicious Minds" by Elvis. Shane? He didn't have a favorite. Not anymore. Songs had stopped having meaning for him. He'd prefer absolute silence, forever.

A man of about seventy walked out of his ground-floor room and into the parking lot, wearing blue boxer shorts, a white V-neck undershirt, and a pair of black sandals, keys in his hand. A Sinatra guy, Shane thought. Probably "My Way" or "Come Fly with Me." Shane made him for the red Buick Regal. It was backed into a space, always the sign of an asshole. Instead, the old man looked up and down the block, which was stone empty, then crossed the street to a one-story office building with storefront-style signs advertising a law office—*Terry*

Kales, Criminal Defense/DUI/Divorce/Immigration—accounting offices, a Mexican bakery, a notary, and a place where you could get your cell phone fixed.

Not Sinatra.

Neil Diamond.

He went inside the law office, came back out a few minutes later holding a manila envelope, unlocked a silver Mercedes using his key fob, the lights blinking twice, disappeared inside, started it up, rolled back across the street to the parking lot. A woman came walking out of the old man's hotel room then—she looked young, maybe sixteen—met the old guy in the parking lot, got in the passenger side of the car, pulled away. Five minutes later, the Benz was parked in the Royal Californian's lot and the old man was headed back into the hotel, which is when he spotted Shane up on his perch.

"You always stand around at dawn watching people?"

"Just having a smoke," Shane said, "while I contemplate which car to steal."

"Why not just get an Uber?"

Shane pointed at the man's Benz. "German engineering has always appealed to me, but as a Jew, it feels shameful. So you're safe." Shane telling him he was a Jew to put him at ease, no one ever felt scared of Jews, but also just to see how he reacted, Kales seeming like a Jewish last name. Shane flicked his cigarette butt over the balcony. It landed, still smoking, a few feet away from the man. "You mind stepping on that for me?" Shane pointed at his own foot. "I'm down a limb."

The old man scratched his stomach absently but didn't make a move to the cigarette. "You here for a court date?"

"No," Shane said. "Not today."

"You need a lawyer, I'm right across the street, as I think you know."

216 // Palm Springs Noir

"How much for a murder defense?" Shane asked, but he laughed, a big joke, two guys at dawn, bullshitting.

"Less than you'd think." Terry walked over to the butt, stepped on it, cocked his head sideways to get a better look at Shane's foot up above him. "Looks like self-defense to me."

"I'll keep that in mind," Shane said.

"I keep office hours at Cactus Pete's." He pointed at the bar attached to the Royal Californian. "Be there until at least six thirty. I'll buy you a drink, we can talk about your case."

"I'm innocent."

"Yeah," Terry said, "that's what we'll tell 'em."

Shane couldn't tell if Cactus Pete's had a seventies kitsch design aesthetic or if it just hadn't changed since that decade. He'd never been in a bar that had shag carpeting. The VIP area, set off from the tiny dance floor and deejay booth by an actual red-velvet rope, had high-backed booths that reminded Shane fondly of the Angus, Terry Kales sitting in the biggest one, sipping on a glass of something brown, papers spread out in front of him, a cell phone to his ear, another cell phone and his car keys keeping his papers from blowing away, the overhead fans working overtime to keep the room cool. He didn't look up when Shane walked in, at least as far as Shane could tell, which was hard because Terry had on sunglasses, the bar's windows flooding the room with bright light.

It was just before three. Tomorrow at this time, he'd be in the clear. That was the hoped-for result. He'd found a 99 Cents Only store two blocks away, limped his ass over there, his foot on fire, picked up a change of clothes, some sunglasses, a Padres baseball cap. Went next door to the Circle K, got his disposable phone. He was about out of cash now, but he'd figure that out. This old man? He'd probably had a good enough life.

On the dance floor, a woman was setting up for karaoke, and for reasons Shane could not fathom, there was a guy dressed as a clown sitting at the bar. Green hair. Red nose. Striped pants. Big red shoes. Stars-and-stripes shirt and vest. Back of the vest, embroidered in rhinestones, it said HERMIETHECLOWN.COM. He had a cup of coffee and a *Desert Sun*, the local paper, reading the sports page. Shane sat down at the bar but kept a stool between himself and Hermie.

"Get you something?" the woman setting up the karaoke asked. She was younger than Terry, older than the clown, somewhere on the plus side of fifty. She had on a tank top that showed off her shoulders—muscular, but lean—and a full sleeve of tattoos down her right arm. Shane saw two names—*Charlotte* and *Randy*—amid flowers, sunsets, and spiderwebs. She had a name tag pinned above her left breast that said *Glory*.

"Was wondering what time the show was," Shane said.

"Six," Glory said. "You sing?"

"Yeah."

"We have a lot of regulars, so sign up early."

"Truth is, I was wondering if I could warm up first." When Glory didn't respond, Shane said, "I'm staying here."

"Room?"

"204," he said. "On account of my foot. Gotta have surgery in the morning. Just trying to have one last good night before I get the knife." He looked over at the clown. "Unless you've got first dibs."

"He don't speak," Glory said, "or sing."

The clown nodded in the affirmative.

Glory leaned over the bar and examined Shane's foot. So did the silent clown, who blew lightly on a whistle he kept around his neck, which Shane found disconcerting. He slid his flip-flop off, wiggled his toes.

218 // Palm Springs Noir

"You can't be in here without a shoe on," Glory said.

"Just letting it breathe," Shane said.

Glory nodded solemnly, like they'd come to some agreement about life. "What's your song?"

"I mix it up," Shane said, and out of the corner of his eye, he saw Terry slide his sunglasses down his nose, "but mostly Neil Diamond."

Shane was midway through "Girl, You'll Be a Woman Soon" when Terry came over and stood next to the clown; Terry had tears streaming down his face. Terry and the clown swayed back and forth together, Shane digging down deep for the end, telling that girl, soooooooooon you'll need a man, giving it some real soul, some real pathos.

"Again," Terry said, and tossed Shane a fifty, so he did it again, Terry breaking down in full sobs this time, clearly going through some shit. When he finished, Terry said, "One more, your pick," and then went and sat back in his booth, the clown following him. Shane went with "Song Sung Blue." When he was finished, Terry motioned him over to his table.

"You really having surgery?" Terry asked once they were all comfortable in the sweaty half-moon banquette, Terry's shit spread out everywhere, Shane eyeing his car keys, his plan coming into full focus, Hermie busy on his phone, answering texts. Popular fucking clown. "I heard you talking to Glory."

"Yeah," Shane said. "At the hospital up the street." He'd seen it in the brochure. It was named for John F. Kennedy, which Shane thought was some bad presidential juju.

"Good hospital," Terry said. "All of my best clients have died there."

"Like the girl this morning?"

"That was my daughter."

"Really?" *Really.*

"Yeah," Terry said, "I've got limited visitation at the moment, so I take what I can get."

"Okay," Shane said, not sure if he believed him. "What about you, Hermie? Any kids?"

Hermie looked up from his phone, shook his head no.

Thank God.

"Can I give you some legal advice?" Terry said. "Jew to Jew."

"Mazel tov," Shane said.

"You've clearly been shot in the foot. In about two hours, when the courthouse closes? This bar is gonna fill up with off-duty cops, DAs, public defenders, judges, and expert-witness types. You should be gone by then."

"That is good advice," Shane said. "Why are you giving it to me?"

"When it all comes down," Terry pointed at a television above the bar, the sound off, running Fox News, "they'll take us both."

"Apart from that."

"You have the natural ability to make a person feel something, you know? That's special." Terry adjusted his sunglasses, Shane thinking maybe he was getting a little teary-eyed again, or maybe he just liked the Jim Jones vibe he was giving off. "Sometimes a song, sung by the right person, it'll touch you. You touched me up there just now. I don't know. Maybe I'm drunk."

Hermie nodded vigorously.

"You saw my daughter? Her mother," Terry said, "won't have me in the house, which is why I'm in this situation over here. 'Girl,' that was our song. Our wedding song. Seems dumb, no?"

"People pick terrible songs for their weddings," Shane

said, and then told Terry about his job working weddings, all the times he sang "Wild Horses" for newlyweds.

"No one *listens* anymore," Terry said. "Words used to mean something." He looked over at Hermie. "No offense."

Hermie shrugged.

"Anyway," Terry said, "you seem like a nice guy in a bad situation. So. Maybe I can help you. Do you want help?"

"I could use a friend," Shane said.

"I could be a friend." Terry reached into his back pocket and pulled out his wallet, slid a business card over to Shane. One side was in English, the other in Spanish, but both were for a dentist named Marco Degolado in Los Algodones, Baja California, right over the Mexican border, according to the thumbnail map printed on the card.

"You got any warrants?" Terry asked.

"No," Shane said.

"That's two hours from here. Two exits before Yuma. Easy in and out of Mexico, all the snowbirds go there for dental care when they're down here. They're liberal with their opiates and antibiotics in Mexico." Shane nodded. "Dr. Degolado knows his way around minor surgery as well. He's a friend too." Shane nodded again. His foot *was* killing him. "Let me make a call."

"You'd do that?"

"You walk into JFK with that," Terry said, "you won't walk out."

Shane looked over at Hermie. He gave Shane an affirmative nod. What the fuck went on in *that* guy's fucking mind?

"All right," Shane said. "Set it for tomorrow afternoon?"

"What's your name?"

Shane thought for a moment. "My friends," he said, "call me Gold Mike."

"What do you want the doctor to call you?"

"Mike Voski."

Terry picked up his cell phone. "Give me five minutes," he said, and then headed outside, which gave Shane a chance to casually snatch up Terry's car keys from the table. He turned and looked out the window to where Terry's Benz was parked, around the corner from where Terry stood, hit the unlock button, watched the car's lights blink twice, set the keys back down.

Hermie the Clown didn't utter a word, so Shane said, "You a monk or something?"

Hermie stared at Shane for a few seconds, then said, out loud, "You ever meet a chatty clown?"

"Can't say I have."

"That's part of the game." He reached over and picked up the car keys. Hit the button. Lights flashed again. Locked.

"How about I give you fifty dollars and we call it even?" Shane said.

Hermie said, "How about everything you've got in your wallet?"

Shane had his gun tucked under his shirt and could have, he supposed, shot Hermie, done him like Han Solo did Greedo, but Shane wasn't yet the unprovoked murdering type. "Not gonna be much more than fifty." He dug out his wallet, pulled out everything, set it on the table, sixty-seven bucks.

Hermie took it all. "Not personal, you understand."

"Just two guys doing business," Shane said.

Hermie stood up then, gathered up all his belongings, then pulled out his own business card, everyone in this fucking place the kings of Vista Print, apparently. It said:

HERMIE THE CLOWN
Parties. Charity Events. Private Functions. Restaurant &

Bar PR.
NO KIDS 18+ ONLY
SEE WEBSITE FOR RATES/CELEBRITY PHOTOS
Hermietheclown.com
Phone: 760-CLOWN-69
E-mail: Hermie@Hermietheclown.com

"I'll be back in a few days," Hermie said. "If you're coming back."

"I'm coming back."

"You'd be good in the clown game. You've got a nice presence."

"Thanks," Shane said.

"I got my teeth capped in Los Algodones. Can't have janky teeth and be a clown. Freaks people out. Terry hooked me up." Hermie went silent again, like he was trying to get Shane to ask him a question.

"And then what?" Shane finally said.

"And then I have to do Terry favors, periodically. Drop things off. Take out the garbage sometimes. Clean up his room. Favors. So, if you're not willing to do that, I'd say keep moving, hoss."

There it was.

"He really Jewish?" Shane asked.

"His brother was a rabbi," Hermie said.

"Was?"

"Died."

"Natural causes?"

"I didn't ask for an autopsy."

"Out here?"

"Las Vegas," Hermie said. "Everyone here is always trying to get to Las Vegas, everyone in Las Vegas is always trying to get somewhere else, no one happy to be any one place."

"You make a lot of sense, for a clown."

"You'd be surprised what a guy can learn by staying quiet." He looked outside, where Terry was still on the phone. "My Uber is here." Hermie stood there for a moment, shifting back and forth in his big red shoes. "He doesn't have a daughter," Hermie said, then closed a giant, exaggerated zipper across his mouth, locked it, tossed away the key, and walked silently back out into the heat of the day. Hermie bumped fists with Terry, got into a waiting Prius, and drove off.

Shane unlocked the Benz again.

Terry came back in a few minutes later. "You're all set, Gold Mike," he said.

"What do I owe you?" Shane asked.

"Doctor will have a couple prescriptions for you to bring back."

"That all?"

"Well," Terry said, "you'll need to go back for a follow-up. In which case, I might have something for you to deliver. Could be you come to find you like Mexico."

"I'm gonna need wheels."

"You beam here?"

"No," Shane said. "Car broke down. It won't be fixed for at least a week."

Terry tapped a pen against his lips. "Okay," he said. "How about I have Enterprise drop off a car for you. Nothing fancy, you understand. What do you have for collateral?"

Shane pondered this for a moment, then reached under his shirt and put his gun the table.

Shane waited until Cactus Pete's was in full swing to make his move. Terry wasn't kidding about the clientele: a steady stream of men with brush cuts and tucked-in polo shirts were followed by men and women in business suits, mostly of the off-the-rack variety, not a lot of tailored sorts doing time in Indio's courthouse. Terry came out a couple times to take phone calls, cops and attorneys greeting him as they passed by, Shane watching from his window as they all glad-handed each other.

Shane took Gold Mike's head, hands, and feet out of the safe, refilled the freezer bag with some fresh ice to help with the smell, zipped the bag back up, and headed downstairs. It was about seven, the sun still up, at least 105 degrees, and Shane saw that there were now anthill mounds rising up through the cracks in the parking lot pavement. The lot was full, a dozen Ford F-150s with American flags and 1199 Foundation stickers in the window, a couple Lexuses, a few BMWs, another five nebulous American cars, a surprising number of motorcycles, a couple Benzes. There was a Mexican kid, maybe six or seven, sitting on the tailgate of an F-150 parked next to Terry's Benz, eating a Popsicle, playing on his phone. Shane's rental, a white Ford Fiesta, was parked next to Terry's Benz.

"You staying here?" Shane asked the kid.

"On the other side of the fairgrounds." The kid pointed beyond the courthouse and jail.

Shane looked down the block. There was, in fact, a giant county fairground right next to the jail and courts. Across the street was an A-frame Wienerschnitzel cut-and-pasted from the 1970s, a fire station, an Applebee's, a used car lot. He tried to imagine what it would be like to grow up here. Figured it was like anywhere else. Either you lived in a happy home or you lived in a shitty one.

"You should go home," Shane said. "It's late."

"My dad works at the jail," the kid said.

"Oh yeah?"

"He's inside having a drink."

"What's he do there," Shane said, "at the jail?"

"Something with computers."

So probably not a cop. That's good. "You see anything weird here?"

The kid looked at Shane for a few seconds, like he couldn't be sure of his answer, then said, "I saw a clown. Like in that movie."

"What movie?"

"I didn't see it," the kid said. "But my cousin? He saw it and said it was fucked up."

Shane looked around but didn't see Hermie. "Recently? The clown I mean."

"Couple minutes, I guess."

Odd.

"You do me a favor?" Shane asked.

"I'm not supposed to talk to anyone," the kid said, "cuz my dad says the East Valley is filled with criminals and pedos and losers and that's just who he works with."

"Yeah, that's smart." Shane pointed at his foot. He'd wrapped it in a towel and then taped his flip-flop to it, so he could walk around a bit better. It looked absurd. "Could you just run over and get me a bucket of ice from the front desk?"

The kid looked at Shane's foot. "What happened?"

"Stepped on a nail."

"Must have been pretty big."

"You do this for me or not?"

The kid slid off the back of the truck and headed to the hotel's lobby, which gave Shane the chance to pop open the unlocked trunk of Terry's Benz, drop the freezer bag in, and then close it.

* * *

Shane got in the Fiesta—it smelled weird inside, like vinegar and shoe leather and wet newspapers—started it up, turned left on Highway 111 out of the hotel, so he wouldn't pass Cactus Pete's, since he'd told Terry he wasn't leaving until the morning, then kept going, driving west into the setting sun, his left foot inside a bucket of ice. He rolled past the presidents—Monroe, Madison, Jefferson—then was in La Quinta—Adams, Washington—and into Indian Wells, then Palm Desert, just another snowbird in a rental car, could be anyone, so he opened the Fiesta's moon roof, let some air in, get that weird smell out. Then he was in Rancho Mirage, passing Bob Hope Drive, then rolling by Frank Sinatra Drive, Shane starting to feel like he'd gotten away with it, so he took out his burner, called the anonymous Crime Stoppers hotline, was patched through.

"This is going to sound crazy," Shane said, now in Cathedral City, passing Monty Hall Drive, a street named for a guy who'd spent his entire career disappointing people by giving them donkeys instead of cars, "but I swear I saw a man at the Royal Californian in Indio chopping up a human head. He put it all into a bag in the trunk of his Mercedes."

By the time he finished his story, Shane was in downtown Palm Springs, rolling north down Indian Avenue. His left foot was numb, but the rest of his body felt alive, sweat pouring down his face, his shirt and pants damp, even though the AC was cranked at full blast, the moon roof just cracked. He'd go back to LA tonight, get all the pills from the storage unit, then torch it, now that he was thinking straight. Then he'd turn around and head to Mexico, get his foot operated on, since he had an appointment already, and Terry was going to be in a jail cell for a good long time, maybe forever. And then he'd just keep rolling east, until he got back to Upstate New York. Find his father at some Indian casino, see if he wanted to start a duo, figure out how to have a life together, Shane thinking, *Whoa, what? Am I high?* Shane thinking his foot was probably infected, that what he was feeling was something bad in his blood, sepsis most likely, and then he was passing the road to the Palm Springs Ariel Tramway, burning it out of town, the fields of windmills coming into view, Shane finally taking a moment to look in the rearview mirror, to make sure there weren't a hundred cop cars lined up behind him, and thinking, for just a moment, that he was really fucked up, that he was really hallucinating some shit, that he needed to get some real meds, because sitting right there in the backseat, a gun in his hand, was a fucking clown.

PART IV

ILL WIND

SPECTERS

BY T. JEFFERSON PARKER

Anza-Borrego

Borrego Springs is a tidy, low-slung desert town surrounded by Anza-Borrego State Park, the largest in California. The town has over three thousand people. The park is one of California's wild places—mountain lions, bighorn sheep, abundant reptiles, birds, and wildflowers spread for miles.

Driving in, I looked out at the pale mountains rising in the west and east, a green splash of distant palms, and a wash of orange wildflowers on white sand. It was already ninety-one degrees on this May morning.

My name is Harold Bear and I'm the sole proprietor of Bear Investigations, an LLC. I'm half Luiseno Indian, which puts me in good standing with my tribe and band, though we—the Bear Valley band—are considered "unrecognized" by the United States. I have four employees.

I'd been hired to find Julie Spencer, who went missing four days prior, her abandoned Porsche Cayenne found on Pala Indian land not far from here. Julie was the wife of Congressman Todd Spencer (R), who represented my district in north San Diego County. I first met Spencer just three days ago—when he hired me—though we had both fought in Fallujah back in 2005. We never crossed paths in that bloody battle.

I found the Desert Springs Motel and pulled into the lot. The motel was owned and operated by Dan Morrison, a platoonmate of then Private First Class Spencer. Spencer had earned himself a Silver Star for pulling Morrison from a burning Humvee. Thus making him able to campaign for Congress as a war hero. Todd and Dan had been part of a convoy attacked in what we Americans called East Manhattan— Iraq being shaped roughly like New York City. I had fought in Queens.

The Desert Springs Motel was classic midcentury modern. Which meant a three-sided horseshoe of freestanding bungalows built around a swimming pool and parking. The aqua neon sign sun-blanched and eaten by rust.

When I got out of the car, the hum of air conditioners greeted me in the heat. The wildflower bloom was over for the year, but the motel still looked busy. Young parents and kids in the pool. Desert all around. House windows shimmering in the hills.

The office was a stucco block with a canvas awning. There were blinds behind the glass front door and an intercom built into the wall. A slot for mail. A camera was recessed just above the doorframe, taking aim at my face from close range.

I tried the door and it was locked. I pushed the talk button on the intercom, said my name, and asked to see Mr. Morrison.

"He's not available at this time." The woman's voice was muffled and soft, sounded like it was a hundred yards away.

"I'd like to come in."

"Why?"

"There's something important I need to discuss with Mr. Morrison."

"But he's not available."

"We fought in Fallujah at the same time."

"Put a business card in the mail slot. It's the way we do it here."

"I don't do it that way. This is important. Please open the door."

I held my PI card toward the camera. The card itself gives me no powers at all, legally, but it is an assuring or sometimes intimidating thing to certain people.

Then I heard a man's voice in the background. I couldn't make out what he said. A beat of silence.

"I suppose you can come in," she said.

The dead bolt clanged open and in I went. The lobby was very small and poorly lit. Nowhere to sit. I'm a big man and unhappy in tight spaces. There was a counter on which brochures stood tilted up in a box—desert activities.

The young woman behind the counter looked late thirties, with tired brown eyes and thinning tan hair. Her smock was tan also and a mini mic was clipped to one shoulder strap. Her name plate said *Abigail*. She looked like people I'd known who were undergoing chemotherapy—pale, braced, and accepting. Making the best of it. She said that Mr. Morrison wasn't in, and they had no vacant rooms.

When Abigail receded into an inner shadow, the man's voice came through a speaker above the closed door behind her. Above the speaker was another camera, aimed again right at me.

"Can I help you, Mr. Bear?" he asked. His voice was thin and unhurried.

"I'm a private investigator working for Representative Todd Spencer. I need just a few minutes of your time."

"Are you part of any media or news organizations?"

"I am not."

"Please give me a few minutes to get ready," said the presumed Dan Morrison. "Abigail, you may offer Mr. Bear some water."

She handed me a cold bottle from a small refrigerator behind the counter.

"Thanks, Abigail. I see the motel is full, or almost."

"For the heat and pool. Excuse me."

She turned away and went through the door behind her. Before that door closed, I glimpsed the room beyond, sunlit through the shades, a plaid stuffed chair, a coffee table, an IV drip station waiting in the corner.

I sipped the water and looked at the brochures. Stared into the camera over Abigail's door. I don't like being maybe watched, but maybe not. The camera lens was about the diameter of a .45-caliber bullet.

"Mr. Bear," the man's voice said through the speaker, "exit the lobby and go right, to bungalow six at the end of the first row. The door is open."

I considered Abigail's closed door, then pushed back outside. The blinds banged on the glass. When I got to bungalow six, the door was cracked.

"Come in."

It was dark inside at first, even with the sunlight following me in. A man sat on a retro orange vinyl sofa.

"Please sit in front of me."

The folding chair was small and wooden, and I wondered if it would agree with my 240 or so pounds. I sat. The chair so far, so good.

My eyes adjusting to the dark, I looked directly at Dan Morrison, his face shaded by a black ball cap, bill tugged down low. Aviator sunglasses. A long-sleeved black shirt buttoned all the way, black pants, black canvas sneakers, black socks. White tufts of hair below the cap.

"I have no refreshment to offer you," he said.

"The water is good."

"Do not look at me with pity."

"I promise not to."

The room focused around me: bookshelves, an old-style TV—possibly black-and-white—in one corner facing a recliner. Blinds on the windows, which faced the parking lot and pool. Framed photographs on the walls, California's natural wonders, mostly.

"How is Todd?" he asked. As through the intercom, his voice was thin and faint, as if coming from a longer distance.

"He would tell you he's running for reelection against some big money," I said. "And campaigning hard. I can tell you he's anxious and worried. His wife Julie went missing four days ago. They found her car abandoned out by Harrah's in Valley Center. There are signs of foul play."

Morrison seemed to think about this. His expression was impossible to read behind the sunglasses and steep black bill of the ball cap. In the shuttered light I could see the flesh coiled on his cheeks, evidence of fire and surgery. His nose and lips looked incomplete, like features that had never matured. Features made for a life in darkness.

"Do you think Todd is responsible for her disappearance?" he asked.

"Should I?"

"I'm not qualified to say. I know little of Todd except what happened in Iraq. I know nothing of his wife. I can't help but think you've wasted your time coming all the way out here."

"Go to the man's character," I said. "I want to know how he behaved that day in Fallujah."

A long, air-conditioned pause. He was considering.

"I was in that city the day your Humvee went up," I said. "Over in Queens, going door-to-door."

"Do you think about it a lot?" he asked.

"Not anymore."

Morrison grunted softly. Maybe a dry chuckle. "I think about it every day," he said. "I admire people like you, who forget."

"Almost forget."

"Do you use alcohol or drugs?"

"Not drugs."

"Being a Native, you must have your issues with the drink. I used to drink oceans of bourbon and eat pills by the handful. Finally overdosed but the skies cleared. A good doctor. She got me through, and I haven't self-medicated for four years. I take aspirin when my skin heats up."

"I admire that."

"No pity, Mr. Bear. I asked you once."

I considered explaining I felt no pity in my admiration, but that would have been a small truth within a larger lie: I did pity him, and the world did too. But why should Dan Morrison have to endure that? Why shouldn't he be able to live in a remote desert motel, unavailable?

"We had to make a run to the palace," he said. "Uday's old place in Volturno."

"I remember it," I said.

"We were on a humanitarian mission that day." I heard the controlled emotion in his thin voice. Forced calm. "We had a transport truck full of food and medical supplies for the friendlies. Not one Iraqi showed up to claim a handout. Not even kids. The imams would have them arrested or worse. You must remember the saying, *If you deal with Americans, you die.*"

"Certainly," I said.

"Spencer and I were part of security. It was a terrible road. The insurgents were thick in Fallujah by then—twenty-four different groups we considered 'hard core.' And even Saddam's enemies were starting to hate us. We'd been making lightning raids every day and there was always collateral damage. Or so the Iraqis claimed.

"No trouble on the way in. We sat in that Humvee like a couple of nervous rats while the rations and first aid kits were loaded out. Todd acted a little above things. Cocky. Like he wasn't born to die or get blown up in this dirty little war. He talked about running for office when he got home. Looking back now, I think he was terrified. I know I was. Our Humvee had just been up-armored with an add-on kit and some improvised stuff. Hillbilly armor. Which made it more prone to roll over. At any speed, a Humvee is a rollover waiting to happen. As you know."

"I saw one do that," I said.

Morrison studied me for a moment, then stood and walked into the kitchen. I heard a refrigerator open and close. He was a wiry man of average height. He moved slowly, with a hint of the spectral in his sunglasses, tufts of white hair and the all-black clothing. He carried himself with heavy deliberation, like an older man, or a warrior who had been wounded once and forever. I knew from my investigation that Morrison was forty-five—three years older than me.

He set another bottled water on the table in front of me. Sat again and picked up a remote to open the blinds on one of the front windows, allowing in slightly more light.

"When we started back, Todd and I were on point, not the rear guard. It's all about seeing, as you know. You're looking for those roadside bombs in anything that looks harmless and common—a ruined tire, a dead dog, a pile of trash, a blown-out vehicle that wasn't there last time. The insurgent bomb makers were crafty. The bombs that worry you most are the ones you never see, the ones set off by phone. And that's what we hit. One of the big boys. Made by Rocket Man himself. Remember him?"

"It was big news when we nailed him."

"Caught him at home, with a bomb schematic up on his computer screen. Anyway, the hajis had dug in after we'd passed through, somehow dodging our patrols and helos and surveillance drones. In broad daylight. I used to think their Allah was a better god than ours, the way they could get away with things like that.

"Then the world blew up and I was upside down. Saw the road through the windshield, smelled the gas. Todd had been blown out of the vehicle. His door was gone, armor and metal blown off at the hinges. A blessing, because the Humvee doors liked to lock up in a blast, could trap you inside, where you'd cook. I couldn't get my restraint off. It was stuck and I had one shoulder dislocated and the other wrist fractured. My limbs would not answer my will. I thought my back was broken. I struggled in place, felt the gas spilling onto my legs. Prayed and screamed. Screamed and prayed. The world went whump and the Humvee shivered, then Todd was back inside but he couldn't get the damned strap off either because the latch had melted. He started sawing away at it with his utility knife. The vehicle was almost fully engaged by then. A pyre. Todd kept crawling outside for air, then back in to help me. Face black and his hair scorched. I remember that. He finally collapsed my bad shoulder and pulled me outside into the dirt. I rolled around like a dog to put the flames out. Heard the sniper fire but I couldn't get my legs under me. Figured my spinal cord was ruined. Todd ran to some K-rails for cover. I felt abandoned. I knew it was just a matter of time until the snipers got me."

I imagined big, confident, above-it-all Todd Spencer proned out behind the K-rails. He'd gotten Morrison out of the frying pan but into the fire. Then barreled away through the sniper rounds to safety. Did that make him half hero and half coward?

"Air support finally showed up and the snipers got blown to kibble and bits," said Morrison. "The convoy circled back to us, got Todd and me into a truck. The pain was not of this world. Nothing compares to being burned. Nothing. It changed my life far beyond the booze and narcotics. I remember the corpsman shooting me with morphine and he couldn't figure out why I was still awake and wailing. He hit me with another pen and the next thing I knew I was in Germany. I wake up in Germany often."

He held up the remote again and opened the blinds a little more, and I saw Morrison's violently cabled flesh. He looked monstrous but somehow undefeated.

"How did the pain change your life?" I asked. "Beyond the bourbon and the pills?"

"It made me realize that character is not fate and fate is not character. I had a high school English teacher who taught us the exact opposite."

I thought about that for a beat. "Spencer got the Silver Star for saving your life."

"I wanted him to have it. I was learning to embrace the life he'd given me, while detesting the man I'd been changed into. This thing you see . . ." He set down the remote on the coffee table and opened his empty hands as if presenting himself to me.

In that moment I wondered if war-hero Congressman Todd Spencer hated himself.

"Todd could have been anyone," said Morrison, reading

my speculation. "The least of my concerns was who pulled me from the fire, and if he could have done better. Could *I* have done better? A burning man cannot always defeat a military-grade body harness that's been soldered shut by an explosion."

"So, your fate was not your character? And Todd's fate was not his?"

"Far from it. And that is a central truth of life. Clearly proven by war."

I thought of Todd Spencer's eventual fate in Fallujah, the IED that blew his foot and lower leg off not three weeks after his act of alleged heroism.

"What do you know about the missing wife?" he asked.

I told him of Julie Spencer's gambling and shopping enthusiasms, the psychotic breakdown she'd suffered two years past, her drinking. I noted the stress of Julie being her husband's reelection campaign manager, and the concerted Democratic efforts to unseat him in the coming election.

"I've donated to Spencer's campaigns over the years," said Morrison, his thin voice shivering in the air conditioner's hum like a stalk of wheat in a breeze. "Modestly. He doesn't stand for my politics, but he's a brother and a marine and he saved what's left of me."

"No contact with him since Fallujah?"

"None. Some memories you don't want to see, face to face." Another dry sound that might have been a chuckle.

"What are your politics, Mr. Morrison?"

"I have none in a partisan sense. It's liberating. It frees one up to begin at the beginning."

"Of what?"

"Everything."

Another long moment of air-conditioned quiet. Morrison

was still, hands on his knees, a black-clad apparition with a voice. Then he slowly reached up and took the sunglasses off. Dark eyes in a face that looked like a heated thing, still melting.

"What did you bring home from the war, Mr. Bear?"

"I left as much as I could over there."

"Oh, but there's always something that follows you back. Like a dog that will do anything to remain with you. It doesn't have to be a ruined face like mine, or a blown-off leg like Todd's."

I nodded and thought back to Queens. Hot and crowded and beginning to boil with hate. The door-to-door searches. All of us hot to find the Blackwater killers, and Fallujah turning against us like a rising tide. I remembered a small home, one of hundreds, the smell of lamb and coriander and cumin. Dark inside. Always dark inside. Then sudden movement, face-close fire, muzzle flash and the air thick with lead and gunpowder and screams. Jordan down behind me. Medina in the doorway. By the time I got back to him Medina was still where he had fallen, floating in blood. It seemed to take us forever to shoot those people. Another forever to drag Medina back inside, out of sniper sight. Forever again to get off his helmet and pack the hole in his chest with a roll of QuikClot. Him staring straight at me as his eyes fogged over and his body seized and went still.

"I lost Medina," I said. "A good man. We entered a dwelling and met heavy fire."

"You lost him?"

"He was lost," I said, picking my words carefully so as not to adjust in any way the memory that I had built for myself. My accounting. My truth. "And I was there. I replay those minutes sometimes. Often."

Medina. Could I have done more?

"You replay them, the minutes, looking for what you did wrong," said Morrison.

"Correct."

"And if you don't find anything at first, you keep replaying them again and again. Looking for something new. The smallest thing you could have done that would have changed the fate of Medina."

I nodded.

"You torture yourself with a changeable truth."

I took a deep breath and shifted in my chair. "I would like for there to be an answer. As to whether or not I was at fault."

"And why it took you so long to do things, while Medina bled out?"

I felt my chest hitting my shirt. I listened to the air conditioner in the half-light of the bungalow. Saw through the blinds fractured images of children jumping into a swimming pool.

"Which leads us to the curse of the living," said Morrison.

"Yes. Why him but not me?"

"Which should be embossed on our motto right beside *Semper Fi.*"

"I thank him in my dreams," I said. "Medina. He always accepts."

"We were the lucky ones," said Morrison. "We have managed to move forward."

I nodded again.

"Please give Todd my best wishes," he said. "Tell him I bear no grudge for what he did or didn't do."

I took a stool in a bar called the Roost, just off Christmas Circle in Borrego Springs. Ordered a double vodka on ice and knew there could easily be more before the sun had set on this day. Who knew? I might even spend the night.

I looked at that drink for a long time before taking the first sip. When I did, the promise was all there for me, as it always had been: strength, confidence, luck. And the wilds, never far away in my Luiseno blood. A mirror behind the bar aimed my face back at me. The TV volume was off as the newspeople discussed the virus. I appreciated their silence.

Especially appreciated it when the screen went to Todd Spencer's somber image from his press conference the day before. There he was, waving a fistful of papers at the press and media. I couldn't help but read the caption on the TV screen: *Republican congressman Todd Spencer refused to answer questions yesterday about his missing wife, Julie . . . Later he renewed the attack on his Democratic opponent, Najat Amir, whom without evidence Spencer has accused of being terrorist-sponsored . . .*

I wasn't sure if I wanted Spencer to be lying about Amir or telling the truth. More to the point, after my talk with Dan Morrison, what could I possibly make of Todd Spencer?

As the vodka took me back to that day in Queens again, I smelled the woodsmoke and the lamb and the cumin wafting through that crowded labyrinth of a street. I thought of Spencer and Morrison and Medina, and how the net of that war had snagged us. And hundreds of thousands more. I tried hard to put all of us into some kind of historical and spiritual perspective, to see us all as just blips of life in a vast universe. But I couldn't. We are not blips. I will not be a blip. Vodka.

I looked at the mirror again, at the reflected snout of one Harold Bear—Luiseno Indian, husband, father, son, and brother. Private investigator. Ex-marine. And I thought: *You are okay. As okay as you are ever going to be.*

I sat another hour. I'm always surprised how far a mind can wander and still find its way back, how many thoughts and memories can race through you in one slender hour of life. Fallujah. My son and daughter. First touching the girl who would become my wife in the San Luis Rey Mission when I was fourteen.

Dan Morrison sent me a text saying he'd let me know if he thought of anything that might help me regarding ex-Pfc Todd Spencer and his missing wife.

The bartender gave me a look. I shook my head, brought out my wallet on its belt chain. Paid up, left a nice tip and the rest of the vodka.

OCTAGON GIRL

BY CHRIS J. BAHNSEN

Desert Hot Springs

Wearing a camo bikini, Blythe stepped onto the octagonal platform and began her stride around the cage perimeter. Above her head, she held a white card with the number three on both sides. The upper rows were mostly empty, but there was still a decent crowd of a few thousand. This was her first gig at the new sports arena. Just opened in Desert Hot Springs, it was already becoming *the* venue for MMA fights in the Coachella Valley.

God, we needed this place.

Many in the crowd looked as if they'd climbed out of a fissure in the crusty ground, skin clay-colored, eyes deeply crow-footed from squinting against the sun glare and the sand pelting in off Banning Pass. Blythe knew them as hard cores of the low desert, who would not leave DHS, damn the crime, the druggies, the hell temps now topping 120 most every summer.

Catcalls and whistles, the heat of many eyes, affirmed that for the one minute between rounds, Blythe was the center of this raucous beer-soured universe. She let each platform heel come down in time with the hip-hop loop bumped on the PA, just firm enough to shake her goods without being herky-jerky—a flaw she'd noticed in other girls from the agency.

She raised the card higher, felt a slight pinch from one of her nipple covers. The only action her body had seen in weeks because her man Sandro practiced celibacy before a

246 // PALM SPRINGS NOIR

fight. Inside the cage, he sat taking instructions from Franco, his trainer. On the opposite side, Musaff Ali panted on his stool, coal-skinned, face goose-egged from Sandro's accuracy of hand and foot.

Blythe finished her lap and stepped down to the floor where a director's chair waited. She smiled at her son Logan, who sat a few yards away in a reserved section, rivers of yellow gold hair over blue eyes. They'd grown bluer with each of his eleven years, about all his father had left behind before drifting on during her third trimester. Logan grinned back at her while sucking soda through a straw.

As she took her seat a buzzer sounded round three.

The two fighters knocked gloves in the center of the cage and began stalking one another. Sandro, carved yet lithe in tight green shorts and fingerless fight gloves, was a fan favorite. Undefeated at 14–0, he wanted to turn pro soon and move to LA, the three of them. Besides his smooth Latin looks and winning record, his growing fan base would also help gain the Ultimate Fighting Championship's notice.

Blythe could see herself moving up with him. The week before, she'd driven to North Hollywood to a casting call for Octagon Girls with the UFC. Invited there based on head and body shots she'd sent in. Her audition went well, she thought. But it would be two weeks before she heard anything. Either way, after popping out a baby at eighteen, waitressing, and co-caring for her father until last year, her time had finally arrived.

Ali tried a takedown on Sandro, who slipped out of the hold and threw a spinning backfist. It struck the right side of Ali's head: he wobbled but kept on his feet.

Watching Sandro's predatory intensity, Blythe smiled to herself. All she could think of was how the sexual tension would boil over tonight in his bedroom. Actually, it was *their* bedroom now, as of five weeks ago when she and Logan moved in.

After a faked front kick, Sandro torpedoed a straight right hand, dead on Ali's glass jaw. The big man bounced off the cage and went down, a felled tree with a canopy of dreads. Sandro charged in, but the ref blocked his attack. Ali lay twitching in his dreams.

Blythe mentally adjusted Sandro's record to 15–0. If he reached 16–0, a fightwear company had offered him sponsorship, *mas dinero*. Good things for him meant good things for her, and Logan. Just one more win.

As Sandro eased his dusty pickup away from the arena, he kept asking, "Who's the greatest?" and from the backseat, Logan chanted, "San-dro! . . . San-dro!" until they all joined in.

Here they were, already becoming a family, and Blythe wished her big sister could see them now. Jackie had been against her moving out. Wanted her to stay put at the Sky Valley house they inherited after their father passed. Logan needed stability, a real home, Jackie said.

"What he needs is a male role model," Blythe had snapped back. "Not my hard-ass sister trying to be one." She still felt bad for saying it.

The night winds of March gushed through the half-open windows. Blythe zipped up her hoodie. On Dillon Road, the pickup had to slow down behind a hulking motor home.

Sandro gestured through windshield. "Fucking snowbirders."

"Snowbirds," Blythe gently corrected. "Hey, they tip good, mister."

Sandro grinned at her, and his right hand took her left. She ran a thumb over his stony knuckles. Such deadly hands, yet nothing but adoring when they touched her body.

* * *

By the time the truck scooped into a dirt-tracked mobile home park, Logan was dozing. Mature palm trees danced to a gust. They passed an empty trailer space, now a community trash depot, heaped with broken pallets, a car seat, stained mattresses. Two scrap dogs sniffed at the spilled guts of a garbage bag. At least it wasn't gang turf, Blythe thought.

In the carport, Sandro draped an arm across the boy's shoulders and steered him inside a dingy double-wide. It was the first time Blythe had seen him in such a fatherly role with her son—more often he acted like an older brother with Logan, playing combat video games with him, or teaching him grappling moves.

After Logan flumped onto the living room couch, Sandro unfolded a sheet over him. The boy would have to sleep there until Sandro cleared the spare room of training gear.

Warped wood paneling covered the walls, bare except for a Bruce Lee poster. Okay, so what if he didn't seem in a rush to make the house family friendly. Why bother, with LA coming? Anyway, this was a big step for him, asking her to move in, and she didn't want to push it. He grew up an orphan in Mexico City. A loner his whole life.

"I remember only my mother take me down an alley and leave me there," he told her. Blythe could relate. When she and Jackie were in junior high, their own mother ran off with their older cousin. It seemed too easy, how people could erase you from their life, as if wiping a soiled shoe on the grass and walking on. But she would show Sandro not all women would bail on him.

Already fast asleep, Logan held his Conor "Notorious" McGregor action figure in one hand. "Why don't they have one of Sandro?" he'd asked her the other day.

The fighter turned to her now.

Blythe stood near the front window in a porch lamp glow and unzipped the hoodie to show him, by the play of shadow and light on her bared form, that the evening had just begun.

When Blythe awoke and brushed her long umber hair aside, she read 9:16 a.m. on the nightstand clock. She panicked, used to waking up way earlier for the breakfast shift at the diner, then remembered she'd traded for the day off.

Sandro stood motionless in the doorframe wearing only boxer briefs. He faced down the hall listening—to what? She said his name. He raised a palm to her for quiet.

Then she heard it too, a *thwick . . . ting . . .*

Sandro's leg muscles flexed, and he stalked down the hall. His hunter's posture unnerved her.

She sprang out of bed.

In the living room, the couch was empty. From the spare bedroom Sandro shouted: "Little fucker!"

She ran to the end of the hall and cut left into the spare room. Sandro stood a few steps inside the doorway. His face burned with anger. Ten feet away, Logan stood rigid beside a wooden training dummy that once belonged to Bruce Lee. His hand was in midgrab of a small, star-shaped throwing weapon lodged in its chest. The dummy had a cylindrical head with two spindles extending from the torso to simulate arms. Sandro had purchased it through an eBay auction for a small fortune. Many times Blythe had seen him bow to it at the start of a workout.

The razor points of the throwing star had made other fresh holes and chips in the wood. Did her boy have any idea how dangerous these things were?

"Where did you get that, Logan?" she asked.

Logan's eyes traveled over her body. Realizing her naked-ness, Blythe stepped farther behind Sandro.

"I found it in the truck, under the seat."

Sandro moved to the dummy. At first, he ignored Logan. His finger probed the fresh pockmarks in the wood.

"I . . . just wanted to make it stick, like Naruto," Logan said.

Sandro pulled out the star and flicked it aside. He snatched Logan by the wrist, yanking him away from the dummy. A wet pop came from Logan's shoulder. He yelped and fell to his knees. Sandro stayed on him and raised a hand over the boy, but Blythe flew onto his muscle-sloped back before it could come down.

"I look that bad?" Blythe asked her sister, who had broken down upon entering the hospital room. Jackie never balled. But then she'd never seen Blythe in a hospital bed, Logan asleep against her with his left arm in a sling. Tenderly, Jackie laid the back of her hand on Blythe's forehead, the only part of her face not bandaged or contused.

After she established that Blythe and her nephew were basically okay, Jackie said, "You can't keep dragging Logan with you every time you shack up with a creep."

Blythe wanted to remind her sister she only lived with one other person, Logan's father. But her nose hurt and her patience was gone. "Jackie, just put a sock in it, okay?" Bad enough she had to deal with questions from the police, and a social worker who tried to bully her into a safe house in Thousand Palms. Bad enough her voice now had a strange bagpipe timbre.

"Did you get my car?" Blythe said.

She had reluctantly called Jackie earlier from the hospital

and asked her to retrieve her Jeep from Sandro's place. Everything else of hers and Logan's would have to be sacrificed. She would not go near him again.

Sporting a butch haircut, both arms sleeved in tats, Jackie nodded. "Where're you going? Can you even drive like that?" She had agreed to trade cars, her nondescript white Toyota Camry for Blythe's burnt-red Cherokee Sport, so Sandro couldn't trace her whereabouts. Since Blythe hadn't pressed charges, he might not be held long. But getting hooked into the system, social workers knocking on her door, no, that was not an option. Neither was going back home like Jackie wanted. Sandro would come looking for her sooner or later.

"What about that special item?" Blythe asked.

"Check way under the front seat."

Earlier that morning, when she awakened in the ER, Sandro had already left her a voice mail. After weepy incoherencies, he actually had the balls to ask if she could bring bail money. She deleted the message.

Jackie moved to her nephew's side of the bed. Softly, so as not to wake him, she ran a finger over his twitching eyebrow. "At least let me take Logan."

Blythe extended her hand. "Keys." The doctor wanted to keep her and Logan another night, but she had her own plans for their recovery.

Dangling the keys out of her sister's reach, Jackie said, "Tell me where you're going first."

"We need the waters."

Chuckwalla Palms was a boutique lodging with only nine units. A bit pricey, but so were most other spa-tels that exploited the natural springs running beneath town. These mini resorts, dotted all over DHS, walled off guests from a city gone to seed.

At the front desk, the gap-toothed man in an aloha shirt didn't so much as blink at Blythe's face, Logan's arm sling, when he handed over the room key. Locals had seen it all in this town, now more of a desert asylum for misfits, swingers, drifters, career criminals, and lately, migrating millennials.

Blythe had booked a suite that came with a private whirlpool, so they wouldn't have to use the public pool. Such a room would drain her savings, but she needed time to think and heal, to keep out of Sandro's reach.

The back room of the suite was a small clay cabana, whirlpool tub sunk below a wooden deck. A tinted sunroof overhead. Logan, wearing blue jammers, a cold gel pack strapped to his shoulder, stepped down into the tub. A sunray lit his hair. Halfway submerged, he stopped.

"Keep going, Logan," Blythe said, standing near twin timer dials mounted on the wall. "But leave your shoulder out."

The scent of cannabis touched her nose, wafting in from god knew where. So-called entrepreneurs, hipster types, were converging on the city to open grow facilities. Maybe it would help bring things up, she thought. Or else invite more dopers.

Tentatively, Logan sat on the higher step. Only his head and shoulders above water.

Blythe turned the dials. The calm pool upwelled into a churning froth.

"Hot," he said.

"Uh-huh, so your pores can swallow those magic minerals." Her words conjured her mother. For every scrape, patch of eczema, or bonfire burn she and Jackie endured as children, their mother would bring them to the waters, and it did seem miraculous, how the natural minerals soothed their wounds, rejuvenated their spirits. She remembered the fun of breath-holding contests with her sister in the warm shallows of a public pool, no eye sting when you went under. Like swimming in holy water. At the deep end, Mama sunbathed like a starlet, sweeps of blond hair pushed back by her shades. Blythe could see her there, propped up on her elbows, pretending not to notice stares from men, or her daughters calling for her attention.

Blythe pointed a stern finger at her boy. "Twenty minutes, young man."

In the suite, she finished unpacking the suitcases Jackie had put in the car for them, then placed calls to her booking agent, her boss at the diner, and Logan's school. Told them the same lie: they'd been in a bad car accident, suffering injuries that would keep them home for a couple of weeks.

Twenty minutes later, while Logan leaned against the foot of the queen bed, eyes drooped, Blythe unstrapped his gel pack and finished drying him with a towel.

"I miss Aunt Jackie," he yawned, lying back in bed.

Blythe said, "Me too." But the boy was already asleep. She slid a cool sheet over him until she got to his hurt arm, the blue sling. Quiet tears overtook her. Yes, she had moved in with a creep, just like Jackie said. Stupid. A stupid, bad mother— that's what she was.

In the kitchenette, she made herself a cup of coffee and leaned against the counter. The late March afternoon had risen to eighty-one degrees. Through the wall glass, in the distance above a windbreak, she found the snowy peak of San Jacinto, a steady companion her whole life. Logan's sun-bleached hair was almost as white as the mountaintop. Looking at his resting face, she feared there would be no father figure for him ever again, no happy family.

She checked e-mails with her phone. Nothing from the

254 // Palm Springs Noir

UFC yet. Most of the women at the audition had been in their early twenties. How many more years could her body, pushing thirty, compete? Not many, but what a way to go, right? Traveling the country to strut the best fight venues, streamed internationally. Even if they didn't take her, Blythe resolved right then to save every penny and move herself and her boy to LA anyway. Grab some casting calls for movies.

Digging out the prescription bottle in her purse, she took a Vicodin and dropped it into the steaming mug to melt it. Her broken nose throbbed. Breathing deeply brought a twinge of pain, a chronic reminder that, once Sandro had released his choke hold, she'd fallen to the floor, her ribs hitting a metal leg of the dummy on the way down, then a face-plant into an iron dumbbell plate. Out cold, like Musaff Ali.

Her phone vibrated on the counter. There were three texts from Sandro:

> i wan 2 die 4 what I don
> u no i lov u
> and logan

So, he had his cell phone now, which meant he was back on the street already. Sure enough, a new post on his Instagram page promoted his upcoming fight, in ten days, at the sports arena again. He was out there, free as a tumbleweed. She wondered if she should have pressed charges. No. Somehow she would handle things her own way. For starters, she blocked his cell number.

While Logan slept, Blythe went out to the Camry, hoodie pulled down around her face, and retrieved the weighted beach towel folded up under the driver's seat. Locking herself in the bathroom, she placed the towel on the counter. Her hands undid the folds from a snub-nosed Diamondback .38 Special, the handgun her father had given her when she turned sixteen. And a box of shells. After loading the weapon, she shoved it into the waistband of her jeans and dropped the tail of her blouse over it. The gun's stability felt good against the small of her back.

First gun she ever fired was her father's Sterlingworth shotgun, in the open desert. She was nine. Got thrown to the ground after an ugly explosion. She didn't want any part of the shotgun after that. But he made her stop crying and put the shotgun in her hands again. Told her to say *I am not afraid* then fire the other barrel. The kick wasn't so bad that time because he showed her how to be ready for it. And she felt proud by his smile, one coffee can blown off its hook.

The gun gave her courage. Since leaving the hospital, she'd been avoiding her own reflection. Now, taking a deep breath, Blythe looked into the cabinet mirror. An apparition stared back. A face with gauze cross-taped over the swollen nose, ruined by the macabre colors of Sandro's rage. She experienced again the incredible pressure of his arm around her neck, a steel bar compressing her carotid, his feral growl in her ear. She had quick-tapped his forearm like she saw them do in the octagon. The gesture meant you'd had enough. But there was no ref to jump in.

When she came out of the bathroom, Logan was awake, sitting on the edge of the bed.

"How's the shoulder, my little man?"

"Aches."

His sling was askew, so she had him stand still while she adjusted it. A bolt of pain made him suck in air. She pulled a

Vicodin from her jeans pocket and held it up for him. "After I get you some water, I want you to take half of this, to make it hurt less."

Logan shook his head. "I don't need it. Pain is good."

The back of Blythe's neck tingled.

Whenever he and Sandro had roughhoused, and Logan inevitably got bonked somehow, Sandro coached him to tough it out, pulled him back from tears, and said, *Pain is good . . . pain makes you stronger . . .* She had loved the way Sandro taught him to be strong.

"Please don't ever say those words again," she said.

"Why? What did I say?"

"I'm sorry. Your mama is just in a strange way right now. Never mind, give me a hug." She pulled him close, careful of his sling arm.

Stepping back, Logan held it up for her, the .38, gripped in his hand. "Is this a real gun?"

Blythe eased it from his grasp, but he still held it with his eyes. Her son deserved a straight answer, she decided. Especially now. She laid the .38 across her palm, barrel pointed to the side. "This is to keep us safe."

"From him?" Logan said.

She nodded.

"But he's in jail now, right?"

"He won't stay in jail, honey. That's why we can't go home for a little while."

Logan reached for the gun again, but she tucked it back in her jeans. "Time to put it away."

The boy's eyes converged on the gauze over her nose. "It's my fault he hurt you, Mom. I know I wasn't supposed to use Sandro's stuff."

"No, it isn't your fault, don't ever think that." Blythe's

voice constricted. "It's my fault. I couldn't protect you, so you protected me instead."

He shook his head. "But I didn't. I ran away."

"So you could call 911." She held his face in her hands. "That was a very smart, awesome thing you did."

He shrugged, then his eyes darted behind her. "Mom, a scorpion!" he said, pointing to the marble floor.

The bug idled only a few feet from them, pinkish exoskeleton a translucent window to its dark innards. The stinger was folded downward into the lowered tail.

"Stay here," Blythe said.

As she drifted toward the invader, it did not back away. The stinger rose. With her boot, she quickly stepped on the tail end. Squatting, she used the butt of the gun as a hammer, twisting each blow into the writhing body. Even after the scorpion went still, she kept on hammering and hammering until Logan touched her shoulder. "Okay, Mom."

Lodge time elapsed in a reel of mindless TV, board games on the bed, takeout and pizza deliveries. Logan, young and resilient, didn't need the sling for long as his range of motion in the shoulder improved. Blythe's rib pain faded enough so she could tolerate sit-ups and some floor exercises. The bruises on her face slowly cleared. Her nose, bandage-free, now had a subtle curve to the left but thankfully wasn't flattened any.

Sometimes Logan cried out in his sleep. He told her he was having nightmares of Sandro chasing him. And he was drifting inward, away from her. Was he shifting blame to her for what happened?

Sandro had done this to her son, to them, and she hated him for that. Yet there were also moments when her mind replayed the good times and she pined for what could have been. It was a maddening cycle that manifested as long late-night soaks after Logan crashed, plus Vicodin, washed down with whatever beer was on special at the liquor store.

She was soaking this way when her sister called just after midnight.

Soon as Blythe answered, Jackie blurted, "Your creep was here."

"Sandro? When?"

"Like three minutes ago." Blythe heard the crackle of a joint being hit, hard, before her sister continued. "Fucker wakes me up knocking on the window of the master. He thought I was you, kept calling your name."

"What happened?"

"Not much. I showed him Dad's shotgun and he got gone like real fast."

"You had Dad's shotgun that handy?"

"So, wait, all this shit's gone down, and you think I wouldn't sleep with it like a lover?"

Anger, its molten lava, gushed from Blythe's chest, up her neck and into her cheeks. Now he was terrorizing her sister. "I'm sorry, Jackie, for all of this. I should've gotten a restraining order."

"Hon, I just showed him two barrels' worth of restraining order." Her joint crackled again. "Just come home. You can have your room back."

"Not yet." Blythe wanted off the phone, to think, to plan, to do what? "Soon though. Love ya loads, sis."

"Do *not* go back to that creep, Blythe, no matter how much he begs."

Next morning, northwest of the valley, past the wind farms where a dirt lane dead-ended into open desert, Blythe stood behind Logan, a hundred yards from the car. His arms were extended, the .38 in his hands. Blythe reached around him and held his wrists to help him aim. He needed both thumbs to cock the hammer.

"Just relax," she said, resting her hands on his shoulders. "Now exhale as you squeeze the trigger like I showed you."

A bull's-eye target, drawn on cardboard from a pizza box, was stuck to the spines of a saguaro cactus twenty feet away. Beyond, the desert raced toward the apron of the mountains. Blythe loved the desert at this hour, how the early sun on its upward arc gave this world a flaxen sheen.

She felt Logan's shoulders tense. The gun barrel flinched upward with a *crack* like a giant whip snapping, followed by three echoes slapping off the distant rock face.

Logan lowered the gun. "Cool."

"Right?" Blythe said, mussing his hair.

"How far does a bullet go?"

"Far, but we want to hit the target, not the mountainside." She positioned herself behind him again.

When he brought the gun up to the target, Blythe spoke into his ear: "Pretend the cardboard is Sandro's face."

Logan's hands tightened around the gun. "Yeah . . . I *hate* him."

"I hate him too," Blythe heard herself say, which immediately brought pangs of guilt, as if she were somehow betraying Sandro.

Three days later, on an unusually cool early April evening, they were at the sports arena. Blythe knew the promoter, so they'd slipped through a staff entrance to avoid the pat downs and security wands. She and Logan sat in a reserved row alongside the octagon. Biggest crowd she'd ever seen, maybe five thousand heads. She had taken extra time with her hair and wore her short black leather jacket over a mauve blouse. Tight jeans. She wanted Sandro to see what he could never touch again. *Never is a long time* came a voice deep in her mind.

"Fuck off," she said aloud.

Embarrassed, she looked down at Logan but he hadn't heard her over the crowd noise.

Logan sat frowning, hands clutching the armrests. He had not wanted to come, but she told him if he did, if he met Sandro in the eye, the nightmares would go away. For herself, she hoped it would reduce her flashbacks of the incident.

The first three fights blew by. Then, impossibly, the emcee was back in the cage announcing Sandro Garcia and his opponent, Hank "Inglorious" Stoddard, also undefeated, for the amateur super-welterweight matchup.

Attacked by nauseous fear, Blythe struggled to hold it together. Logan sat low, head sunk into the neck hole of his sweatshirt. She pulled it back down under his chin. "C'mon, Logan. Show him you're a brave boy, not a turtle."

He sat up and repeated the word *turtle*, and for the first time since the assault he actually laughed. The music of it filled her with relief and she laughed with him, thankful for this momentary lifting of a long dark stretch.

Both fighters were in the cage now, loosening up as Chicano rap pumped through the house.

Against her nervous fear, Blythe felt the excitement of fight night coming back.

Sandro shadowboxed and shuffled in her direction.

Blythe stood. *Look at me, asshole*, she willed, even as her knees trembled.

When he saw her, his hands dropped.

"Stand up, Logan, and look at him," Blythe said, reaching her hand down for his. "C'mon, Logan." But her boy had slumped into his chair again.

Through the mesh of the cage, Sandro smiled at her. Blythe did not smile back. She felt untethered, light-headed.

The fighters were called to the center of the cage for instructions from the referee. In a neon-orange sport bikini, some redhead walked the octagon perimeter hoisting a round one card. Decent legs but no flow in her stride, Blythe thought.

When the buzzer sounded round one, she sat, letting herself breathe again.

Inglorious, a muscled slab with a shaved skull, charged in and went for a hip toss. Sandro evaded it and they both ended up on the mat, bodies grappling like angry crabs. Sandro's panther speed allowed him to slip behind Inglorious and throw his right arm around his throat. He wrenched Inglorious back and cradled him between his knees, trapping his neck in the vise of his forearms. In a lion-killer choke, Inglorious was at Sandro's mercy now.

The crowd cheered, and up came the chant: "San-dro . . . San-dro . . ."

Blythe knew what it felt like to be Inglorious, and it reminded her how easily Sandro could have killed her, or her beautiful boy.

"Can we go?" Logan said.

"Not yet, honey."

Any moment now, Inglorious would tap, or black out. But for some reason Sandro released him. Both men jumped up and faced off again. Boos erupted at Sandro for not finishing the job. Why would he do that? Blythe wondered. He *never* gave his opponents a break.

Sandro's feet planted. He looked right at Blythe and

winked, doing nothing when Inglorious threw a right hook that connected solidly against his jaw. The crowd moaned with the impact.

Inglorious went on throwing hooks, uppercuts, elbows to the face, knees to the body. Almost everything landed, the crowd roaring. Yet Sandro, staggered, one eye badly cut, threw nothing back.

Boos and jeers. Plastic beer bottles struck the cage.

The fighters stood slightly apart now, gathering their breath.

Sandro dropped his hands again and stood, as if waiting for a bus.

Reflexively, Blythe shot to her feet. "What the fuck, Sandro!?" she shouted through her hands. Others nearby stood and repeated, "*What the fuck! What the fuck!*" and soon, the whole arena joined, even Logan. Blythe's body vibrated with the energy of the crowd.

This was her city, these were her people, in all their raunchy glory, who bled Mojave sand, bathed in the lustful winds, who were durable as cactus against the changing climate of their lives. Jackie was her people, the coolest, most giving person Blythe knew. Didn't she and Logan need a person like that by their side for the long haul? *Fuck yes we do.* Fuck if the three of them weren't a happy family whose love for one another ran pure as the waters beneath them. So fuck LA anyhow.

I'm a hard core of the low desert, like my father, my sister, and now, my son.

The WTF chant faded and everyone sat back down. Looking over at her boy, Blythe grew teary-eyed, his tender profile bracing her decision.

When she looked toward the cage again, Sandro met her eyes. He nodded as Inglorious rushed in and delivered an uppercut into Sandro's chin. Backed against the mesh of the cage, face a smear of blood, Sandro seemed doomed as Inglorious kept on swinging, Sandro's head getting banged side to side. After what seemed like eons to Blythe, Sandro broke away, so quickly that for a moment Inglorious punched at nothing but mesh, until he looked left: Sandro's fist blazed in striking Inglorious's jaw, hard enough to send his mouth-piece flying.

Inglorious crumpled to the canvas.

A roar swelled from the crowd.

With seconds left in round one, the ref stopped the fight.

Inglorious lay brain-rattled. Sandro wasn't much better off. He stood swaying, fingers grasping the mesh to hold himself up as he gazed toward Blythe. Franco got in his face, screaming angrily. The trainer didn't understand what had gone down.

But Blythe did now.

Sandro had taken a horrendous beating, nearly ruined his perfect record, and possibly his whole career, for her. That meant something, didn't it, his willingness to risk his UFC dream? What other man would do that? Since growing up wild on the mean streets of Mexico City, Sandro had known no other way than the fist. Violence was his currency, his language, and now, his apology to her.

The emcee announced Sandro the winner by knockout to fresh boos and cheers. Entourages of both fighters swelled into the octagon until Blythe could no longer see Sandro.

"Can we go *now*?" Logan said.

In the concession area behind the bleachers, Blythe bought a draft of PBR then leaned against the sidewall. Logan beside her, they watched yabbering men line up to order schooners before the next fight.

"You said we were going, Mom."

As if not hearing the boy, Blythe popped half a Vicodin, chased it down with gulps of beer. By the time she drained the plastic cup, she knew she had to see him. To finish things, one way or another.

A familiar security person walked past and said hello. Blythe smiled, asked if he could do her a tiny favor.

When the *Staff Only* door clicked shut behind them, Blythe lingered in the long bright tunnel. The left tunnel branch, she remembered, led to the men's locker room. To the right, the arena.

Propping Logan against the wall, she lowered her face down to his. "I want you to wait for me right here."

"No! You said we were going!"

"Stop it, right now. Give me one minute. And while I'm gone you do not move from this spot, understand?"

Logan's eyes went wide over her shoulder, toward the sound of shuffling footsteps. Blythe turned, and there was Sandro, head hung down, limping along with one arm slung across Franco's shoulders.

Sandro's head lifted. His dusky eyes gleamed at the sight of her. He spoke Spanish to Franco, who then retreated down the tunnel.

Then it was just the three of them again, like the family they'd almost become. Blythe saw it up close now, the damage of Sandro's self-punishment, his face like a cubist portrait, nostrils stuffed with cotton. A butterfly bandage sealed a cut over his right eye.

He limped to within a few feet of Blythe and dropped to his knees.

Bawling, he sputtered, "*Lo siento mucho* . . . so sorry I hurt you . . . and Logan . . ."

Blythe's own tears came, and she went to him. Sandro

threw his arms around her legs and buried his face in her stomach.

"Shhhh, it's okay." Blythe stroked his sweaty hair. "It's okay, baby."

From her right side, Logan's hand swung down sharply and rapped Sandro on the head. The fighter grunted. His face turned to find Logan standing with the butt end of the .38 raised to strike again. The hatred in the boy's eyes was far beyond his years.

"Logan, no!" Blythe said. Before she could reach for the gun, Sandro's left hand lashed out and knocked it away. The gun skittered along the tunnel floor. Snatching the boy by the throat, Sandro rose from his knees, fresh blood dripping from his hairline. He pushed Logan backward until the boy was pinned against the opposite wall, then began to lift him until his toes left the ground. Logan, choking, clutched at the fighter's hands, unable to budge them.

Sandro's growl rose, more lupine than human.

A contained explosion flashed in the tunnel, Sandro thrown sideways to the ground. Released, gasping for breath, Logan ran down-tunnel to his mother, who stood with the Diamondback hanging at her side. She hugged him tight. Fifteen feet from them, Sandro pushed himself off the floor. A hole in his left shoulder spewed blood down his arm.

Blythe moved in front of the boy and pointed the .38 at the wounded mess lurching toward them. She cocked the hammer, and exhaled.

THE LOOP TRAIL

BY KEN LAYNE

Joshua Tree

The Mojave Desert eats a couple of tourists every summer. It's the nature of the place. More people die around Joshua Tree from car crashes and pill overdoses and trying to run across Highway 62 in the dark than will ever die from a day hike, even in the oppressive heat of monsoon season, but it's the amateur hikers who make the headlines.

A couple of years ago, Joshua Tree became a destination. Not just as a weird desert wilderness a couple of hours from LA, but a weird desert wilderness that had become very popular on Instagram. You see it in music videos, in fashion shoots, the twisted arms of our signature yucca trees turned into backdrops for various celebrities and social media influencers. If everybody is coming out here, it must be all right.

A place with decent cell service and well-stocked grocery stores and stylish Airbnb cabins on every sandy road seems pretty safe to the modern visitor. And if you're used to the easy green paradise of Yosemite, you probably think national parks are all like that: woodsy campgrounds and friendly rangers in Smokey Bear hats.

But the campgrounds in Joshua Tree National Park are just sand, hard-packed sand surrounded by boulders and cactus and scrub brush. There are rattlesnakes coiled on the trails and cholla lying in wait for bare ankles and suburban dog snouts. Most of the campsites close for summer because it's just too hot, but people come anyway and feel lucky to be there at all.

Three seasons of the year, you can walk around in relative comfort. Summer is not one of those seasons. Summer is hard in the desert, even the high desert, where it's fifteen degrees cooler than Palm Springs—and that's still a hundred-plus in July and August.

Besides, it's a haunted land. Desert wilderness is like that.

When the young couple vanished on the Loop Trail at the end of July, it was the Airbnb owner who reported it. They hadn't checked out; their luggage was still in the vacation rental, beer in the fridge, toothbrushes on the sink. And their car was gone.

It was easy to assume they'd been dumb about things. Got lost, got confused, wandered the wrong way, hit one of those canyons without a phone signal, and that was that. The annual human sacrifice to the Mojave. Take them, oh desert gods, so that the rest of us might be spared.

Search & Rescue was out the morning after the pair had been reported missing.

I heard the helicopter rumbling over my little house up near the national park entrance and figured it was a Marine Corps chopper, because those noisemakers liked to fly low right over my dirt-road neighborhood, going back and forth between Camp Pendleton and Twentynine Palms. Always practicing for invading some unlucky country in the Middle East. But this one was making circles just inside the park boundary, maybe two miles away. That had happened a couple of times in recent years, when some amateur rock climber had learned about the reality of gravity and had to be flown out on a stretcher. The chopper would set down and take the injured party to the local hospital. Or to a better hospital if the situation was dire.

Making circles meant lost tourists.

It seemed ridiculous—lost tourists in sight of houses and cell phone towers and the highway—but it was the hottest time of year, when the humidity gets sucked up from the Gulf of California, producing a few good thunderstorms and flash floods once in a while. People get confused in the heat.

Out at Amboy Crater, an hour north of Joshua Tree alongside Route 66, there were a couple of deaths every year. People parked their cars and followed the sandy trail through the lava rock and maybe hiked up to the rim of the old volcano and snapped some pictures of each other. And then they became disoriented on the way back, a way back that is much more treacherous in the midday sun. Even in late springtime. There's no shade. The path that seemed so clear on the way in becomes confusing. Soft bodies and weak hearts don't know how to respond, so they overreact, overheat. With pounding pulses and sweaty faces, the frightened tourists become distraught. Which look-alike sandy path between look-alike piles of black lava rock leads to the rental sedan with the air-conditioning? So many day hikers have died at Amboy Crater that the federal Bureau of Land Management had to put up some big colorful flags to show people the way back to the parking lot.

Just as I was making coffee, I got a call from the little radio station where I work. Nighttime, mostly, although I fill in a daytime shift when necessary. But nighttime is the good time, just me and the airwaves and whatever souls might be listening. Community radio is a different animal than the soundalike FM and AM corporate channels still around at this point in the fractured media environment.

It was Gary, the news editor. "You see the Search & Rescue over there?"

I did. Would I maybe go over and check it out? I said I would. Not my regular duty but I'd done enough of it. Enough to know I preferred the late shift, taking calls from Landers and Sunfair and Yucca Mesa and Pipes Canyon and the base, wherever people listened. Lots of calls about UFOs and meth shacks. Desert stuff. I played a little music between the calls. If you've got a community radio station in your town, you know what I'm talking about.

Professionally equipped with my one necktie and a travel mug, I got in the truck and drove down Quail Springs to the ticket booth of the park's entrance. Marla was in there, scowling out at the world. I nodded hello and showed my annual pass.

"They're at the Loop Trail parking lot," she offered. "Couple of kids."

"Little kids?"

"Young people." She rolled her eyes. I said thanks and drove off before she could get started on the superintendent, or the RVs, or how many months until she could get full retirement. They must've put her in the booth to discourage people from visiting at all.

It was weeks before Labor Day, so the road was mostly empty. I hardly ever drove into the national park. The road was really just a loop that came out at Twentynine Palms, although you could keep going south and eventually come out at the 10, in the low desert. From October to June it was mostly a traffic jam. The people in my rural neighborhood just walked in, when they bothered at all. I loved the park best as my backyard view. It stopped Palm Springs from crawling up the hill, stopped the Inland Empire from spilling all the way up from the San Gorgonio Pass. And it was still full of mountain lions and coyotes and bobcats.

Joshua Tree National Park was mostly lacking in the Joshua tree department. The southern half of the park had none, in fact. Back when it became a national monument—thanks to a well-connected desert-loving Pasadena socialite named Minerva Hamilton Hoyt—it was going to be called "Desert Plants National Monument." Accurate, if not very poetic. Instead, FDR's Department of the Interior named it after the *yucca brevifolia*, or what the Mormon pioneers called the Joshua tree. Imagine having religion so alive in your head that even a raggedy-ass yucca tree full of spikes and spiders reminds you of a biblical hero.

There are a lot more Joshua trees in Mojave National Preserve, another several hours' drive to the northeast, but it's too far from Silver Lake and Echo Park to get much visitation. Which makes it my favorite. But there's no work out there. No radio stations. No listeners. Just a lot of wild and beautiful Mojave Desert.

When I came around the bend, the helicopter was landing in the trailhead parking lot and an NPS cop was standing in the road. There was no place to pull over; so many dimwits had driven off the pavement and into the raw desert that the park service had to build curbs along the whole way. It was like the old Autopia ride in Disneyland. So, I waited until the yellow rescue chopper had lifted off again and the Smokey Bear let me through, although he wasn't happy about letting me turn into the parking lot.

"Trail's closed." He was new. Not young, but new. I fished around the glove compartment for my expired KCDZ press pass and he relented.

A burly retired marine named Miguel was the Search & Rescue captain. He was yelling into a walkie-talkie and pointing at various volunteers with his free hand. They were *all* volunteers. They all looked like hell.

"The dogs gave out," he said. The scent-hound handlers were loading a couple of overweight old dogs into a van. "They couldn't make it back."

It was just an easy loop, maybe three miles total. But boy was it hot, and sticky. I loosened my tie and wiped the sweat off my sunglasses.

"I just need some basics to bring to the station," I said. He didn't have much, but it was enough. I wrote down the names and the ages and then I noticed a cream-colored Acura parked by the pit toilets.

"That's their car," Miguel said. "The dude's car. You can't touch it."

"I don't want to touch it," I said. "Just show me the registration. Or anything else that's interesting."

He shook his head and went back to the dogs and the handlers. What a sorry crew. I took a phone picture of the sedan's license plate and got back in my truck.

Of course I wound up driving to the station in Joshua Tree and typing up the story and recording it for the afternoon news because the morning crew was already home for the day. By the time I'd finished all this unintended work, it was only a couple of hours until my night show. So I went over to the saloon and had a bad early dinner and sweated some more, because Girard refuses to put in air-conditioning and the swamp coolers don't work this time of year.

The press loves a missing-hiker story. And our missing Joshua Tree tourists got the full treatment. From a distance, I mean.

272 // P<small>ALM</small> S<small>PRINGS</small> N<small>OIR</small>

It's the kind of police-beat story you throw together in the newsroom back in Los Angeles, mostly taken from our station's website, with some new bits from the sheriff's department press release and the usual heartfelt statements from the families.

And this one had the bonus of an Instagram-era cautionary tale: They really were just kids, from suburban Orange County, both barely of drinking age. It was the girl's twenty-first birthday weekend. Emily Tran, from Irvine. The boy was half a year older, Francis De Leon, from Fullerton. High school senior portraits were printed on the *MISSING* posters that immediately started showing up in restaurants and tourist shops around town. They looked like nice kids, as people say. Both from second-generation immigrant families, Vietnamese and Filipino, respectively. Her family was wealthy, all doctors and lawyers and bankers. His was middle class, small businesspeople. Both success stories of the kind America doesn't produce too many of anymore.

That night on my shift, a lot of people called in with theories and ideas. Of course nobody had seen the kids, or knew them, or even knew much about where they'd disappeared. To a lot of the old-timers in the high desert, the ones who washed up here decades ago, the national park was as mysterious and distant as Los Angeles.

"I bet they were on drugs," one of my regulars said, calling in from a mobile home park in Yucca Valley. "Most of these tourists are on drugs."

By September, the Search & Rescue missions were a Saturday-only affair, at the insistence of Francis De Leon's father. He owned a couple of restaurants in the OC. But every Saturday he was back in Joshua Tree, with a dwindling supply of volunteer searchers. And like my night callers, most people around town had just forgotten about it. Which is only natural, when the missing people are abstractions.

By then I had a weird feeling about the whole thing. And it became a lot weirder when a college friend of Emily Tran's sent the radio station an e-mail that wound up being forwarded to me. She didn't want to talk, didn't want to use her name. But she had an angle nobody else seemed to know: Emily Tran and Francis De Leon had broken up three months before her birthday trip to Joshua Tree. Emily had broken it off, put Francis in the friend zone.

They had dated in high school, fell in love it seems. But then she got accepted to UC-Irvine and he sort of drifted. Some community college classes, a fight with his father over the family business. Nothing sinister, on its own. Still, you could sense a narrative: She was on her way up in the world. He wasn't. Her life was expanding. His was shrinking. When Emily broke it off, Francis took it hard.

Sometimes a story gets inside you and then you have to see it through. Because nobody else is bothering with it. I started to feel like maybe Emily Tran got a raw deal.

The radio station is not the kind of enterprise that could afford to send its nighttime host on goose chases to Irvine and Fullerton and wherever else the trail might lead, so I did it the cheap way: by phone, on the Internet, collecting names and information from cached web pages and those sleaze-ball operations that sell public records to nervous spouses for thirty-five dollars. I figured out that Francis was training to become a rent-a-cop. That he'd qualified for a concealed-carry permit, as part of this training. And that he didn't have a whole lot of friends—but he did have one friend in particular who still had a presence on social media, as they say on the cable news. Danny Mendoza. And Danny Mendoza still had a Facebook account.

There was a picture of Danny and Francis on the Loop Trail in Joshua Tree National Park, in a post dated two weeks before Francis and Emily vanished. I knew that trailhead pretty well; it was an easy mile-long walk from my cabin. No caption or location data necessary. It felt weird though it wasn't terribly suspicious on its own. Three million people visit the park every year, most from Southern California.

But there was an interesting fact about Danny Mendoza that I learned about on his Facebook page—he had apparently enrolled in nursing school in Manila, at the beginning of September. He'd flown the coop.

By the time October rolled around, I had a pile of information. None of it compelling enough to bring to the sheriff, or to NPS law enforcement. The National Park Service has its own federal police, but in our present national dystopia it is underfunded and understaffed and mostly embarrassed to exist. The county sheriff's department is, at best, indifferent to both the national park and the high desert. Which makes a kind of sense, as it's based in the faraway city of San Bernardino. Another world from Joshua Tree. The kids had vanished barely a mile from the entrance station where millions of cars entered and exited every year, where scores of federal employees roamed on a regular basis, and where search teams had put in hundreds of hours specifically looking for these kids. People vanish in national parks. It's a thing. And the National Park Service would rather not discuss such things.

The final search took place on the last Saturday in October. The weather was nearly crisp, the days short and the shadows long. Only two volunteers made the loop with Mr.

De Leon, but this time they wandered behind a big desert willow that had shed most of its leaves and dried flowers. There was a narrow path behind it, no more than a jackrabbit trail. I've been there since and it's a surprise anyone ever followed it, because it clearly didn't go anywhere. But just before the wall of granite boulders, the searchers spotted the faded wrapper of a granola bar and the lid of a plastic water bottle. A few steps beyond, in a nook that barely fit them both, lay the baked remains of Emily Tran and Francis De Leon.

Francis was on top of her, his pants around his knees. His Heckler & Koch .40-caliber pistol was loosely covered in sand and dead leaves. Emily's shorts were pulled down. The Search & Rescue volunteers—unidentified to this day—immediately backed out and radioed the sheriff's department. They had to physically restrain Mr. De Leon, who was weeping and moaning and seemed determined to correct the crime scene.

I was, of course, out of town that day. At the dentist in Palm Springs. And then afterward I'd gone to Paul Bar because it's on the way home, and by the time I got to the radio station everything had gone nuts. *Inside Edition* and *People* were calling. KTLA wanted me to show them the site, which I hadn't yet seen for myself. Gary had done a good job on the story for our own station and all I could do was listen and learn.

That night on the air I thought I was saying the obvious: That Francis De Leon had raped and murdered his ex-girlfriend after luring her out to Joshua Tree as a "birthday present" and then turned the pistol on himself. That he'd scoped out the high desert two weeks before he brought her into the national park, close enough to see the traffic on Highway 62 from atop any boulder, and stolen her life. That he'd brought a loaded handgun on a short day hike and used it on the girl he claimed

276 // <small>Palm Springs Noir</small>

to love. And that his own father had a hunch all this had happened and had spent three months of weekends closely following the search volunteers, so he could be there when the bodies were found and have a chance to spin the story. Not out of any culpability in the crime, but for honor. Family honor, the family name, the family business.

Rape/murder/suicide. And Francis got away with it, by killing himself. And he used our national park, my backyard, as a slaughterhouse.

It was a total outrage and when I finally fell asleep late that night, at least it all seemed obvious.

I couldn't have been more wrong.

The headlines were all the same, in the days and weeks to come. Mr. De Leon not only didn't get arrested for trying to fix the crime scene, but he managed to write the sheriff's press release.

The couple was found "in a last embrace," the TV news said, with the gun only being used as a last desperate way to end Emily Tran's suffering. And then Francis had taken his own life, tragically but also maybe heroically (with his Acura parked an easy mile's walk away).

They'd been dead for months and were so decomposed that proof of rape or anything of the sort would never appear. So the ding-dongs at the sheriff's department just went with the sob story. After all, they didn't have anybody to rough up and arrest, and the DA had nobody to prosecute, so what the hell.

Boy, I wonder who did the embracing. Probably the ex-boyfriend, who murdered his ex-girlfriend, considering that he killed her first, before turning the gun on himself. And after pulling down her pants and raping her. I wonder if she was already dead by then.

The park service public affairs office had the gall to repeat this garbage: *The sheriff's department concluded that Francis De Leon had no intent to harm Emily Tran and that the use of the weapon was an unfortunate result of the couple's desperation after having been lost for an unspecified amount of time and losing hope.*

That's the dumbest damned thing I've ever heard, and I used to cover the police beat full time.

He was her ex-boyfriend, the ex-boyfriend of a beautiful girl who was going somewhere in life, somewhere that didn't include a security guard and gun nut. He got put in the friend zone. Then he scoped out Joshua Tree, the beloved weekend getaway, dragging his buddy along for the ride. And then Francis De Leon convinced his ex to take a little holiday together in the nice national park, just spend some time together, as friends. He brought a loaded handgun. And once they were a short mile or so down the Loop Trail—which might seem like a very remote location until you remember the little cabins and busy dirt roads and bachelorette parties just beyond—he shot her through the skull and crawled on top of her and shot himself. No harm intended! Just another day hike gone wrong.

This county is something else.

THE SALT CALLS US BACK

BY ALEX ESPINOZA

Salton Sea

It was one of ours who first found her things, along the gray silt and dried-up fish bones near the edge of the Salton Sea. They were simple articles—a pair of sandals decorated with jeweled tortoises climbing along the leather straps, a straw hat with a wide brim, a coin purse with a few dimes and pennies rolling around inside like errant thoughts.

Stuffed in a striped canvas bag, the boy found a thin piece of fabric stained with drops of blood, broken sunglasses, and an envelope with the name *REBECCA* scrawled in blue ink followed by a string of numbers and letters, dashes, and periods: *68-12.00W-87.01.02.RYZ.* She was a woman, no doubt about that. Because of the sandals and the bag, the indiscriminate piece of fabric the boy said was neatly folded.

"Like this," he told us, mimicking the motion of someone folding laundry. "Very neat. It was a perfect square."

We wondered how he knew about these things. About perfect squares, how the numbers written on the envelope were strange enough to remember. We wondered all of this to ourselves but stayed quiet as he went on, his sticky hands smelling of maple syrup, his red forehead beaded with sweat we could see as clearly and plainly as the date palms lining the perimeter of the lot where we parked, the place we called home. For now.

"Who is this boy's mother?" one of us whispered.

Some among us shrugged their shoulders. "I don't know."

"*Yo no sé*," the old woman with the raspy voice and blood-shot eyes replied.

A few of the men smoked and paced back and forth, nervous in that way men always are.

"Go on," we implored him. "Tell us more. What else?"

None of us ventured out much anymore. We preferred the cool darkness inside our trailers. We drew the blinds, turned fans on, the generators humming along like a swarm of giant hornets. We ate little. We listened to the preachers on the radio and waited for the end to come, just like we'd been taught. Now this boy was telling us a story about these mysterious items left along the banks of that salted sea. Was it a sign? Had she been sent to us by the Divine Presence? Was it a test? Was this boy even real? None of us were certain we even knew where he came from. Maybe he was making it up. Maybe he was lonely and looking for attention. When we asked him where he lived, where he came from, he pointed toward the opened doorway.

"Over there," he said. "My father and I walked for days. We found your trailers. The gray man in the green truck took clemency on us. Invited us into the flock once was passed the Test."

We knew the Test. Some of us in that very room had invented it. It was a way of knowing if a person was on the Righteous Path. If they passed it, then they were part of our movement.

"And your father?" one of us inquired. "Where is he?"

"Last seen eating some of the wild weed on the other side of the highway."

We nodded collectively. The man had gone on a pilgrimage. He was probably deep into the desert now, seeing visions and talking to the ghosts of his past.

"How long has he been away, your father?" we asked.

"A few days now."

We sympathized with the boy then. We knew that the pilgrimage was only supposed to last a few hours at the most. The father not coming back at that point meant he never would. He would be lost now, speaking in riddles to the hot wind and cacti.

The boy was our responsibility. That's how it works among our clan. And his father missing and now this discovery his boy had just made, well, it was clearly all connected. We just didn't know how yet.

Some said it was the salt and brine that brought her back. We thought it was something else entirely. We saw it as the omen we were waiting for. A dead body floating in the polluted water like that? What else could it be?

A sacrifice.

The Divine required it.

And we were meant to bear witness. To watch it all unfold.

To tell it then wait for the next sign to reveal itself: the Fire that would cleanse.

She had once been blond. That was for sure. That we knew right away. The yellow strands of hair were visible through the water's grit. We gathered around our television sets, and some of us even went so far as to venture out, stumbling over the sand and silt. We stood at the edge of a broken dock jutting out toward the fetid sea like a severed finger. She surfaced in the middle of the afternoon, when the sun is the hottest and blanches the entire area. Everything is white, the moisture sucked dry from every living thing roaming out there, among all that nothingness, terrifying and beautiful at once.

The body bobbed up and down, and we could see the arms extended out as if they were in supplication, begging for something only she could see. Her back was pale, wrinkled as tree bark, and her toenails were painted pink. Some of us thought of rose petals, the soft kisses of the children we were forced to abandon once we heard the Calling that led us out here. Still others among our group laughed and cursed, said she was a sinner. A filthy whore who got what she deserved for not heeding the signs the way we had.

"The police," someone stated.

A line of cars, sirens blaring, flashing red and blue, came up over the small embankment. Then there was an ambulance and a white van.

"Who called them?" the boy asked.

"The hippie artists," we said.

They began appearing with more frequency over the past few months. They smoked pot and had tattoos and piercings all over their faces and bodies. They dressed in rags and built elaborate bonfires and danced naked in circles in the middle of the night. Those of us designated to do the shopping saw them at the small grocery store on the southeastern edge of the lake. They bought cases of water, rolls of toilet paper, matches, twine, canned beans, and neon-colored energy drinks.

"Vagrants," the store clerk told us. "Don't like these artists. Ever since they been coming around, things in these parts have gotten funky." He looked at us, smiled. "You folks are all right. God-fearing. Make no trouble. Call no attention to those of us out here who'd rather be left alone."

We smiled. The men adjusted their suspenders, smoothed out their button shirts. The women pressed their skirts down and tightened their white head scarves.

It was one of them, for sure. They were probably out on

the lake at sunrise, paddling along in one of their makeshift rafts constructed of discarded driftwood and frayed bits of twine. They probably saw her body, panicked, pulled out their cell phones, and called the authorities.

This was why we kept such distractions—things like phones and computers—to a minimum. They only worked to pull us away from the important tasks of prayer, fasting, and preparing for the Day.

We only had our television and radio with the one station we were instructed to listen to. There, in secret codes delivered by the preachers, we received our information.

The police officers stepped out from their cars, their guns clipped to their oversized belts, their black boots slick as oil. They wore puffy jackets even though it was hot. They strung up yellow tape. The medical examiners wheeled out a gurney from the back of their van as two men in a boat paddled toward the shore. Among the folds of the tarp we could make out her wet strands of hair, the web of veins poking from the thin pink membrane of her scalp.

The two men jumped out of the boat as it reached the shore. They wore rubber boots and gloves, and they hoisted the tarp containing the body out and onto the shore.

Her mouth was agape, her eyes open, the sockets empty, no doubt picked out by the wild birds who sat on the rocks and splintered telephone poles, watching us with sinister intentions. Her breasts were pale and flat, and the flesh made a rhythmic slapping sound as the men inched her farther and farther away from the edge of the water and up a small embankment, not too far from where we stood, clustered together, peering at the strange and foreign spectacle. Her belly was distended. Exposed like that, under the glaring desert sun, it looked like a giant egg, something a prehistoric creature would have laid. A series of black bruises dotted her arms and her right index finger was missing.

"The missing finger," one of us muttered.

"Yes," said a few others.

"It's a sign," said the first one. "Something's coming."

We bowed our heads then lifted them, closed our eyes, and turned our faces to the sun before walking across the gravel lots, past the abandoned homes and boarded-up shops toward our settlement.

They identified the body. Her name was Judith Arnold. Sixty-three years of age. A widow with a son and daughter. We heard them on the radio, their voices low and quivering. They asked the public for help in finding their mother's killer.

"We are distraught," the daughter said, in between sobs.

"We are begging you," the son added. "If anyone knows anything, please come forward."

More information surfaced as the days passed, as we listened and tried following the clues, looking for the sign we needed that would indicate our final departure.

She had been stabbed repeatedly in the stomach, chest, and back. The coroner's office said there were strange words carved into her thighs: EROT, VALKUM, MEDCOLIUM.

"Evidence suggests the victim was assaulted and killed elsewhere and then brought here in an attempt to hide the crime."

The medical examiner spoke, said the water in her lungs didn't match what was typically found in the waters of the sea. "We discovered different minerals suggesting she wasn't drowned here," he explained.

There were trace elements of iron oxide, barium, copper, and magnesium.

"The victim was drowned, stabbed repeatedly, and had her skin lacerated. All of this postmortem," the examiner said.

Police presence grew in the area in the days that followed. We saw the squad cars parked out in front of the grocery store, by the gas station and convenience store, and out near the empty unpaved streets.

"I'm telling you," the store clerk said as we did our shopping, "it was one of those artist freaks. Likely did some ritual bloodletting. Now the cops are all up in our business. Who knows what else they'll find? Who knows how long they'll be here?"

He was angry.

"They said she was killed elsewhere," we explained. "They dumped her body here."

"Bullshit," he replied, then apologized. "I shouldn't have said that to you holy types."

We smiled and forgave him.

Who here among us has not sinned or committed an afront to His Holiness, after all?

The police continued their inquiry. We watched as they kept patrolling the area. They, in turn, watched everyone and everything going on around us. They must have been pressured by the woman's family. A private investigator was hired, a young man with a pair of thick-framed glasses and neatly ironed collared shirts was seen wandering up and down the lakeshore. He took pictures on his phone and spoke into it from time to time. We wondered who he was talking to.

"He's recording what he sees," the boy told us.

"How do you know?" we asked.

"I was standing a few feet away, behind a pile of rocks, and I listened," he said, shrugging his shoulders.

"Any word from your father?"

"No," he replied. "It's like he vanished into the air."

He wasn't a bother, and we all cared for him. We fed him, made sure he had clean clothing and that he attended the sermons we held each Friday evening in the tent.

Of course, we were bothered by the fact that his father had not come back. And some of us even went so far as to suggest that a search party be formed so that we might go out there and try to figure out where the man had gone. But we were not equipped to take on such risky endeavors, so we left it at that. And we tried never to talk about him.

We saw that investigator roaming around outside our property. He stood by the front entrance we'd erected when we first came. It wasn't really an entrance. It was just two piles of stones stacked together. It was clear, though, to anyone passing by that this was a residence, a specific location, maybe even a home. He waved at one of us.

"Hello?" he hollered. "Can I approach?" He held his arms up as if he were surrendering.

We stopped what we were doing, and one of us said, "You may pass, young man."

He was sweating, and we could see damp circles of perspiration underneath his armpits. He said he'd been hired by the victim's family and was working closely with the county sheriff's office to investigate the death of the woman named Judith Arnold.

"What a tragedy," we said. We shook our heads and lowered our gazes.

"What do you all know?" He held a small pad and pencil.

"Only what we've heard on the radio. That's all."

"Yeah," he said. "Yeah. A real tragedy. Shame."

"May He bring her peace."

The man glanced around, taking in the trailers and vans where we slept, the old chairs and rusted drums, the broken crates and strips of tarp we'd found and made our own. We had our washbasin, the small tubs where we bathed, the outdoor firepit where we sometimes cooked our food or sang hymnals and spirituals to His Holiness.

"So, am I to understand that your group is something of a religious sect?" he asked.

"We are an order," we explained. "We don't like terms like *sect* or *cult*. Of which we are neither."

"I see. I apologize," he said.

"What is it you seek?"

The man cleared his throat and said, "How many of you are there?" He waved with his pen.

We blinked, paused, thought for a moment. We could see the suspicion in his eyes. "Our numbers are great. We are many working as one."

"Okay, okay." He scribbled things down in his little notebook. "Do you all live here?"

"We've lost some along the way, but yes. All of us here make up the congregation."

He nodded, took a handkerchief out from his shirt pocket, and wiped the sweat from his pink forehead. "Is everyone accounted for? Nobody missing?"

We thought of the boy, his father.

The investigator waited for our answer. Some of us shuffled our feet. Still others glanced away.

"Everyone is here."

"Interesting," he said. "Interesting. So, you can account for every single person then?"

"Yes." We started getting annoyed. "Look. We have nothing to hide here. We're quiet. Law-abiding and God-fearing."

"I apologize," he said. He could tell we were becoming angry. "I'm just trying to do my job. Just trying to get down to the bottom of things."

And that was it.

He left.

We breathed a collective sigh of relief and continued on with our work.

He showed up again a few days later, holding a stack of papers in an envelope. We led him to a table, placed a cloth atop it, and poured him a drink of iced tea.

"Why, thank you," he said, evidently stunned by the gesture, given the tone of his voice.

"We are civilized," we replied.

"Of course." He laughed, took a sip, and cleared his throat. He had a habit of doing this. It annoyed us.

"What can we do for you?" one of us asked.

He opened up his folder and pulled out a few slips of paper. They contained a series of sketches and drawings that looked like symbols. It was a language, perhaps. We didn't know. But whatever it was, it appeared ancient, primordial.

"Ever seen symbols like these anywhere?" he asked.

We shook our heads. "We have not."

"You sure about this?"

"Of course, yes."

He told us no one knew what they meant. He'd asked everyone he could think of, ran them through the police database, sought advice from anthropologists and university scholars versed in local lore. Everywhere he turned, though, he came up with nothing.

"If that's the case," we said, "then why do you think *we* can help you?"

"Friend of mine studied religion," he answered. "Ancient sects."

"We are not a sect."

"Didn't say you were. Just—"

"We don't know any of this."

He sighed. "Says this looks like something ceremonial."

"What does this have to do with your investigation?"

He finished his iced tea. "Glad you asked. This little bit of information wasn't released to the public, but it seems that these symbols, these bizarre-looking little stars and crosses and figures that could be letters and whatnot, well, they were carved into the skin of the dead woman."

"And because we are a religious organization, you assume we have something to do with this?"

"I didn't say—"

We pointed in a vague direction toward the horizon. "Why don't you go and bother those crazy artists who come here and do drugs and dance around naked? They're probably the ones that did it."

"I'm only trying to gather information. That's all."

None of us noticed him standing there, just a few feet away, listening to everything the investigator was saying. It was only when the young man got up to leave, handing over his empty glass and excusing himself before walking over toward his car, that the boy came forward.

"What is it?" we asked.

The boy stared down at the ground. There were rocks and small pebbles littered about. He kicked at some of them with the tip of his dirty shoe.

"Those symbols? The ones that were drawn there on those papers?"

"What about them?" we asked, leaning in now.

"I seen them before. In a book my father carried with him."

"Show us," we implored. "Show us now."

The camper was cramped and hot, and there were flies buzzing around inside, bumping against the torn mesh of the door screen, hovering over the dirty dishes in the sink, piled up for who knew how long. Stacks of paper filled the ground, and it was hard for us to move in there. In a section of the tiny laminate kitchen counter, next to the stove, its four burners charred black as the desert night, was a picture of a woman. She wore pants, and her hair was tied in a bun. Her left hand rested on her hip, and her other was placed on the window of a blue van. Her mouth was open, a tiny red O, as if she were in the middle of saying something. The woman's eyes were radiant, glowing. This we could feel, even as we stood there, in that forsaken space. There were a handful of pebbles and a lit candle near the photograph.

"Your mother?" we asked.

"Grandmother," the boy responded, as if knowing the next question already. "She raised me. My real mother . . . she left. When my father came back from the service, he took me with him."

"Where?" we asked.

He shrugged his shoulders. "All over. We slept in motels. Once we met some men on motorcycles. Followed them for a while. They gave my father drugs that kept him up for days. That was when he started seeing things. He started writing in his book."

The boy riffled through a plastic bag and pulled out a spiral notebook. He held it out and told us to open it, to look through the pages. Inside there were scrawled images of distorted faces and scribbles, phrases, and words that made no sense.

"Witchcraft," one of us muttered.

"Who is this devil?" someone else asked.

"The back," the boy urged. "They're in the back."

They did look similar, though the marks on the dead woman's body were distorted and blurred in the photographs the investigator had shown us. There was something sinister about the whole thing, something that made us feel as though we'd stumbled upon a situation not meant for us.

"Call the investigator back," one of us said.

"No," someone else replied. "They'll think *we* killed her."

"Let's leave all of this alone. Pretend we didn't see any of it," still others insisted.

"I think he did it," the boy said. "I think *he* killed her. That woman."

They had stopped, he said, one night. A long stretch of road. Past the giant windmills churning their big, wide blades. He was fast asleep. His father had been driving for days. Without sleep, he explained.

"The squeak from the brakes woke me. I felt the camper stop. The engine turned off." He took a deep breath. "I could see out the window." He pointed toward the back of the camper. "Red lights flashing."

"Was it the lady?" we asked.

"There was a voice I didn't recognize." He began to shake. "Then a scream."

After that, there was nothing. He heard a loud thud, saw his father's red, shaking hands, noted the look in his eyes.

"He was mad," the boy said. "I tried asking him if everything was okay. But he stayed quiet."

He only partially saw the name of the city where they

were. Someplace with the words *Hot* and *Springs* in it. We knew then why her lungs were filled with water that had different mineral contents than the Salton, why she looked the way she did. She'd come from one of those expensive spas tucked away in the hills, those places that rubbed you down, sprayed your face with fragrant mists, where you could splay out under the hot sun and bake your skin until it itched and bubbled.

After driving for a long while, the car engine gave out. Steam hissed from the hood. His father beat his fists against the hot metal. He gulped down the last of their water, told the boy to take whatever he could carry, and they set off on foot.

"That was when we met you all. My father went back for our camper, somehow got it fixed, and brought it here."

"Did you see a body?" we asked.

"No," he said. "I only saw the blood."

That was how we knew. We talked among ourselves. We held counsel and decided what steps we needed to take when it came to the knowledge we'd gained, this strange boy we'd inherited. Our scripture taught us to care for others and ourselves, but it also taught us to make sacrifices in order to fulfill the plan He had in store for us. Many of us argued over the proper solution.

Hand the boy over to the authorities, some felt.

Leave him to fend for himself. We could travel farther east into the desert. Get lost and prepare for the final days, still others said.

We prayed.

Finally, the solution presented itself.

We had very little. It was easy for us to pack up and leave. We were, after all, not tied to material things. We needed none of that. We gathered at the center of the wide clearing, followed the lead car out. We were a caravan of God-fearing souls lost in the dry wilderness. All we were looking for was hope, a home, a place where we could hang our hats, put our Bibles down, and rest. Finally, to rest.

We imagined lakes. Jagged granite peaks. Waterfalls cascading down boulders and rocks. The sound of the water, that beautiful and gloriously rich sound. We smelled pine-scented air. We heard owls and hawks screeching in the sky. There would be wide fields of wildflowers all around us. We wanted to live again. We wanted to breathe clean, cool air. We didn't want our lungs to feel scalded by the hot desert wind that bit and begged and took so much.

Out. Somewhere far. Miles from the main highway that led us out of the state. We found a desolate road. We followed the main car leading the caravan—that car where we knew the boy rode.

There was nothing out there. No buildings or houses. No sign of anyone anywhere.

He looked confused. He must have been sleeping, because when he was ordered out of the car, he rubbed his eyes. He bit his lip and wiggled a finger through the hole in his shirt. "Are we there?" He glanced around.

"Yes," one of us said.

He looked around again. "Where?"

One of us, an old man with a long beard and glassy eyes, said, "See that ridge? It's there. Just past it. On the other side." He held something in his hand. Some of us couldn't see, though. It looked like a green duffel bag. The old man picked this up, and he led the child up a thin path, cutting through wild sagebrush and thorny cactus up and over the ridge.

We waited.

We prayed.

The Holy Spirit entered some of us. We spoke in tongues. *Ashohala. Ere al om tah collah.*

The sun had set by the time he returned. The green duffel bag was gone. He held a long wooden club. The end looked as though it had been dipped in red paint, the color thick and dark, menacing. We pretended not to know what it was.

"I suppose we should get going now," the old man said.

It was taken care of. We must push on.

Somewhere out there was our rightful home.

The place promised to those like us.

ABOUT THE CONTRIBUTORS

Debra Cross

CHRIS J. BAHNSEN is known as a "zebra" by his Chicano uncles, in that he is half Mexican and half white, and thus walks the strange and sometimes precarious edge between cultures. His work has appeared in the *New York Times*, the *Los Angeles Times*, the Smithsonian's *Air & Space*, *Hobart*, *River Teeth*, and *Hippocampus*. He is an assistant editor with *Narrative* magazine, living biresidentially in Southern California and Northwest Ohio.

Mark Krajnak

ERIC BEETNER has been called "the twenty-first century's answer to Jim Thompson." He has written more than twenty novels, including *All the Way Down, Rumrunners*, and *The Devil Doesn't Want Me*. When not spending the weekend vacationing in Palm Springs with his family, he cohosts the podcast *Writer Types* and the Noir at the Bar reading series. For more information, visit ericbeetner.com.

ROB BOWMAN moved to the desert several years ago from Denver, his longtime home and setting for his upcoming detective novel. His fiction has appeared in the *Coachella Review* and the *Donnybrook Writing Academy*. Additional credits include *Modern in Denver, Book and Film Globe*, and others. He cohosts the film and pop culture podcast *Reel Disagreement*. When not immersed in these things, he is with his wife Mindy and their sons, Jetson and Rocket.

Tim Courtney

MICHAEL CRAFT is the author of seventeen novels, four of which have been honored as finalists for Lambda Literary Awards. His 2019 mystery, *ChoirMaster*, won a Gold IBPA Benjamin Franklin Award. In 2017, Craft's professional papers were acquired by the Special Collections & University Archives at the University of California, Riverside. He holds an MFA in creative writing from Antioch University Los Angeles, and lives in Rancho Mirage, California, near Palm Springs.

Adele Peters

BARBARA DeMARCO-BARRETT spends time in the desert whenever she can. She hosts *Writers on Writing* on KUCI-FM, and her book *Pen on Fire* was a *Los Angeles Times* best seller. Her short story "Crazy for You" was published in *USA Noir: Best of the Akashic Noir Series*. She has also published in the *Los Angeles Times*, the *Los Angeles Review of Books*, *Inlandia, Shotgun Honey, Partners in Crime*, and *Paradigm Shifts*.

ALEX ESPINOZA is the author of *Still Water Saints, The Five Acts of Diego León,* and *Cruising: An Intimate History of a Radical Pastime.* He's written for the *Los Angeles Times,* the *New York Times Magazine, VQR, LitHub,* and NPR's *All Things Considered.* The recipient of fellowships from the NEA and MacDowell as well as an American Book Award, he lives in Los Angeles and is the Tomás Rivera Endowed Chair of Creative Writing at the University of California, Riverside.

Cat Gwynn

JANET FITCH is the best-selling author of *White Oleander, Paint It Black, The Revolution of Marina M.,* and *Chimes of a Lost Cathedral,* an epic of the Russian Revolution. Her short stories and essays have appeared in a variety of publications. Two of her novels and her story "The Method," from *Los Angeles Noir,* have been made into feature films. The Palm Canyon mobile home in "Sunrise" belonged to her grandmother.

TOD GOLDBERG is the *New York Times* best-selling author of more than a dozen books, including *Gangster Nation, Gangsterland,* and *The House of Secrets,* which he cowrote with Brad Meltzer. His journalism has appeared in the *Los Angeles Times,* the *Wall Street Journal,* and *Best American Essays.* Goldberg is a professor of creative writing at the University of California, Riverside, where he founded and directs the low-residency MFA in creative writing and writing for the performing arts.

Mark Davidson

J.D. HORN is the *Wall Street Journal* best-selling author of the Witching Savannah series (*The Line, The Source, The Void,* and *Jilo*), the Witches of New Orleans Trilogy (*The King of Bones and Ashes, The Book of the Unwinding, The Final Days of Magic*), and the stand-alone Southern Gothic horror tale *Shivaree.* Originally from Tennessee, he lives in Palm Springs and San Francisco with his spouse, Rich, and their rescue Chihuahua, Kirby Seamus.

Bill Green

KEN LAYNE, editor and publisher of *Desert Oracle,* a pocket-sized field guide to the mysterious Southwest desert, hosts *Desert Oracle Radio* and its companion podcast from the Mojave high desert. Once a month he leaves his home alongside Joshua Tree National Park to tell eerie campfire stories at the Ace Hotel & Swim Club in Palm Springs. Farrar, Straus & Giroux's MCD Books recently published his first hardcover collection, *Desert Oracle, Volume I.*

T. JEFFERSON PARKER is the author of twenty-five crime novels, and numerous short stories and essays. He was born in Los Angeles, grew up in Orange County, and now lives north of San Diego. He has won two Edgar Awards for best novel, an Edgar for best short story, a *Los Angeles Times* Book Prize and a Seamus Award. When not at work he enjoys fishing, hiking, and beachcombing.

Bruce Jenkin

ROB ROBERGE, from Wonder Valley in the high Mojave Desert, is the author of four books of fiction and one memoir, *Liar*, selected for the Barnes & Noble Discover Great New Writers program. His short fiction and essays have been widely anthologized, and he is currently at work on a novel.

EDUARDO SANTIAGO's first novel, *Tomorrow They Will Kiss,* was an Edmund White Debut Fiction Award finalist. His next book, *Midnight Rumba,* won the New England Book Award for best fiction. His short stories have appeared in *ZYZZYVA, Slow Trains,* and the *Caribbean Writer.* His nonfiction was featured in the *Los Angeles Times,* the *Advocate,* and *Out Traveler* magazine. He is on faculty at Idyllwild Arts Academy, which sits high above Palm Springs.

Dalmiro Quiroga

KELLY SHIRE has published work in numerous journals, including *Brevity*, *Entropy*, and the *Coachella Review.* Her essay "Beautiful Music," about long-standing Cathedral City radio station KWXY, appeared in *Full Grown People.* As a half–Mexican American, third-generation resident of Southern California, her writing often explores themes of place and identity. She lives south of Palm Springs with her children and husband, and is completing a memoir.